MISTRESS OF THE AIR

S. NANO

Mistress of the Air
Published in 2024 by
House of Erotica
houseoferotica.uk

an imprint of
Andrews UK Limited
West Wing Studios
Unit 166, The Mall
Luton, LU1 2TL
andrewsuk.com

MISTRESS OF THE AIR

S. NANO

HOUSE OF EROTICA

Contents

HOUSE OF EROTICA

1

Captain Wyndham had the tail of the bi-plane in his sights. He had the measure of his adversary. He knew Delagrange's plane wasn't capable of matching his speed. He knew he was a more skilful aviator than his opponent. He could have led the race from start to finish if he chose, but he preferred to give the crowd a show. That's why he stalked the tail of his competitor, waiting for the right moment to take him.

The crowd in the grandstand on the ground below rose to their feet. Wyndham heard their roars even above the spluttering of the planes' engines as they raced across the sky.

He didn't need the injection of dimethyl aether into the fuel to give him added propulsion, but he wasn't going to forgo the chance to impress the spectators. There were around five hundred yards to the finish line. He pushed the throttle and gripped hard onto the joystick.

The engine roared, and the propellers buzzed, drowning out the noise from the crowd. The captain accelerated with a burst of speed, zooming past his rival's bi-plane, leaving it in a trail of smoke as he overtook the hapless Frenchman.

The crowd went wild with excitement at the daring manoeuvre on the finish line.

After they both landed, Delagrange came up to shake Wyndham's hand and congratulate him. He was now in the final of the bi-plane time trials.

October 1910 would go down as a landmark date in British aviation history. This meeting at Doncaster Aerodrome and Airship Station was the first of its kind in the British Empire. It was a gathering of the pioneer aviators of the era to test the new-fangled bi-planes to their limit in a series of races and time trials. The captain believed with passion he was in the vanguard of a new movement. This event was proof of it, with aviators from the British, French, Prussian and American Empires.

As he walked back to join the other pilots, he received numerous slaps on the back. He glanced up at the grandstand. One figure stood out from amongst the crowd. His eye was drawn to a woman in one of the boxes, dressed in claret velvet, watching the event with keen interest, her arm outstretched as her maid poured a glass of champagne out for her. The image registered for a fleeting moment before he moved on.

He joined the group of other pilots. He was proud to be counted amongst this band of intrepid, pioneer aviators. Many were his friends and colleagues such as Charles Theobald and Edward Milnes with whom he had worked closely in developing their bi-planes, especially the adaption of their engines to use dimethyl aether for added propulsion. There was Monsieur Saunier from France, Wyndham's hated rival, and his compatriots Monsieurs Le Blon and Delagrange, Count von Schreck from Germany, and finally John Burch who had travelled from the United States to attend the meeting.

They formed a distinctive group. Captain Wyndham cut a striking figure dressed in his trade-mark flying dress of a black, fedora hat, white polo-neck sweater, long beige, canvas coat and flying boots, with huge, brass goggles hanging around his neck. The other aviators wore the attire of country gentlemen in tweeds as was more the style of the period.

He noticed Saunier, in particular, looking suave and dapper, reeking of expensive French cologne, chatting amiably with a group of young, attractive girls. He envied the Frenchman's social ease and good looks, conscious he was not the most handsome of men with his long face, pointed chin hidden by a goatee beard, and dark, deep-set eyes.

He knew he was a skilled and daring aviator though, and now he faced his rival in a fly-off for the speed-trial. Monsieur Saunier was a better pilot and possessed a faster machine than Delagrange and had beaten Wyndham narrowly at a recent meeting in Paris. The captain was desperate to beat the Frenchman, hoping the adjustments to his engine might give him the advantage. He waited patiently until the completion of the airship altitude trials before preparing for what was the final event of the meeting.

It was a close fought flight as he expected. It came down to the last lap of the race with Captain Wyndham on his competitor's tail. He had a manoeuvre up his sleeve. He had read the speed and direction of the winds and, taking his bi-plane high into the sky, let the wings get caught in the slipstream of the wind before adding the extra propulsion, swooping at enormous speed to surge past the Frenchman. The captain was just a few hundred yards from the winning post, and a satisfying triumph over his rival, when his engine misfired and his plane lost power, diving to the ground.

Wyndham was furious. He was so close to winning the event, only to be robbed of it at the final moment by an engine failure.

He shook his rival's hand, trying not to do so too grudgingly. The disappointment still left a bitter taste in his mouth when he stood on the platform with the other aviators, awaiting the distribution of the prizes for the competitions.

The compere stood on the stage and announced, "It is with great pleasure I introduce the sponsor of the prize for the fastest bi-plane, Lady Sally Rudston-Chichester."

Lady Sally's reputation went before her. She was well known as an extraordinarily wealthy and powerful lady, and the rumours she was also a severe dominatrix to the rich and influential were widespread. Captain Wyndham did not mix in those circles, his first sight of her being at this flying meeting.

The imposing figure of Lady Sally swept onto the platform. All eyes were drawn towards her. She stood upright in a claret, velvet jacket and matching skirt, the longest leather boots Wyndham had ever seen, decorated with silver buckles and black laces, and a fox-fur around her neck, the snarling teeth and startled eyes of the fox's head glaring out at the crowd. A matching fascinator with a black ostrich feather sticking out from it completed the outfit.

She was undoubtedly a formidable woman. Her alert eyes glittered with confidence as she cast a glance over the crowd. Her waist must have been constrained in the tightest of corsets as it was impossibly thin, and this only served to accentuate her breasts and hips, which were beautifully rounded and voluptuous. The men in the audience looked on awe struck at this statuesque, ravishing figure of a woman as she towered over them from the platform.

Her voice carried confidently across the expectant crowd with a clipped, pronounced enunciation, indicative of her aristocratic upbringing.

"Ladies and Gentlemen, we are on the cusp of a new era…"

The crowd hushed, hanging onto her every word.

"We are entering the age of the flying machine. I have a vision of a sky filled with airships and teeming with bi-planes. And these brave gentlemen, but regrettably no ladies," she added tersely, "are in the vanguard of this movement. I pay tribute to these intrepid pioneer aviators at this, the first flying meeting in Britain, here at Doncaster Aerodrome. I assure you, I shall be at the forefront of this new age, and will soon amaze you, for at this very moment, just a few miles from here, my team of skilled engineers are using their arcane knowledge to construct the most magnificent airship the world has ever seen.

"But to turn to today's events, it's with great pleasure I present the Rudston-Chichester prize for fastest aviator to France's Monsieur Saunier."

There was a burst of applause. Captain Wyndham gazed on enviously as he saw his hated rival kiss Lady Sally's leather-gloved hand and receive his prize. It should have been his. If only his machine hadn't failed him at the last moment. He knew he was faster than the Frenchman. Just as

3

Saunier turned away to give his acceptance speech, Lady Sally's eyes met the captain's. There was the merest flash of dazzling, white teeth as she offered an acknowledgement, and the slightest hint of a smile. Perhaps Wyndham had imagined it and, if it was there, he realised with disappointment it probably meant nothing.

It was not the last encounter he had with Lady Sally that day, nor the event that was about to turn his world upside down. In the evening, the competitors at the flying meeting were invited to a ball in their honour. Captain Wyndham felt distinctly uncomfortable in his formal dinner-jacket and starched, white shirt with its winged collar and bow tie. Of course, Lady Sally was there, dressed in a magnificent, turquoise ball-gown.

She had a servant in attendance too, a strange figure in a black and white French maid's dress with layer upon layer of petticoats. There was something not quite right about Lady's Sally's maid, then it struck him... she was a man. There was no question about it. Captain Wyndham was shocked. He had heard of such things though never encountered them in the circles he mixed in. How terribly risqué he thought, openly flaunting a transvestite maid. She carried a fan and, every so often, wafted it past Lady Sally's face to cool her.

Captain Wyndham stood in uncomfortable isolation in the corner of the ballroom tugging at his starched collar, contemplating how early he could politely take his leave, when suddenly he was conscious of eyes peering at him. When he looked up, there was no doubt, Lady Sally's piercing gaze penetrated to the far end of the room.

She glided in his direction, the enormous train of her ball gown behind her, her strange maid following in her wake making sure it didn't get snagged. *Was she coming towards him?* As she made her stately progress across the ballroom she got blocked by somebody who started fussing around her. It was Monsieur Le Blon, one of the French pilots, looking elegant in his smartly tailored dinner-jacket and his curly moustache, waxed and perfumed. *Damn, trust him to interfere.* He strained to hear the conversation.

"Ladee Salee, it ees such a pleasure to meet you, I 'av urd so much about you. If I may be so bold as to compliment madam on her décolletage, I urv never seen such breasts, they are *trés magnificentes.*"

"No, you may not, Monsieur. If you had heard anything about me, you would realise how provocative your puerile comments are. You dally with a strict English dominatrix at your peril, monsieur."

At that, and in full view of the guests at the ball, her gloved hand drifted to his crotch and grabbed his cock and balls tightly, squeezing and twisting them. Monsieur Le Blon let out a squeal of surprise and pain.

4

"So, let that be a lesson to you, Monsieur Le Blon," Lady Sally emphasized, squeezing even harder so that, even from his corner of the ballroom, Captain Wyndham saw him wince, and heard another squeak of pain and embarrassment. Wyndham smiled to himself, admitting to being amused at the spectacle.

Lady Sally was detained for just a moment before she brushed him aside disdainfully and continued her progress across the ballroom floor. Wyndham realised she really was heading towards him. *What could she possibly want?* Having seen how she dealt with Le Blon, he anticipated her approach with trepidation.

"Captain Wyndham," Lady Sally announced boldly.

Despite being above average height, broad shouldered and a heavy build, the captain felt small and insignificant alongside her. Lady Sally could only be an inch or so taller but, with her high heels, she appeared to tower over him.

"Lady Sally," Wyndham muttered in embarrassment.

"Jolly bad luck on the final race, Wyndham. It was a daring move and deserving of greater reward."

The captain's face lit up at the compliment. He looked up but couldn't help but be distracted by the sight of Lady's Sally's breasts. Seeing them at such close quarters he could well understand Monsieur Le Blon's misguided comment on them. Lady Sally's dress was cut daringly low, and the magnificent orbs of white flesh were pushed up enticingly by her corset and the cut of her gown.

And then she spoke. If Wyndham was embarrassed over what to say, he needn't have worried. She commanded the conversation and Wyndham listened, bewitched and mesmerised at the vision she laid before him. There was no escape for him. He was pinned into the corner by Lady Sally's heaving breasts with no escape. He tried to concentrate on what she was saying, conscious of the treatment meted out to Monsieur Le Blon, all the time urging himself to focus on her face not her chest, but it was an enormous effort of will when they were practically thrust under his nose.

She spoke of her airship. She described how vast it was going to be, how fast, how powerful, and how high it would fly. She described how sumptuously it would be fitted out. She extolled the virtues of her ocean liner of the air. Wyndham nodded enthusiastically as her breasts swelled and subsided with every excited explication of her venture. She enthused about her designers and engineers who were working on it, of the technical challenges they faced and how they had overcome them. Wyndham stood trapped in the corner of the ballroom like a frightened rabbit in headlights, all the time trying to distract himself from the sight of Lady Sally's enormous décolletage as it heaved up and down in front of his eyes.

Then she proceeded to explain how, as he must certainly know, she was the foremost dominatrix of her age. She described with great enthusiasm the dungeon that would be fitted out on the airship, and how excited she was about the adventures she would have, and the whippings, spankings and punishments she would administer to the carefully selected group of submissive gentlemen who would accompany her on the airship's maiden voyage.

"It's my ambition, Captain Wyndham, to be the *Mistress of the Air*, yes… a veritable *Mistress of the Air,* and I envisage you playing a vital role in fulfilling my vision."

Wyndham's ears pricked up at those words but he only had the slightest moment to interject with a nervous, "oh really," before the enormous breasts backed him even further into the corner. Lady Sally continued by praising his aviation skills and the daring manoeuvres she'd witnessed at the flying meeting. Wyndham flushed with pride. She went on, much to the captain's delight, to say how those French aviators were all show and no guts, and she needed somebody who would take risks for her, to serve her loyally and selflessly. Finally, she wound up her diatribe and came directly to the point.

"Now, captain. I pride myself on my instincts and judgement of character. You see, the matter is I need an airship pilot. I need someone who can share my enthusiasm for air flight and is a skilled aviator. I believe you are my man Wyndham."

Lady Sally continued extolling the excitement of the new age, how she was going to take her airship on a grand tour across Europe and how he, Captain Wyndham, would be her pilot.

Finally, she concluded, "So that's settled then, Captain Wyndham. I can assure you the financial rewards will be considerable. It's good to have you on board. I'm sure we will share many adventures together. You can report to my airship station at Howden in Yorkshire. My maid, Victoria, will give you all the details."

With one dismissive wave of a lace-gloved hand she breezed off, leaving the hapless Wyndham gaping in astonishment. He had been swept away by her charisma. He had barely uttered a word. At no point did he agree to the venture yet he knew in his gut he wanted to accept the challenge. He felt strangely compelled to help Lady Sally fulfil her vision of travel in the largest and fastest dirigible ever to be built.

2

"I'm very disappointed in you brigadier... very disappointed."

Lady Sally was back at Rudston Hall, 'entertaining' one of her submissive gentlemen, who was secured onto a whipping bench in one of the rooms dedicated to domination and punishment.

Indeed, most of the rooms of the house were put aside for that purpose, rendering it a playground for the expression of Lady Sally's dominatrix persona. Except the kitchen. Cook had stood firmly to her ground, insisting none of her mistress's strange goings-on take place in her domain. "It's disgusting, milady," she said. "Quite unhygienic. I can't have those bodily fluids around where I'm mixing cakes!"

Lady Sally circled the whipping bench menacingly, the brigadier following the sound of her heels clicking on the parquet flooring until they came to rest in front of him. The scarlet silk of her corset brushed against the hairs of his handlebar moustache. The firm, white flesh between the straps of her black suspender-belt were before his eyes, allowing him to stare down at her elegant legs in their black stockings. The smell of her, musky and sensual, was intoxicating. As he glanced up from his restrained position, he noted the wooden paddle cradled in her silk-gloved hand.

"I'm sorry, mistress. I'm disappointed myself. I should have loved to join your adventure, but I've been called back to my regiment."

"Huh," Lady Sally sniffed. "All that pointless marching and parading. You should send your soldiers to me. I'd soon instil some discipline in them!"

"I don't doubt that, mistress."

Brigadier Trumpington was left helplessly exposed. The regimental uniform of the Rutshire Hussars was left draped over a velvet chair, and he was now naked, kneeling on the bench, his ankles and wrists shackled to its wooden frame with handcuffs, his arse sticking up invitingly into the air.

It was too tempting a target for Lady Sally to ignore. She lifted her arm and whacked the paddle against the brigadier's backside. There was a thud, then a yelp of pain. His flabby arse wobbled like the jellies cook created with the hundreds of brass moulds in her kitchen.

She fixed her gaze on him, peering through a black mask which highlighted her penetrating eyes lined by dark kohl.

"It's your loss brigadier. This will be an adventure like no other; I'm so looking forward to it. I shall be a *Mistress of the Air*, floating in the clouds whilst administering cruel punishments to a select group of helpless slaves. And I have all manner of new dastardly devices to experiment with. There will be clockwork and steam-powered implements of torment. My workshop has been working over-time to get them ready. And you will forgo all the excitement..."

"I'm so disappointed, mistress. I know what a privilege it is to be invited, and I should love to be joining you."

"Well, it's a poor show, brigadier, that's all I have to say. I am of the opinion you should prioritise service to your mistress over these military shenanigans. What have you to say to that?"

"I'm truly sorry, mistress, but if I don't return to the regiment this weekend, I'll be court-martialled."

"It would be a small price to pay for displeasing me. You would just have to tell them you simply had to serve your mistress, and she insisted on taking you on an adventure." Lady Sally hesitated, a subtle smile spreading across her lips, "But tell me, brigadier, if you were subject to a court-martial, what punishment would it impose?"

The brigadier was disconcerted by Lady Sally's smile–it was a bad omen. From bitter experience, it usually meant she was having a fiendish idea. A trap was being laid for him.

"Well, mistress, if it were deemed to constitute desertion, then it would be a treasonable offence, and the punishment would be execution by hanging."

"But taking into consideration the mitigating circumstances of having a mistress to submit to, what punishment then?"

"I don't know. I doubt such a case has come before the military tribunal, mistress."

"You think not?"

The paddle came crashing down on the brigadier's arse again. He howled in pain. He hadn't prepared himself for the heavy stroke. The tingling pain spread across his backside like spiky tentacles.

"Yet, I know how many of the officer class indulge themselves of chastisement from a strict mistress. Come now, you are raised on corporal punishment–a strict governess, public school, Sandringham, the barracks. You cannot resist a good caning... and if it's from a sexy mistress, skilled in the arts of sadistic punishment, like yours truly, then all the better."

"Yes, mistress. Of course, mistress. It's true, who could not resist the magnificent Lady Sally Rudston-Chichester."

"I know what sentence a court-martial would pass. They would give a full judicial punishment, would they not?"

The brigadier gulped, "Yes, mistress."

"So there, the dilemma of how I should deal with your disobedience is resolved. For failing to join my airship adventure, the punishment is a judicial flogging and caning," Lady Sally announced triumphantly.

"Thank you, mistress. That's very fair, mistress," replied the brigadier, hints of both anxiety and anticipation in his voice.

To get him warmed up for what was to follow, Lady Sally gave him another almighty whack with the wooden paddle. The brigadier groaned. His arse throbbed.

"That is merely the beginning," warned Lady Sally. "A military tribunal would expect the most severe punishment to be inflicted for dereliction of duty... the duty in this case being servitude to me."

Brigadier Trumpington was completely in her control. He was used to this, had attended Lady Sally on many occasions and willingly subjected himself to all manner of punishments, but he was nervous. He'd deeply offended Lady Sally by not joining her airship adventure, and he was not going to get off lightly.

There was a clunk of wood upon wood as she dropped the paddle onto an occasional table behind her. He followed the trail of Lady Sally's footsteps as her metal-tipped heels clicked across the floor, visualising her statuesque figure as it surveyed the implements of corporal punishment on display. She pondered over which to choose.

Lady Sally had the largest collection of antique whips, canes, riding crops, floggers and straps in the country. She had built the collection up over many years, having poured through specialist magazines forwarded to her from her favoured bookseller in Drury Lane to seek out new acquisitions to her collection. She corresponded with collectors from all over the world, arranging for implements to be shipped to her from far-flung parts of the globe. She attended auction sales and, such was her determination to acquire every antique or unusual tool of corporal punishment... and such was her wealth, that she would outbid anybody for an implement she'd set her heart on.

She possessed the riding crop used by the Duke of Wellington at the Battle of Waterloo, the cat of nine tails from 'The Bounty', a rattan cane used by a Moghul emperor, a set of leather straps from Han Dynasty China and a bull whip from Commander Cody's wild west show. Anything distinctive, or with a unique history, she purchased for her collection. The most precious items were kept in a glass fronted mahogany cabinet. She only used these on special occasions. The more everyday tools for corporal punishment were arranged in rows on brass hooks around the room. There was a myriad of options available to her.

It was to the objects hanging freely available to which she turned. After all, the type of judicial punishment she had in mind for the brigadier might break skin and draw blood... and she certainly didn't want to stain any of her precious canes and floggers with a slave's blood. That would simply not do.

She pulled a leather flogger off its hook. She ran its thongs through her silken fingers to assess their feel and weight. The leather bands were heavy and thick and would deliver a suitable whack on Brigadier Trumpington's arse. She nestled the flogger's handle in her hand, and her fingers wrapped around it in comfort. *Yes, that would do nicely for warming him up.*

Now to the canes. She had a huge collection of them; several hundred in this room alone, but many more scattered throughout the house. *After all, one never knew when one would need a cane, and it was essential to have one to hand wherever one was.* Each cane was a different length or thickness and had its own balance and weight. She picked several from the wall to try them out, swishing each one through the air to test how it handled.

She wanted to deliver a severe judicial punishment in keeping with the sentence she had imposed, and to give vent to her genuine annoyance that the brigadier chose futile military service over attending *her*.

She had a clear vision for the select party of submissive gentlemen she wanted on her airship–a duke, bishop, banker, judge, and a military man. She had secured the first four from the many men who attended her, only too happy to pay a handsome sum to sponsor the expedition and join her adventure. That it was the brigadier's duty to return to his regiment, and that he may not be exaggerating the consequences if he failed to return, mattered not to Lady Sally; she expected to be placed first above all. The punishment for not doing so must be severe.

She had made her decision. She opted for a *kendo* stick. The brigadier was privileged. This implement was a gift to her from the Crown Prince Taisho. It was an antique *shinai* from the Edo dynasty dating from the late 17th century and had belonged to Emperor Higashiyama. It was rare she used one of her antiques, but Lady Sally felt the circumstances merited it.

She slid her silk gloves off and wrapped her fingers around the handle. It felt perfect. The *shinai* did not have the flexibility of a regular cane, but its weight and strength would deliver a hard whack. It was made of slats of dried bamboo strengthened by resin and bound tightly together by leather thongs. Lady Sally considered it highly appropriate; after all, kendo was an ancient means of instilling discipline in the human character, which was precisely what the brigadier needed.

She strode around to the front of the bench to tease him.

"Are you ready?" she asked, dangling the thongs of the leather flogger before his eyes.

"Yes mistress," he muttered.

Lady Sally looked magnificent in her scarlet corset over a black, silk blouse, thrusting her ample breasts up and making the distinctive phoenix tattoo on her left tit clearly visible. An ivory cameo hung from a black, silk choker around her elegant neck.

Despite the fear of the threatened punishment, or perhaps because of it, he couldn't help but get an erection.

She stepped back behind him. She ran the strands of leather across his backside. Their warm touch was deceptively sensuous. She twirled the flogger in her hand to warm up, and the brigadier listened to the thrashing of the thongs through the air.

Then she struck. The flogger swished through the air. Four rapid slashes across one of his bum cheeks, followed by another four on the other. The leather straps stung with a prickly pain.

Lady Sally ran her hand across his backside. On top of the earlier whacks with the paddle it was just starting to blossom into a red glow. The touch felt soft and cooling though the brigadier was aware it was only a brief respite.

The flogger whipped against his buttocks. This time the strokes were harder.

Lady Sally leant over to inspect his backside.

"You have a nice rosy arse there. But, of course, this is a judicial punishment, and the flogger is only to warm you up."

She went over to the table to pick up the *kendo* stick.

In a piece of showmanship, she posed in front of the brigadier. He lifted his head up to see Lady Sally, her stunning figure squeezed into the silken corset, her ebony hair flowing over her milk-white breasts, a look of steely determination in her blue eyes. She was in a crouching position, holding the *kendo* stick over her head in position, preparing to strike.

She fixed her gaze on him.

"Look upon this, slave, a *shinai*, a Japanese bamboo sword. I don't believe I've ever used one on you. It's thicker and harder than a cane. I rarely use them because they are so vicious. But, in your case it's appropriate and deserving, is it not?"

The brigadier's heart jumped a beat, "Yes, mistress."

She practised a few strokes to impress her slave and instil a sense of fear in him. The force of her stroke as it sliced through the air was like a gust of wind against his face. It was, indeed, a fearsome object

"I received this as a gift from my travels in the Far East when I was younger. The Crown Prince Taisho gave it to me and taught me how to wield it properly himself."

Lady Sally lowered the stick and offered its end to the brigadier to kiss.

"Now I will deliver a just penance for your snubbing my invitation."

She took up the crouching position again, this time behind the brigadier where his arse still hung invitingly in the air, presenting the perfect target for Lady Sally.

"Kiai!" She screamed. Whack!

The blow was so fierce, the brigadier's eyeballs nearly popped out. It drove right through him and sent waves of pain reverberating through his body. Out of the many beatings he'd taken from Lady Sally, this was one of the hardest strokes he'd ever received.

"Kiai". Whack!

"Argh!" the Brigadier shouted, tears welling up in his eyes.

"Kiai," Lady Sally screamed again, like a Samurai's war-cry. Whack.

"Please Lady Sally," the brigadier pleaded. "Please, that hurts so much, mistress."

She lowered the *shinai*, "Well, of course it does. Mayhap you have forgotten what the punishment is for. Remember, this is a judicial punishment, so there is no safe word and I will not yield to any pleas for mercy. I will deliver exactly the number of strokes I think proper for the offence."

"Yes, mistress," he whimpered.

"Kiai!" Whack. "Kiai!" Whack.

Lady Sally continued. So engrossed was she with her punishment of the brigadier she was oblivious to the two figures who entered the room. It was Victoria, Lady Sally's transvestite lady-in-waiting in a French maid's outfit and, behind her, Captain Wyndham, who had a meeting with Lady Sally to report on the progress of her airship.

They were spectators as Lady Sally rained fearsome stroke upon stroke on the brigadier's exposed derriere. Victoria was used to this. This counted as normal behaviour in the daily routine of Rudston Hall, though even she had to admit it did appear a particularly ferocious beating, even by Lady Sally's high standards.

Victoria shuffled nervously, waiting for the right moment to intervene to let her know the captain had arrived.

Captain Wyndham looked on wide-eyed, and open-mouthed.

Eventually, after countless strokes, Lady Sally paused to catch her breath. Victoria chose this moment to speak.

"Captain Wyndham is here. You asked me to inform you when he was here, madam."

Lady Sally was indignant. "Really, Victoria. You can see I'm in the middle of a thrashing... and you choose to interrupt me now!"

Victoria looked crestfallen. "But madam, you did ask me to bring the captain to you."

Lady Sally was having none of it, "Victoria, you should know by now that the art of serving me is not necessarily to do what I say, but what I don't say!"

"But..." spluttered Victoria.

"And stop shuffling around, Victoria. Do you need a wee or something?"

"No, madam."

"Very well, Victoria. It's nearly tea time, so you may take Captain Wyndham out to the terrace where we will partake of some tea. I should not be much longer now."

"Very good, madam," replied Victoria as he ushered the gob-smacked Captain Wyndham out of the room.

Lady Sally returned to her hapless victim. The brigadier's backside was crossed with red marks and dark bruises. Her punishment had been unrelenting, and his arse was a mess. The pain was excruciating though by now he was in such a daze he was beyond caring.

"The final five strokes, brigadier, then I will have received satisfaction."

"Kiai," she screamed like an enraged dervish as she brought the last five strokes down on his throbbing backside.

The brigadier howled, but was relieved the punishment was finally over.

"Oh, and one more, just for the hell of it." Whack.

The brigadier groaned. That was the hardest corporal punishment he'd ever taken, no small achievement given Lady Sally's justified reputation as a strict English dominatrix.

"There now, brigadier. How do you feel after that?" asked Lady Sally as she unlocked the handcuffs.

The brigadier thought carefully how to respond, "Thank you, mistress. That was a well-deserved thrashing. You excel in the sadistic arts, your ladyship and I submit to your judgement and skill."

"Ha, at last a little contrition from you, brigadier," she sniffed.

Having untied him from the whipping bench, Lady Sally led him across the room where there was an iron cage. She opened the door and beckoned him in.

"I shall have my meeting with the captain and return in due course. You will wait here until I come back, in case I feel like giving you a few more strokes," she said, locking the padlock on the door and dropping the key into her cleavage.

"Yes, thank you, mistress."

3

Victoria hustled a shell-shocked Captain Wyndham out the room.

Lady Sally did nothing to hide the fact she was a strict dominatrix, indeed positively flaunted it, but seeing her in action was an eye-opener for the captain. She was oblivious to their presence, unaware of how long the pair of them stood watching the spectacle. And what an awesome sight it was. There was Lady Sally, her breasts bulging out of the corset, her black hair fanned around her as she swirled the bamboo sword like a vamped-up version of a Samurai warrior. It was the savagery of the beating that shocked the captain though.

"Victoria, I hope you don't mind me asking, but is that normal behaviour?" he enquired.

"Oh yes, that's fairly typical. And that was only a beating to be fair, I've known her be more sadistically wicked."

Captain Wyndham stroked his goatee beard, "More sadistic? Oh really."

The captain was concerned about his commission. Strangely drawn to Lady Sally's powerful, exotic presence, as he gathered most men appeared to be, he didn't consider himself submissive, let alone a masochist.

Victoria, picking up on his hesitance, clarified, "She has plenty of submissive gentlemen who come to her. I'm sure what she wants from you is your skills as an aviator, to be captain of her airship."

"Oh," Wyndham laughed nervously, "that's a relief."

"Though once you get captivated by her, there's no telling where she might take you," she added ominously. "I mean look at me... I used to be an engineer. I installed the steam-powered hydraulic water pumping station at Rudston Hall. I wore overalls all the time and wouldn't have been seen dead in women's clothes. But look at me now." She shrugged, with a bemused but kindly look in her eyes.

"Indeed." The captain was somewhat disturbed by this, but decided not to question Victoria further on the matter.

It had to be said that Lady Sally's maid was immaculately turned out. The threat of punishment was ever-present if her appearance did not meet her mistress's exacting standards, as a poorly presented maid reflected poorly on Lady Sally, which, quite simply, would not do. The captain noted how neatly her blonde wig was brushed and tied back with her maid's cap perched on top of it. Her closely shaven skin was applied with blusher, her eyes with eye-liner and shadow. The transvestite transformation was impressive, but left enough doubt in the viewer's mind to raise the suspicion she was not quite what she seemed.

Victoria led Captain Wyndham through the grand entrance hall with its marbled columns, cast-iron balustrade and teak fittings, past Lady Sally's collection of jade figurines, and onto a paved terrace. This looked across a wide lawn through an avenue of lime trees towards the ornamental lake. It was a spectacular vista.

Victoria invited the captain to take a seat at a cast-iron table with a view overlooking the park.

"I'll arrange for tea to be brought out for you. It's three-thirty. Lady Sally will join you soon. She won't miss afternoon tea... she never misses afternoon tea."

"Thank you, that's most kind of you," Captain Wyndham replied.

Wyndham sat back and waited patiently in the afternoon sun. He was relieved he'd changed out of his working clothes for his visit, anticipating, correctly, that his oil-stained, canvas coat would not be appropriate for the grandeur of Rudston Hall. He wore the light beige, woollen suit with a light blue check pattern and burgundy velvet waistcoat he reserved for special occasions.

He sat there reflecting on the magnificence of the stately home, the broad sweep of formal gardens before him and the park in the distance. His thoughts turned to his unusual employer, the remarkable Lady Sally Rudston-Chichester.

He was pulled from his reflections by Lady Sally's distinctive, crisp tone of voice.

"It's magnificent, isn't it? The fifth Earl of Rudston commissioned Capability Brown to landscape the park."

Captain Wyndham stood up to greet her and gave a little bow. Lady Sally offered her hand to him, and the captain leaned forward to place a delicate kiss on her silk gloves, which she had put back on. She had not changed, appearing still dressed in her scarlet corsetry.

She ceremoniously laid a riding crop on the table and took up a seat opposite him.

At that moment, Victoria arrived, teetering on high-heeled ankle-boots, carrying a silver tray laden with a huge tea pot, scones and patisseries.

Lady Sally waved her hand, "Victoria, would you do the honours please?"

Her maid laid out crockery and poured the tea out into the delicate china cups.

"Lapsang Souchong, from my very own plantation on the foothills of the Wiyi mountains in China," she explained.

"Tea or lemon?" enquired Victoria.

"Lemon, please."

"Sugar?" asked Victoria holding silver sugar tongs with a lump clasped between their claws.

"No thank you," said the captain.

The tea was deliciously refreshing on a warm spring day.

"Victoria. Don't be such a dilatory dolly. Captain Wyndham is my guest. You should offer him a scone. Really!" She explained in an aside to the captain, "she can be so inattentive. She needs a good reprimand to keep her on her toes."

A plain scone with a spoonful of homemade strawberry jam and another of clotted cream was placed on a plate for the captain.

Lady Sally got down to business.

"So, captain, how is work progressing on my airship?"

"Very well madam, the fit-out is nearly complete. She should be ready to launch for the summer season as scheduled."

"And the experiments with the dimethyl aether propulsion, are they successful?"

"Yes, they've been incorporated into the engine's design. There's no doubt your airship will be the fastest in the sky."

"Excellent, and my airship designer, Mr Barnes-Wallis, I trust he's well?"

"Yes your ladyship. He's so young though, but a brilliant technician and designer. He bamboozles me with his technical knowledge of airship construction. He's quite a genius."

"Yes I know, Wyndham. I have an intuition about people. He has a first class honours degree in engineering and did his PhD on geodetic design. He was an exceptional student who came highly recommended. That young man will do exceedingly well. He will go on to great things, I'm sure–dam busting things, I dare say," she laughed.

Captain Wyndham proceeded to explain in more detail how work on the airship was progressing.

"We shall be ready for a test flight in May and, provided that goes without any hitches, your ladyship will be able to set off on her adventures in late June."

"That's excellent, captain. I'm so excited, I can hardly wait. I shall attend her official launch of course. And there's such a lot of packing to do. Well, that is to say, Victoria has a lot of packing to do for me. You will love it won't you my maid?"

"Oh yes," she concurred. "Will madam be taking all her corsets with her?"

"Well, of course, Victoria. One can never have too many corsets. If I don't take them all, then the very one I have a fancy for might not be there."

There was one matter that intrigued Captain Wyndham, and he plucked up the courage to raise a somewhat delicate matter.

"Excuse my asking Lady Sally, but the expense of your airship must be enormous, yet you are a young woman. How can you finance such an extravagant project?"

"No, I don't mind you asking in the slightest, captain. I came into my inheritance when I was only eighteen and I've accumulated many business interests over the last decade. As to the costs of my airship project, it's very simple. I own a brass mine in Zanzibar and I dedicate the profits from this venture, which are considerable, to the building of my airship. As I'm sure you'll know the demand for brass has gone through the roof in recent years."

"A brass mine? But surely..."

"Dare you question me, captain?" Lady Sally intervened, her eyes flashing with indignation.

"Well, no Lady Sally, it's just that surely a brass mine..."

"...must be a most singular and unusual object. Indeed, it is, captain!"

Captain Wyndham decided against entering into a discussion on metallurgy and the nature of alloys with the formidable Lady Sally.

He smiled politely, "Oh yes Lady Sally, indeed it must be."

"Come captain, you must sample a patisserie. I understand from cook they are passion fruit eclairs."

The captain examined the plate, and the cakes did look delicious. They were long and plump with light-brown, flesh coloured, choux pastry, covered in a similar coloured icing. Lady Sally put one on his plate and took one for herself.

Lady Sally attacked the patisserie with relish. Her pearly-white teeth bit into the soft pastry so firmly the cream oozed out the other end. There was cream over her red lips too, which she licked off sensuously. Captain Wyndham was transfixed as he watched Lady Sally roll her tongue around her lips before taking another bite. Realising he was staring, he turned attention to his own éclair.

As he bit into it, cream squeezed out of the pastry over his fingers. They were, indeed, exceedingly good cakes. The combination of sweet choux pastry, tangy fruit icing, and rich cream was perfect.

"I simply love messy food," remarked Lady Sally before sliding a finger between her lips to lick cream off. "I wanted to bathe in whipped cream

17

once but cook said there wasn't enough cream in the dairy to cover my breasts, which I think rather impertinent of her, don't you think?"

"Yes, Lady Sally," mumbled the captain through a mouth full of éclair.

"Well, I must say cook has surpassed herself today. Those eclairs are delicious. You must pass my compliments on to her, Victoria."

Her maid looked askance, "Is that wise, madam? After all, you don't want her getting too full of herself..."

"...she's too full of herself as it is. Yes, I know. Perhaps you are right... on this occasion."

Lady Sally finished off by dabbing her lips with an Irish, damask napkin, which, as she explained to the captain, made for the highest quality table-linen. She continued with her business.

"Now, you must come to my workshop. There's something I need to show you that is most pertinent to my adventure, indeed to your role as my airship pilot. It is the main reason for our meeting."

They strolled along a gravel driveway, Victoria holding a parasol over Lady Sally to shield her alabaster skin from the glare of the sun. They came to a series of single-storey, brick outbuildings.

"These are my workshops," Lady Sally announced.

On entering, Captain Wyndham looked around; everywhere the benches were strewn with sprockets, circuits, conduits, brass dials, copper pipes, cogs, gears and pistons. The walls were covered with the tools for working them.

Drawing the captain to one side so her maid didn't hear, Lady Sally explained what went on here, "This workshop is where my artificers and arcane engineers have been building dastardly devices to take on my adventures."

"Dastardly devices?" queried Wyndham.

"Oh, don't be so naïve captain. Toys for me to play with."

"You mean, like dolls?"

"Oh really, captain... sex-toys! Though, in a manner of speaking you are not so far from the mark. These are of a clockwork, electrical or steam-powered variety, built by my team of engineers to my own design, naturally. After all, I have a natural flair and expertise both in sexual arousal and corrective punishments.

"See those two crates over there," she said pointing to the corner, "they contain the objects I want to take with me. Take them back with you today. I will arrange for you to use my charabanc to convey them to the airship station.

"But hide them and, on no account, tell my maid. Victoria is so nosy, she'll go snooping around opening them. I want them to be a surprise. And besides, she'll get over-excited if she sees what I'm taking... and that's not good for her."

Captain Wyndham gulped. Crates of mechanical sex toys; he wondered what sort of venture he was letting himself in for.

"Of course, Lady Sally. I won't say a thing."

"But this isn't what I've come to show you. Come and take a look at this," she said, beckoning Victoria to join them. "You will both find this interesting, though for differing reasons, I expect."

Lady Sally led them over to a crate, about the same height as her, standing upright against the wall. She pulled open its front to reveal a brass figure. She was a thing of beauty, expertly moulded in shiny brass. The detail in the figure was exacting. The curve of her breasts with the circle of their areola was just perfect. In the place where her nipples should be, there were two red bulbs. Her brass features had a wistful expression which managed to appear both robotically detached yet sensual at the same time.

"This is Clarissa."

"Blimey," gasped Victoria. "She's wonderful, madam. Is she a plaything?"

"No, she's not, so don't get excited, Victoria."

"No," exclaimed Captain Wyndham. "This is an automaton."

"Not just any automaton, an automaton pilot. Open her up, captain."

He released the panel in her abdomen from its catches. It swung open to uncover an array of dials. The captain stroked his goatee bear as he examined them closely. There was a compass, an altimeter, a statoscope, chronometer, a speedometer, the devices necessary for measuring distance, speed and direction. He gasped. This was the latest in airship technology.

"Do you see her nipples," said Lady Sally, pointing to the red bulbs. "They will light up in an emergency. A little touch of my own I found rather amusing. I have to confess, even my workshops do not possess the skills for such sophisticated technology. Clarissa was made in Germany, as you will discover, because the factory where she was manufactured will be our first port of call."

"She's amazing," said Captain Wyndham.

"She's so sexy," exclaimed Victoria, reaching out her hand to run it across Clarissa's shiny, brass tits, so perfectly formed and realistic looking.

Lady Sally rolled her eyes, "Oh really, Victoria, do control yourself."

"Can I dress her, madam? Please let me dress her. I can find her a wig and something nice from madam's wardrobe to put her in."

"Oh, if you must Victoria. If it will amuse you, but you must keep the control panel accessible, so no corsetry I'm afraid."

She turned to Captain Wyndham.

"You must take her back to the airship station, captain, and install her in the cockpit. I have an instruction manual for you, which has been translated into English." There was a twinkle in her eye, "Of course, this will mean you need not be confined to the control room for the whole voyage, captain. During normal operation Clarissa will be able to do the routine flying, leaving you free for other things…"

Lady Sally left the last sentence hanging ominously in the air.

"So, captain, until the day of the launch. It will be a wonderful occasion. I had better return to my slave now. It's tiresome, I know, but I suppose I ought to release him from the cage I confined him to, and let him get on his way."

"Thank you, Lady Sally. Like you, I can't wait to see your airship in flight. It's been a remarkable afternoon, your ladyship… in more ways than one."

"Adieu captain. We will meet again soon."

4

It was a momentous day in this sleepy, rural backwater of Yorkshire. The enormous zinc-plated shed erected many months ago, and the mysterious comings and goings beyond the perimeter fence had aroused the curiosity of the locals. Few local people were engaged in the construction of Lady Sally's airship, and those who were had been sworn to secrecy. The steady flow of deliveries and visits from a succession of tweed-suited scientists, designers and engineers had caused much speculation. The local labourers believed it was a giant wheat harvesting machine that would put them out of work. Others believed it was a secret weapon for the war threatening to break out across Europe.

There was no hiding something special was to be revealed on this day. Lady Sally had engaged every shire horse from farms for miles around. Word spread like wild-fire that the giant shed doors would open to expose the unknown contraption. Work on nearby farms stopped for the day. Everybody dressed up in their finest Sunday clothes, the men in their best suits and ladies in dresses and bonnets. They brought picnics with them; huge baskets laden with freshly baked bread, butter churned that morning, chunks of cheese and the finest cuts of ham. The men brought barrels of the strongest ale and their pewter tankards. There were no children in school as every child from far and wide appeared. The event topped every fair, wake and celebration held in the area for decades. The huge throngs sat outside the perimeter fence enjoying themselves, eagerly anticipating what might be revealed when the doors of the giant shed finally opened.

There was great excitement when Lady Sally arrived. She came in a chauffeur driven charabanc laden with trunks and hat boxes, accompanied by her strange transvestite maid. The midday sun reflected off the vehicle's olive-green paintwork and polished chrome, dazzling all who followed its passage through the gate of the airship works. The side of the charabanc was decorated with Lady Sally's coat-of-arms, a purple and black shield with the letters 'L', 'S', 'R' and 'C' in its quarters surmounted by two crossed whips.

Captain Wyndham waited at the road-side to greet Lady Sally with Barnes-Wallis, the chief designer of the airship. Victoria opened the door for her and she alighted from the charabanc. She looked elegant and summery in a fine cream cotton-linen dress and magnificent wide-brimmed hat tied under her chin in an extravagant bow. The farm workers strained to catch a glimpse of Lady Sally, whose reputation had spread before her; and they were not disappointed. Her perfect hour-glass figure enhanced by the tightest of corsets was striking, even from the distance of the perimeter fence.

Despite wearing stiletto heels in cream calf-skin she glided effortlessly towards Captain Wyndham and stretched out her hand towards him.

"It's good to see you again captain, you may kiss my hand."

Wyndham leant over to take Lady Sally's hand into his and offered a gentle kiss. He was no longer surprised by her flamboyant behaviour. Her hand was also offered to Barnes-Wallis, who was more embarrassed at kissing Lady Sally's hand but who nonetheless did not hesitate in deferring to her wishes.

"I am thrilled. It's wonderful to see my project come to its fruition. I take it everything is ready for the maiden flight of my airship."

"Yes, Lady Sally," replied Wyndham, "she's ready. She's a magnificent machine; I'm convinced your ladyship will be impressed by her."

"I don't doubt that, captain, after all the interior fittings have been made to my exacting specification and design."

"I see you've brought your luggage, madam," said Wyndham, gesturing towards the charabanc laden with trunks.

"Oh, but that is merely one or two trifles, my corsetry and some of my antique whips and canes. I have engaged the services of several horse and carts for the remainder of my wardrobe, and the heavier bondage and domination equipment is already installed. My maid has spent several weeks packing for my escapade, haven't you Victoria?"

"Oh, yes madam, I certainly have!"

"Come Victoria, don't pretend it hasn't been anything but a labour of love for your mistress."

Victoria's wistful look conveyed that it had indeed been just that.

"Follow me Lady Sally," said Wyndham, leading the way. "Barnes-Wallis is going to give you a tour of the airship and explain the technique of its construction. It uses many unique materials and design features, but he's the expert on that."

As they entered the shed Lady Sally gasped. She had a vision of how her dirigible might look, of course, but her breath was taken away by the sheer scale and magnificence of her creation. The airship was the size of an ocean liner and dwarfed the diminutive figures as they stood on the ground gazing up in awe at the vast expanse of linen fabric enclosing the gas bags and duralumin frame. Barnes-Wallis led them onto the walkways from which they could view the intricate internal structure.

Now in his element, the normally diffident Barnes-Wallis began his enthusiastic explication of the construction of the airship.

"Each transverse frame consists of a hard girder in the form of a stiff, sixteen-sided polygon with the flats at top and bottom; this massive hard girder is twenty-seven inches deep and up to a hundred and thirty feet in diameter. Sixteen steel cables penetrate the centre of the polygon to the corner points, bracing the polygonal girder against deflections and making it erect…"

"…And, of course, erect girders are essential to the structure, are they not?"

"…One half of the transverse frame is divided by a vertical plane passing though the axis of the ship, consisting of a stiff arched rib with oiled ends that are free to slip towards each other, and this arched rib is braced by eight radial wires, which go flaccid through the deflection of the arched rib under the applied loads. Normally four or five wires remain in tension…"

"And how have you calculated the torsional load bearing capacity of my airship?"

"The forces and bending movements in the members are calculated by the solution of a lengthy simultaneous equation containing up to seven unknown quantities. In the solution, we had to find the correct compression force for the radial wires to achieve the required load bearing. This geodetic type of construction for the airframe makes use of a space frame formed from a spirally crossing basket-weave of load bearing erect members. The principle is that two geodesic arcs can be drawn to intersect on a curving surface in a manner that the torsional load on each, cancels out the other…"

"…Well that is simply amazing," commented Lady Sally, "but perhaps I ought to take a look at the living quarters now…"

"…but I'd love to show you my calculations, your ladyship…" called Barnes-Wallis waving a wad of foolscap sheets with closely pencilled figures at the three receding figures.

"Oh, fascinating I'm sure," she called back, "but I've such a busy day ahead of me and I ought to be moving on."

Captain Wyndham smiled as Victoria bustled Lady Sally away.

"He's a genius you know. From my knowledge of aeronautical design, I know the construction of this airship is truly remarkable."

"Indeed, I chose him for his brilliance in structural engineering, captain, though I must confess the 'how' is not always my strong point. I merely tell people what I want and they do it for me… isn't that so Victoria?"

"Oh yes, madam, indubitably, yes."

Captain Wyndham continued the tour by taking Lady Sally to her personal quarters and dressing room. They walked through her sitting room lined with teak panelling and brass fittings with a solid oak writing desk in the corner and opened a set of doors.

"This is your dressing room, Lady Sally…" Wyndham gestured with his hand into the room.

"Oh really, I thought it was the ballroom," muttered her maid.

"Very droll, Victoria. For that piece of impertinence, I expect you to have my trunks unpacked and my clothes put away whilst we are on the test flight."

Wyndham couldn't help but wonder whether that was what Victoria wanted.

Lady Sally cast her eyes across the expanse of teak doors and took one of the shiny brass handles in the shape of a unicorn's head into her hand and opened one to look inside.

"Besides, you know the extent of my wardrobe. It would never do to be unprepared. We are venturing to far-flung corners of the continent, and one can never predict what one might need."

"Of course, madam," Victoria concurred.

The briefest of tours of the airship having been completed Lady Sally was led to the door of the vast shed from which the dirigible would emerge for its official launch. The assembled crowds around the perimeter fence looked on in eager anticipation of the hanger finally revealing its secret.

The doors parted and, pushed by the bulbous tip of the airship, gradually opened as the head of the ship became slowly unsheathed. The crowd expelled a collective gasp. Connected by wires to the bridles of scores of shire horses the airship was pulled out of the manufacturing shed to the nearby mooring tower.

Revealed in all its magnificent glory, the airship was a wonder to behold. Its length was massive, its girth huge. Its surface was covered with lines of ribs formed by the duralumin framework of the ship. It stood firm and erect on the field, globules of black, engine oil hung from its bulbous tip, glistening in the May sun before dripping onto the ground.

It was an object of beauty. Its linen outer cover was painted silver and was lined by wires around the circumference to prevent the material from blowing off.

Written proudly along the length of the airship was her name, *The Corseted Domme*.

The crowd watching from the perimeter fence looked on in amazement. Nothing like it had been seen before. The rumour spread that this contraption was intended to be a flying machine. Wise old codgers nodded sagely muttering that such a thing would never get off the ground. A group from the local Primitive Methodist Chapel exclaimed it was an abomination and a challenge to God, saying that man was never meant to fly and this would end in disaster.

The children had no such reservations. They loved it. They believed it would fly, and Lady Sally's flying machine, a game in which children ran around with airship shaped objects, became a popular playground pastime in local schools for many years. They would never forget the momentous event they were witnessing. For decades, even after they had become parents or grandparents themselves, they would still tell the tale of when Lady Sally's giant flying machine was launched. On that one day Lady Sally's name became written into local legend, never to be forgotten.

The name of the airship created confusion. Ignorant of Lady Sally's sexual predilections they did not know what to make of it.

"Corseted Dome? And a' thought 'er ladyship'd know 'ow to spell now wouldn't thee? Eeeh, even I know 'Dome' is spelt wi' one 'm' and, 'ow can a dome have a corset?"

"Eeh, I dunno, Jack, it's fair flummoxed me," replied his friend, who was somewhat worse for wear, having drunk a gallon of strong ale.

The moment finally arrived when the airship took to the air for the first time. Lady Sally and her maid Victoria stayed on the ground for the launch ceremony while Captain Wyndham took his place in the control car with Clarissa, his automaton co-pilot, and crew. The airship was going on a test flight on a circuit of several miles around the villages then flying along the estuary of the River Humber to the North Sea before turning back.

Lady Sally's voice boomed out across the air field.

"Today is a momentous day. Today is a day you will remember for the rest of your lives. Today the age of airships reaches the zenith of its achievement. Today you are witness to the largest and most magnificent flying machine ever to take to the skies. May the Goddess bless her, and all who sail in her."

With that, Lady Sally Rudston-Chichester smashed a champagne bottle against the side of the passenger coach. The crowd waited expectantly. The power cars fired up, the engines hummed, and the propellers whirred. The wires were released from the mooring tower and docking station and the massive dirigible took off from the ground. Some ran away in fright believing the devil himself had been unleashed, others gasped in amazement. The children leapt up and down in sheer delight. Gradually a ground swell of astonishment and approval rose up amongst the farmers and their families as they stood and gave an almighty cheer, throwing their hats up into the air as the airship soared up to several hundred feet.

Lady Sally Rudston-Chichester was right. They had just witnessed one of the wonders of the age.

5

After her official launch, Captain Wyndham took *The Corseted Domme* on a few more test flights so the crew of riggers and engineers gained experience of handling her before embarking on Lady Sally's more ambitious travels. She was a dream to fly. The captain expected such a vast airship to be unwieldy, but she was a dream; her sleek, bullet-like, frame slid through the sky like it was lubricated, penetrating the puffy folds of cloud with ease.

The airship was loaded with all the necessary supplies for Lady Sally's travels. The kitchens were crammed with fresh vegetables, fruit and herbs from Rudston Hall's kitchen garden, fresh meat from the farm, exotic spices from the east and such jars, packets and tins as required. Cook supervised this though not without grumbling about how she was expected to maintain her high culinary standards whilst floating in the sky.

Lady Sally's vast wardrobe was unpacked though the two mysterious crates with her dastardly devices were secreted in her private quarters for when she decided to produce them. Her 'play area' was ready, and fitted out with all manner of strange equipment.

The day for Lady Sally to set off on her adventure soon arrived. She, along with her maid and her invited guests, and Captain Wyndham and his crew, boarded the airship.

The living quarters were situated in the gondola attached to the bottom of the fuselage. The quarters for the crew and Lady Sally's gentlemen friends were modest but perfectly commodious. However, her own suite of rooms and the 'public' areas, consisting of a dining room, sitting room, study and, most importantly, the dungeon and playroom, were appointed in a manner as luxurious as a *White Star Line* ocean liner. The doors and wood panelling were in teak with brass fittings, and there were cut glass chandeliers powered with electricity generated by the engines. Lady Sally boasted that *The Corseted Domme* was the largest airship ever to take to the skies, and that was unquestionably true, not that anybody dare dispute it with her.

The captain took up his place in the cockpit at the front of the gondola, alongside Clarissa, the automaton co-pilot. Victoria had dressed her in an auburn wig (which complemented the golden hues of the brass well), a peaked cap, a military style jacket with epaulettes, a short, pleated skirt (which would never be seemly in decent society) and laced ankle-boots. It was a task she got far too much pleasure from, having been reprimanded constantly by Lady Sally for fondling the brass automaton with such relish she got a hard-on. The panel in the automaton's abdomen was open, and numerous copper wires were connected from there to the control desk. Captain Wyndham felt strange at having such an unusual co-pilot, but during the test flights Clarissa proved herself to be a highly effective assistant.

There was a steering wheel in front of them, similar to one on a ship which controlled the rudders, and a tiller to adjust the elevators. The presence of the captain was essential for complex manoeuvres such as taking off and landing. Although an amazing feat of engineering, the automaton wasn't capable of flying the airship solo. But, once they were in flight, Clarissa could be loaded with the co-ordinates of latitude and longitude for their destination and plot the airship's course.

The captain considered it a marvel that a device could plot a route merely by entering a few numbers! The pace of technology in this new age never ceased to amaze him.

The control cabin was full of shelves stuffed with charts and maps containing detail that Clarissa was unable to interpret. Thus, finding mooring masts and safe landing places was the captain's role, and he still needed to rely on charts and visual inspection.

Lady Sally had a list of relatives she wanted to 'drop in on' in various empires across the continent and told him to get charts for most of Europe… and Russia. Captain Wyndham pointed out that they needed to plan stops at decent airship stations to re-inflate the hydrogen bags. She dismissed the problem with a wave of her hand.

"Oh, don't be such a fuss-pot, captain. I'm sure I can rely on you to find a bit of hydrogen along the way. Besides, I might pop over to India to inspect one of my tea plantations and, whilst over that way, I could drop in on my Malaysian rubber plantation," she teased.

Whilst Captain Wyndham remained in the control room to prepare for take-off, Lady Sally set off for her private quarters with her maid to grapple with the important matter of what to wear.

"It's so hard to choose, Victoria. I do so want to make a striking impression on the first day of my travels."

"Well, there's no lack of choice," muttered her maid

They both stood surveying the rows and rows of wardrobes containing wear for any season or climate, corsetry, fetish wear, hats and bonnets, boots and shoes, in a myriad of styles, materials and colours.

"Well, one must be prepared, Victoria. One never knows where one might end up, or what the weather might be. After all, we are going to far-flung places so I must have the full range of my wardrobe to cover every eventuality."

"There is your favourite purple and black, silk corset, madam, in the colours of the family coat-of-arms."

"Yes indeed, but I suspect my submissive gentlemen will be expecting a corset, and I want to shock them. The idea of purple appeals, but I prefer to opt for a rubber suit as I don't believe any of my guests have seen me in the rubber yet."

Lady Sally had been instrumental in developing latex material. She owned a rubber plantation in the hills outside Taiping in Malaysia, and her manufactory there had spent years perfecting the production of a thin rubber material, which could be cut into tight-fitting clothing. There were rolls and rolls of it in the workshop at Rudston Hall where her personal couturiers, skilled at working the new-fangled substance, designed outfits for Lady Sally.

Victoria was thrilled. She felt the swelling in her cock at the mere expectation of handling the wonderfully shiny, rubbery material, let alone helping her mistress into the outfit. This was a work of art as the one-piece latex suit Lady Sally chose covered her whole body and was remarkably tight-fitting. It required the maid to pull the rubber over her mistress's naked body for her to wriggle into it. Victoria approved of mistress's choice of outfit.

Whilst Lady Sally was squeezing herself into the purple latex, Captain Wyndham was giving the final orders for take-off.

The riggers had checked the gas bags in the bowels of the airship were fully inflated, and they were now in a position to set off. One team was at the slit in the tip of the airship to release the line securing it to the mooring mast, whilst another was on the ground, preparing to release the guy lines tied around the bulbous, erect frame holding the giant dirigible in place.

The engines started up with a roar. The propellers began to whirr. Captain Wyndham gave the orders to the team of riggers to free the cables. *The Corseted Domme* slowly reversed away from the mooring tower before swinging around and lifting up into the sky.

The airship rose into the air. They were heading for the Rhur, the industrial heartland of the Prussian Empire. This was Lady Sally's first destination, where she needed to pick something up for the journey. *The Corseted Domme* had a cruising speed of 80 mph, but could reach a top speed of 120 mph, incredibly fast for any airship, let alone one of her size.

But the first stage of the journey was a leisurely flight across the country at low altitude so the people of England could look up and admire Lady Sally's gigantic, beautiful dirigible.

The captain was delighted; it had been a perfect take-off. *The Corseted Domme* was on her way.

6

Lady Sally was ready to make her appearance. She squeezed into the rubber outfit, complementing it with a pair of shiny, black stiletto shoes with narrow, pointy tips. She looked and felt fabulous. There was something empowering about the touch of tight rubber clinging to her skin.

Her guests were waiting for her in the lounge, having been served tumblers of twenty-year-old matured Scottish whisky from Lady Sally's distillery on the Isle of Islay. Having never met before, they were chatting amongst one another nervously, both because of their lack of familiarity but also in anticipation of Lady's Sally's entrance, knowing they must soon submit themselves to whatever her wicked imagination might subject them to.

There were four invited guests, a duke, a bishop, a judge and a banker, carefully selected by Lady Sally from the many aristocratic or powerful personages who availed themselves of her very particular services. They were regular submissive gentlemen of hers, and had paid handsomely, either in money or special services, for the privilege. It was a once in a lifetime chance for submission to the premier dominatrix of the age whilst floating several thousand feet in the air on a dirigible. It was an opportunity that did not occur often, indeed not at all.

The teak doors pulled open, and Lady Sally showed herself. There was a collective gasp from the gentlemen. She looked stunning.

The purple latex clung to her skin, accentuating every voluptuous curve of her body. Her breasts had been squeezed into the tight rubber, making them firm and rounded, whilst her nipples stood out proud like little buds. Her sleek, black hair cascaded around her shoulders and looked striking against the purple rubber. Her blue eyes, heavily made-up with black kohl, threw a piercing gaze across at them.

They stood up to greet her, complimenting her effusively on her remarkable attire and distinctive look. They could not take their eyes off her.

Lady Sally smiled. It was remarkable how men dissolved into submission at the sight of her in rubber... at the sight of her in anything, really.

"Victoria, you must go to the cockpit and invite Captain Wyndham to join us. Now we are cruising, he should be free to leave Clarissa to pilot.

Tell him that, as my airship pilot, it's fitting he should be acquainted with my guests."

Her maid scurried away to fetch the captain.

"Welcome to *The Corseted Domme,* gentlemen. I promise you an amazing expedition on the most magnificent flying machine of the age."

"With the most remarkable woman of the age too. You look fabulous, my dear," praised the man in a purple cassock and dog collar.

"Absolutely stunning, milady!" exclaimed another.

"You have excelled yourself, mistress."

"It's an incredible outfit, mistress. What is it made of?"

"I've informed you of my business ventures in the far east," she scolded. "Well, this is the material the *Rudston-Chichester Incorporated Rubber Company* produces at my Malaysian plantation. It's rather wonderful, don't you think?"

"It's incredibly sexy, mistress," the duke interrupted.

Lady Sally returned the compliment with a hard stare, and savage words, "I will not be insulted by such impertinences, slave. And look at that bulge in your trousers. I'll soon punish that out of you."

The humiliated gentleman was rescued by the arrival of Captain Wyndham, who looked anxious. He was an aviator and engineer and felt uncomfortable amongst Lady Sally's aristocratic circle of friends. He felt out of place amongst such finely dressed gentlemen in white jumper, flying trousers and boots, though he didn't sense Lady Sally was bothered.

"This is my airship pilot, Captain Wyndham. His skill in flying, and the technical wizardry of my design team, are what have made this day possible."

Captain Wyndham flushed with pride at the acknowledgment given by Lady Sally.

She introduced her guests to the captain.

There was the Bishop of Wetwang. Wetwang being a Peculier jurisdiction within the Province of York, which allowed the part of Yorkshire where Rudston Hall was situated to have its own bishopric. Naturally, on his institution, one of the Bishop's first calls was to the principal landowner and richest inhabitant within his jurisdiction. Needless to say, he soon succumbed to Lady Sally's charms. The fact she declared herself not to be a Christian but a follower of Paganism, a faith that believes in the divine feminine and the Goddess (which Lady Sally considered all men ought to adhere to), did not prevent him making regular visits to Rudston Hall under the pretence of trying to convert her.

There was Mr S T Medlicott, manager of the British operation of the Shanghai, Hitachi, Ipowima and Tokyo Bank. This bank managed Lady

Sally's portfolio of multifarious investments across the world, from her brass mine in Zanzibar to her chain of bars and brothels in the wild west; from her many tea plantations in India and China to her silk emporium in Samarkand. Lady Sally had business interests across the whole world. Obviously, on being introduced to her wealthy client, it was not long before Mr Medlicott was serving Lady Sally's desires in other respects.

Of course, Lady Sally considered it most propitious in pursuing her interests to have contacts with the legal profession. Mr T W Staple Firth was a judge in the High Court. It was mainly through Lady Sally's influence he attained such a position. He had acted as her barrister over several years. It was terribly tiresome for her, but she did have a habit of getting entangled in slander cases as she was rather outspoken. On occasions things got out of hand, so it was useful to have a barrister on hand to protect her reputation.

Finally, there was the Duke of Westminster, who was fourth in line to the throne of England no less. She was related to the duke through the Chichester line of the family. These were the circles Lady Sally mixed in. The duke was so rich he didn't need to work, so he kept himself gainfully occupied by indulging his taste for all manner of perversions. Indeed, there was a rumour that, whilst at Brasenose College, Oxford, as a member of an infamous dining club, he had put his cock in a dead pig's mouth and fucked the poor beast, neatly combining bestiality with necrophilia in one fell swoop. Her reputation as a strict mistress having spread before her, it was the duke who approached Lady Sally with an ardent desire to experience such debaucheries as she could offer. He was younger than the other men and, it has to be said, Lady Sally found him quite 'hot'.

If she allowed any of her submissive gentlemen to fuck her, it would be him; after all, satisfying her own sexual desires was part of the expedition. It would least likely be the bishop because of his declared commitment to celibacy though Lady Sally had never quite understood how his faith permitted him to indulge in flagellation and buggery.

They were a strange group defined by the variety of body shapes and assortment of facial hair they possessed. The bishop was tall, thin and angular with a freckled balding head. The banker had a ruddy, round face with ginger whiskers, and was exceedingly fat. The judge was of medium build with a serious expression, bushy black eyebrows and a long beard. The duke was the youngest of the group and had a well-toned body, smooth skin and a pencil thin moustache, giving him an effeminate look.

Lady Sally was disappointed the brigadier could not join her as a military man would have fitted her vision of gathering the most powerful men from all walks of life rather well. It amused her to have these leading representatives of church, business, law and aristocracy submit to her every whim. The more powerful the better. She would have liked a Member of Parliament and newspaper proprietor too, but there was a limit to the number of submissive gentlemen one could deal with, even for her. There was a reason this combination worked well though as she would explain to them in due course.

Having made the necessary introductions, Lady Sally was getting frustrated. She was itching to put *The Corseted Domme* to the uses she had been designed for, desperate to fulfil her vision of becoming *Mistress of the Air*.

"Enough of this idle chatter." Lady Sally ordered, the level of her voice raising to one of imperious command, "You have come here to serve to your mistress. I will take you on a journey, not only to far-flung and exotic places, but into submission. You have offered to give yourselves up to me, and there will be no respite in your servitude to your mistress.

"I will turn *The Corseted Domme* into a world of domination, flagellation and sadism worthy of the *120 Days of Sodom*. For was not that orchestrated by a duke, a bishop, a judge and a banker, but in Lady Sally Rudston-Chichester's world, it's you who will be subject to me. You will now remove your clothing; hand it to my maid, Victoria. It will be returned when I have completed my travels. Leave the worlds of power, wealth, law and religion behind, and enter into my domain of submission."

At Lady Sally's strident tone, the four gentlemen jumped into action. They proceeded to strip off, knowing their mistress well, and realising it would not be wise to procrastinate in complying with her command.

Captain Wyndham looked on bemused, hoping the order could not apply to him, after all he was needed to pilot the airship. He had to admit, he had been drawn into Lady Sally's world, and was fascinated by her; *but to strip off and submit yourself to dastardly beatings?*

When they were naked, Victoria put studded, leather collars around their necks, and attached leads to them for Lady Sally to hold. She ordered them to get down on all fours and led them crawling, like her pets, into *The Corseted Domme's* playroom.

Lady Sally gestured for the captain to follow, "You must see my dungeon in action. You will find it interesting."

The dungeon playroom was a huge space taking up the whole of the rear end of the gondola. It was designed to be spectacular. One end of the room, from floor to ceiling, was taken up with a display window, which opened out to the sky, and there were large portholes along the sides. There were blinds to plunge the room into darkness and create a gloomy atmosphere, but now the light shone through the glazing to flood the space with light.

It was fitted out with all manner of heavy equipment: bondage chairs, whipping benches, bondage wall, rack and cages. Much of it was made from mahogany with brass fittings and, where required, fitted with padded leather in purple and black, the Rudston-Chichester family colours. Facing the equipment, with its back to the viewing window, was her throne, an ornately carved mahogany chair upholstered in tapestry with the family coat-of-arms embroidered on it.

Her favourite implements of punishment hung from brass hooks and fittings lining the side of the airship. There was an array of tools for sadistic flagellation available: canes, whips, riding crops, floggers and straps in a range of materials and sizes, each one capable of administering its unique quality of beating.

Lady Sally grasped the leads in her latex gloves, and led the men over to the window on all fours, the rubber suit creaking and squeaking as she strode forward. She stood there, a vision in purple with four men at her heels, gazing out. They were at about 2,000 feet and, from Captain Wyndham's position behind them, it truly looked as though Lady Sally was standing in the clouds.

"Now let's administer some punishment," she spat.

7

Lady Sally got down to business. She soon had the bishop and duke strapped onto the whipping benches, the banker secured face forward against the bondage wall and the judge tied face down on the rack. There would be time for more tantalising play, and to try the devices engineered in her workshop, but now she itched to inflict serious punishment on her men. She also wanted to set a marker for her guests of what was in store for them during her travels.

She selected a range of different implements and laid them out on a table in the order she intended to use them. Her maid, festooned, as ever, in layers of petticoats and her French maid's dress, was on hand to pass the next implement.

She started with her bare hand to warm them up, besides there was nothing like getting a feel for the arse of a submissive than testing their reaction to a slap from bare flesh. She removed the elbow length rubber gloves from her fingers, delivering hard strokes with the palm of her hand. There was nothing quite like the sound of a slap on a bare arse. That contact of flesh upon flesh never ceased to provide Lady Sally with a feeling of dominance, not to mention a tingle of erotic pleasure.

The men were arranged so they could see the punishment being meted out to the others, a nice twist, which Lady Sally felt would enhance their sense of anticipation. She decided to start with the flabbiest arse, which belonged to the banker (stuffing himself at too many business lunches no doubt) and work her way up to the tightest, the duke's, which was firm and muscular.

After ten strokes delivered to each of the men with her bare palm, Lady Sally put her gloves back on, ensuring her fingers were stretched firmly into the tight latex. She reached out for Victoria to pass the first of her chosen tools of punishment. This was the wooden paddle. She gave the banker several hard whacks with this. It amused her to see his fat arse wobbling like a jelly. He took his punishment well though, probably because he had so much flesh to protect the nerves. Never mind, she would find a suitable implement to make him squeal. It was the judge who groaned with pain the most. Ironic, really, given how many sentences of corporal punishment he must have handed-out.

Following the paddle was her favourite leather-thonged whip. Lady Sally was warmed up now. Raising the implement high above her head she whipped it down on their backsides in a succession of fast strokes, her black hair flailing with the movement of the leather thongs. She was an expert at wielding the whip, twirling it around and striking with strokes varying in pace and strength to exert the utmost torment. The groans from the four men built up into squeals of pain as the whip cut into their backsides. After countless strokes, Lady Sally was panting with the exertion.

"A-hem," Captain Wyndham, still in the dungeon, and fidgeting uncomfortably at the sight of the punishments, tried to attract Lady Sally's attention.

She looked up, flushed and breathless.

"What is it captain?" she demanded, annoyed at being interrupted.

Wyndham shuffled nervously, not wanting to upset her, "I'm sorry, your ladyship, but you'd expressed the wish to fly low over London. We need to be descending soon, and Clarissa won't be able to negotiate the airship traffic around London, so may I have permission to return to the cockpit, please?"

"Yes, by all means. I want to fly as low over London as possible. I want the whole metropolis to look up in admiration at the *Corseted Domme*. And go slowly so people can truly appreciate her."

"We have to in any case Lady Sally. There are strict speed limits because there's so much traffic. I promise you, madam, your dirigible will amaze the whole of London."

"Excellent, captain. Send message to me when we are on the outskirts. I may be so absorbed in whippings and beatings I forget to notice, and I don't want to miss it."

"Very well, Lady Sally," the captain assured, relieved to be able to return to the safety of the control cabin.

Lady Sally turned her attention back to the four arses thrust out and offering such agreeable targets for her. They were glowing red now. The spiky pain of the whip had spread, penetrating every nerve in their bodies.

Victoria passed Lady Sally the next implement.

"Ah yes," she exclaimed. "This one has been moulded in the manufactory at my rubber plantation."

She handled the tool admiringly. It was, as she called it, her 'hedgehog'. The flogger was flat on one side, but had rubber protrusions on the other, making it capable of delivering two different styles of impact.

Lady Sally started to mix things up. This time she started with the bishop. She alternated three strokes of the flat side with three of the spiky side. One delivered a delicious slapping noise whilst the other was silent, but more deadly. The bishop let out a loud yelp at the first strike of the spiky 'hedgehog'. It delivered a sharp pain that penetrated right through the flesh. The other three men looked on in trepidation at his reaction to the object.

Lady Sally was satisfied with the results. She inspected the bishop's arse and admired the little indentations the rubber spikes created. In fact, she was so pleased, she gave him another three strokes with the hedgehog side, then proceeded to repeat the treatment on the other three.

Next was the cane. Lady Sally selected a nice bendy one. She held it between her rubber-gloved hands and flexed it, testing the tension in the birch. She swished it through the air, a sound she loved to hear.

She set upon the four arses with venom. Three slashes there, five on another backside, another four elsewhere. She gave up counting or ensuring the strokes were evenly distributed. She was in her own zone where she just wanted to inflict pain and here were four arses offered up to her for just that. The air was filled with moans and groans, squeals and shouts as each of them responded to their beatings in different ways. Lady Sally was enjoying herself.

She had also got very hot. The skin-tight rubber, along with the exertion of the thrashings, was causing her to sweat profusely. Lady Sally wore no undergarments underneath the suit. The sexiness of the latex against her skin combined with the excitement of delivering the punishments to her submissive men aroused her, making her cunt wet.

She paused for breath as one of the rigger-men entered with a message from the captain. The young man looked shocked at the naked arses glowing red, but was soon sent on his way by Lady Sally. She unfolded the paper and read the message that *The Corseted Domme* was approaching the outskirts of London. This was perfect timing as she was ready for a break, and needed to do something both to cool off, and to satisfy the sexual needs welling up in her crotch.

She stepped over to the window. By now the airship had dropped in altitude considerably but was still gently descending. Below, she could see the metropolis laid out before her, the factories and foundries spewing out smoke, the hustle and bustle of its streets and its sky-line of iconic buildings. Looking around, she gazed upon a sky filled with commercial and passenger airships of varying sizes. It was as if the air was awash with floating phalluses, *The Corseted Domme*, the longest and the thickest of them all; a mighty tool, dwarfing every other dirigible in the sky. They were close enough for her to see the amazed expressions of their crew and passengers as they caught sight of her dirigible.

The airship was travelling at a crawl as the captain skilfully weaved its massive bulk through the traffic. She descended to as low an altitude as he dared take her.

Lady Sally beckoned her maid over, "Victoria, stop lazing around and come over here and help me out of my outfit."

"Yes, madam," she replied with relish, teetering over in her high-heeled ankle-boots.

Her mistress needed help to unfasten the rubber suit at the back and peel the pliable material from her body. It was a task Victoria thoroughly enjoyed. The feel of the rubber, and the brushing of her bare flesh against the maid's finger (simply unavoidable to undertake the task effectively) aroused her. Lady Sally's skin, and the inside of the suit, was damp to touch, being covered in beads of sweat. The smell, a mixture of rubber, talcum powder, and the earthiness of bodily odours, was all the sexier for it.

"Victoria," Lady Sally scolded, "get on with the job in hand, please. I hope you're not getting turned on there! And you must stand behind me at all times. If I catch you trying to sneak a peek at my privates, you will be severely punished."

Lady Sally's hands stretched behind her into Victoria's petticoats, seeking out her cock hidden amongst layers of lacy material. When she found it; it was hard. She wrapped her fingers around his penis and squeezed hard.

"Really, Victoria, you are incorrigible. I can carry on from here."

She pulled the rest of the suit down until, losing its shape without Lady Sally's body to sustain it, it lay like a pool of shimmering, purple water at her feet.

She stood there naked, save for her purple gloves. Lady Sally's slaves who, despite being in different positions of bondage, were able to crane their necks to catch a glimpse of her, looked on in astonishment. Her naked back and the perfect curves of her hips and backside were in full view. She had the most beautifully proportioned arse, balanced on top of long, stately legs.

The cool of the air was nice after the sticky rubber clinging to her flesh. But her need was still great, and she felt the moisture between her lips. There was nothing for it; she would have to do something. She did not care who saw her, indeed the idea of people in the metropolis below watching rather turned her on. The airship was now floating over London so low there was every possibility an unsuspecting stranger might look up and see Lady Sally, naked, framed in the great, glazed focal point of her magnificent dirigible.

Her hands strayed to her crotch. Her fingers sought out her slit and one slid into her slippery hole. She moaned with pleasure and desire. She really needed this; she gasped as she slid a second finger into her cunt. She scooped up the wetness, pulling her fingers out to find the throbbing nub of her sex and began rubbing it frantically to the sound of her gasps and moans.

An airship floated alongside *The Corseted Domme*, its passengers staring open-mouthed at the exhibition of Lady Sally floating in the air, masturbating. It was simply too much for the more genteel ladies, who swooned into a faint at the sight. Their husbands remained transfixed though. People on the streets, looking up to admire the giant silver airship, received a shock as they got an eyeful of a naked Lady Sally, her fingers up her crotch.

There was a tinkle of china cups.

"Tea's ready, your ladyship."

"Bugger off cook, can't you see I'm busy," Lady Sally countered, too absorbed in her pleasure to turn around.

"Well, I declare, there's no need for bad language," huffed cook. "Besides, it's unlike you to miss afternoon tea."

"Cook, there are some things that take precedence... even over tea, I'm afraid," Lady Sally gasped as the pleasure welled up inside her.

They floated over the Palace of Westminster, Lady Sally with two fingers up her slit. They hung over St Paul's Cathedral, Lady Sally frantically rubbing her clit, getting ever closer to a climax. She came as they hovered over the Tower of London, bursting into the most delicious orgasm as she floated through the air. There were shocked Beefeaters on the wall of the Tower, who gazed upon Lady Sally's naked body, her tits pressed against the glass, as wave after wave of orgasm rippled through her.

8

By the time the airship had flown over the London conurbation into the Thames estuary on its way to the North Sea, Lady Sally had belatedly got her reviving cup of tea. She sat in her throne, now dressed in an Egyptian cotton dressing gown decorated with a winged Isis, sipping from a delicate china cup, her four submissive men in collars and leads at her feet, taking it in turns to kiss her toes.

"Ah, this is the life," she sighed. "Victoria, it will soon be time to get dressed for dinner. Go ahead and get my gown ready."

"Yes, madam."

"Of course, there will be no need for you to dress for dinner," she said to the men at her feet, "I may permit you to have scraps from my plate... if you're lucky."

They muttered their appreciation of her exceedingly generous offer.

It was dusk before Lady Sally sat in the dining room in an indigo gown, the table laid out with the Ming dynasty china and crystal glasses ready for dinner to be served.

"You see why I needed to bring such a large wardrobe, Victoria. It's only the first day of my travels and I'm already on my third change of attire."

"Only the third?" She questioned, "I make it six."

"Really, Victoria, how insolent of you to count."

"Sorry, madam."

Lady Sally turned to Captain Wyndham, invited to dine with her on the first night of the inaugural flight of *The Corseted Domme*, "And how have you found the flying, captain?"

Thankfully, she had not asked him to wear formal evening wear, so he was in the same suit and velvet waistcoat he wore on his visit to Rudston Hall, which he felt tolerably comfortable in.

"She's a dream to fly, your ladyship, especially for such a large airship. The steering wheel is so responsive, and the joystick for the elevators reacts to the slightest caress."

"Do you like to have the joystick in your hand, captain?"

Wyndham went red, "Well yes, Lady Sally, only in so much as it's necessary to work the elevators."

"Yes, there's nothing like having a firm grasp of one's joystick, is there not?"

"No, your ladyship," he spluttered.

"Let us have champagne before food is served. Victoria, go and fetch a bottle of the 1898 Krug. We will have a special vintage to toast *The Corseted Domme*."

Victoria soon returned, a dusty bottle with an elegant, gold-embossed label in her hand. She stripped the foil from its top, pulled off the wire and eased the cork out of the bottle. A stream of white bubbles foamed out of the bottle. Victoria poured a glass out for Lady Sally, and another for Captain Wyndham.

"You are permitted to join me in a glass of bubbly, as it's such a momentous occasion."

"Thank you, madam."

"But first, hand me that cut-glass jug."

Lady Sally took the jug and, placing it under the table, hitched up her gown. Captain Wyndham wondered what on earth she was doing; to his surprise, she released a stream of her hot piss into the vessel. Handing the full jug back to her maid, she gestured for her to fill four glasses up with *her* golden champagne, which were distributed to the four submissive men on their knees at the other side of the dining table.

Lady Sally stood up, "A toast. To *The Corseted Domme*, and all who fly in her."

"To *The Corseted Domme*," echoed around the dining room, the champagne and golden wine being downed by them in one slug.

"An excellent vintage," complimented the bishop, raising his glass to Lady Sally.

"Thank you. I have often considered fermenting my golden waters, and bottling them under my own label, *Lady Sally's Golden Elixir*. Fill the glasses up again, Victoria."

She turned to her airship pilot, a wicked glint in her eye, "You're not tempted to try a glass, captain?"

Wyndham shuffled uncomfortably, as he certainly didn't want to offend his employer yet neither was he ready to partake of the still steaming, yellow waters, "I think, your ladyship, I'd prefer to stick with the champagne."

"A shame. You don't know what a treat you're missing... perhaps one day I can persuade you. Do I shock you, captain?"

"Do you not set out to shock, Lady Sally?"

"*Touché*, captain. But no, I don't believe I do. This is merely how I am."

Wyndham was treading carefully. His own feelings towards Lady Sally were conflicted. What man would not be drawn to her, serve her... fall in love with her? Yet, was he ready to submit in the way those slaves did, or was he content to remain her airship pilot?

"You are a remarkable woman, your ladyship. It's a privilege to be on board for your adventure, but we do need to discuss the next stage of the journey…"

Lady Sally laughed, "How very coy, captain. Hmm, how delightfully challenging for me. I enjoy a challenge."

Captain Wyndham was saved by the arrival of starters, and a discussion about the route to their next destination. The airship was over the North Sea, heading south in the direction of the Rhur region, the industrial heart of the Prussian Empire.

"It would not be a destination of my choosing, except that I have an object to collect from the same automaton manufactory which built Clarissa. I believe you will find it interesting, captain."

Dinner was served: roast quail, dauphinoise potatoes and asparagus. Lady Sally scooped up a piece of asparagus from the silver salver on which they were served and looked at it with disdain.

"Victoria, go and fetch cook for me," she ordered.

Cook soon made an appearance, her round face looking ruddy and flustered, with a mob-cap perched on her head. She had clearly broken away from something as she was still drying her hands on a frilly apron.

"Yes, milady."

"What do you call this cook?" announced Lady Sally, holding an asparagus tip between her fingers. The vegetable hung there, its bulbous tip dripping butter.

"Well, I call it asparagus."

"Don't be impertinent, cook. Yes, of course, it's asparagus, the very finest English asparagus from the vegetable garden at Rudston Hall. But look at it. It's soft and flaccid. Asparagus should keep its firmness, not be limp and overcooked. When I sink my teeth into it I expect resistance… it should be stiff when I put it between my lips. Let me demonstrate."

Lady Sally took the piece of asparagus, drawing it towards her mouth. Her red lips parted to receive it, but it was soft and drooping, with melted butter glistening on its tip. She threaded it between her lips and took a bite off the end.

"You see, it should be firm enough to suck, not just dissolve in one's mouth."

Cook crossed her arms indignantly. "Well I'm doing my best, but it ain't easy, milady. It ain't natural, cooking in the sky. What am I meant to do when this… this thing is juddering and me pots and pans are sliding off me cooker? I can't be doing with this airship malarkey…"

"Cook, all I'm demanding is stiff asparagus. I've a good mind to replace you with an automaton."

Cook snorted, "Ha. You'll never get an automaton to make Yorkshire puddings like I do, and you know it. It's an art and there ain't no machine will ever be able to do it properly. Yorkshire puddings, milady, golden, crispy batter drizzled with onion gravy or even better, golden syrup. They's always been your favourite, milady, ever since you was a child. What would you do without yer Yorkshire puddings!" she exclaimed triumphantly.

"Well, yes, there is that I suppose," said Lady Sally, rather deflated.

The captain smiled, amused to find the old cook get the better of the mistress for a moment.

Lady Sally picked herself up, "Very well, I won't get an automaton... yet. But I won't put up with any impertinence, and you are going to have to get used to cooking on the airship... and I expect stiff asparagus next time. You're dismissed now cook."

"Very well, milady," replied cook before marching back to the kitchen to finish preparing the *Charlotte Russe* for pudding.

"Well, I'm bloody well not eating these floppy things," said Lady Sally when cook had gone, beckoning the judge to crawl over on his hands and knees to her side.

He instinctively opened his mouth and put his tongue out. The asparagus tip drooped over his salivating tongue, globs of butter dripping onto it. Lady Sally threaded it into his mouth, and his lips closed around it, sucking on the flaccid vegetable. She pushed the last piece of the stalk into his mouth.

"Thank you, mistress," he said, once the thing had been consumed.

"Victoria, pour me another glass of champagne."

When the meal was finished, and the table cleared, the slaves retired to their rooms for the night. Lady Sally savoured the moment. She looked out of the viewing window into the night sky, bathed in the luminous light of a full moon, and gazed at the stars. The first day of her airship adventure had been just perfect, everything she could have hoped for.

9

By morning, after flying through the night, *The Corseted Domme* was deep into the Prussian Empire, starting her descent into the Ruhr. Lady Sally, after a little early morning flagellation to get her going, took up a place alongside Captain Wyndham and Clarissa in the control cabin.

Lady Sally looked askance at the automaton with her sleek, auburn wig, short skirt and peaked cap, "Clarissa's dressed very sexily, I see."

"Yes, that was Victoria's doing," explained the captain.

"Yes, she's quite incorrigible. I know I shouldn't encourage her but it amuses me to give her these little pleasures sometimes. Now, captain, you must follow the line of the river."

Lady Sally was guiding her pilot to the airship station where they needed to land, as she had visited these workshops before, and was familiar with the terrain.

They were flying low over the manufacturing nucleus of the Prussian Empire. Lady Sally and the captain looked down upon a concentration of coal mines, factories and foundries. The air was thick with smoke and grit spewed up from the chimneys on the ground. This was where steam-powered vehicles, trains and weaponry were manufactured. The area was a hive of activity; people and goods were on the move everywhere.

Whatever the technical advances of this region, it had still never seen an airship on the scale of *The Corseted Domme*. She attracted curious and excited looks from people on the ground as she slowly steered towards the airship landing station on the outskirts of the city of Essen. Viewing him first hand, Lady Sally was impressed with the skills of her airship pilot as he manoeuvred the cone at the front of the massive dirigible into the gaping hole in the landing stage so it could be fixed onto the mooring mast by the landing wires. The riggers soon set out the guy ropes to secure her, and Lady Sally was ready to disembark.

She was met at the foot of the mooring mast by a steam-powered carriage. Lady Sally looked positively demure in a royal blue velvet dress and black mantle, which covered her décolletage.

"I'm not a fan of these steam-powered vehicles," she explained to Captain Wyndham, who was accompanying her on this outing, along with her maid. "They are so noisy and smelly. I much prefer my charabanc. I believe the combustion engine will be the vehicle of the future when its engines are perfected."

The carriage delivered the group outside a factory, proudly bearing the name *Ernst von Siemen und Unternehmen, Hersteller von Automaten.* Lady Sally was greeted with enthusiasm by an elderly gentleman with white hair and whiskers in overalls, brass goggles dangling around his neck.

"Lady Sally, it's a pleasure to zee you again," he said, giving her a big hug before ushering them into the works.

"Ah, vud you like a glass of *Schnapps*?"

"That's very kind, but no thank you Herr Siemen. I fear I drank rather a lot of champagne last night to celebrate the inaugural flight of my airship and am somewhat feeling the effects of it this morning. A cup of tea would be lovely though."

"Ah, ze English ladies and their teas," laughed the German.

This workshop was obviously an assembly room. There were broken moulds scattered on the floor, and parts of automatons stored on the shelves… brass heads, arms, legs and torsos, indeed every part of the human anatomy moulded in brass, including the male phallus. Captain Wyndham noticed a line of crates against one wall, stamped with the words, *Rudston-Chichester Brass Company Incorporated–Zanzibar.*

"Can I say how impressed the captain and I are with your automaton co-pilot. I have named her Clarissa."

Mr Siemen acknowledged the compliment.

"It's good to visit your workshops again. How are you… and how is business?"

"Business is booming, but for ze wrong reasons. I'm afraid I have bad news for you, Lady Sally. I've been ordered by the *Ministerium* to convert all my production over to ze war effort."

"Oh, how very tiresome."

"Zey consider my other lines of production to be, how do you say in English… frivolous."

"Frivolous… how dare they! Your ground-breaking work is of the utmost importance, and will bring unimaginable pleasures, as I intend to prove on my travels," she said with a mysterious glint in her eye.

"I'm sorry Lady Sally, but it is the way ze world is going. I have no choice in the matter, inspectors have been placed in the foundry to make sure all production is dedicated to automatons that contribute to ze preparations for war."

"How bothersome. I will not put up with that. I'm sure you understand, but if you are not producing automatons for pleasure, or for the benefit of ladies like myself, I cannot possibly supply any foundries in Prussia with brass from my mine."

"I know Lady Sally. I warned them this was likely."

Captain Wyndham, looking a little bemused, attempted to interject, "But surely brass is…"

"And the brass from your mine in Zanzibar is of ze highest quality. Many of my creations would be impossible without brass with such outstanding properties. I fear she," said von Siemen, gesturing to a crate stood upright against the wall, "may be the only one of her kind for many years."

Victoria's eyes lit up, "Is it another female automaton, madam? Can I open the crate up and touch her?"

"Certainly not. You are not to go near that crate without my permission, and if I catch you trying to sneak a peek inside, then you will be punished severely."

Victoria looked crestfallen.

"Ve must keep in touch Lady Sally, whatever the future holds. Your projects have always been the most interesting ones to work on."

"That's very kind, Herr Siemen, I'm sad our business relationship has to end in these circumstances, and wish you personally all the best for the future."

Victoria and Captain Wyndham loaded the crate onto the steam-powered carriage as Lady Sally and Herr Siemen said their farewells.

They arrived back at the mast where *The Corseted Domme* was moored to be met by a moustached gentleman in a bowler hat and pin-striped suit.

"Lady Sally Rudston-Chichester?" he enquired.

"Yes, that is me. What can I do for you?"

"I'm from the British Consulate in Essen. I am to deliver this letter to you from the Ministry of War. I've been directed to accompany you back to England with your airship, it's being requisitioned by the Ministry."

Lady Sally opened the letter and read it. It basically reiterated the message the gentleman had just conveyed. She passed it to Captain Wyndham to read.

"I'm sorry, Lady Sally," he said, with genuine sympathy and disappointment. "And so soon after you'd set off on your adventures."

She fixed the captain with a piercing and meaningful gaze.

"Indeed. Leave this to me captain. I shall discuss the arrangements with the gentleman from the Ministry here. In the meantime, I suggest you take the cargo aboard and fire up the engines *so we can make as quick a departure as possible…* for the benefit of the man from the Ministry, of course."

She was plotting something, "Of course Lady Sally, I'll have her ready to set off *as soon as madam is aboard.*"

"Thank you, captain," she said, turning back to the gentleman as Wyndham and Victoria heaved the crate into the lift in the mooring tower.

"Well, I can't deny I'm not disappointed, sir, but never mind, these things happen. Stiff upper lip and all that, what? You are most welcome on *The Corseted Domme*, I'm sure you'll find me most accommodating."

Lady Sally did indeed have a plan.

Stage one: play for time and lure one's victim into a false sense of security.

"Let it not be said Lady Sally Rudston-Chichester is not a hospitable host. We must partake of some tea when we board. I'm sure you must be parched waiting out here for so long. How tiresome for you. I recommend a nice cup of Darjeeling. It makes a very refreshing brew. Did you know the leaves come from my own plantation in the foothills of the Himalayas? I am something of an expert on the subject and take pride in ensuring only the most fragrant of leaves are used in my teas..."

Lady Sally proceeded to describe her plantations in great detail and the flavours of the teas grown on them. She gave a lecture on the benefits of tea drinking (so much more invigorating than that horrid, bitter coffee stuff) and explained how the British Empire was built on tea drinking.

Eventually, after a ten-minute diatribe, Lady Sally heard the engines fire up.

Stage two: make best use of one's assets

"Oh dear, all this talk of tea has made me quite hot and bothered."

She removed the velvet mantle from her shoulders. Her breasts, pushed up by the corset under her dress, were beautiful orbs of white flesh. The man from the Ministry, being somewhat shorter than Lady Sally, had a view right down her cleavage. It never failed. Lady Sally had found that every male, when faced with a pair of such magnificent boobs, would lose all concentration and sense. Throughout her life this was a weakness she had learnt to exploit.

Stage three: act swiftly.

She brought her knee up into his testicles. Lady Sally's aim was very precise; it came from years of practise. She knew the exact spot to cause the most excruciating pain. The man from the Ministry doubled up in agony.

Stage four: press home one's advantage.

With the gentleman bent over clutching his aching balls, Lady Sally wasted no time in pushing him against the metal frame of the mooring tower. She produced coils of thin cord from within the confines of the velvet dress, and within seconds had the man's wrists secured to the tower. She soon had his ankles tied together. The man from the Ministry did not know what had hit him.

"You dally with England's strictest dominatrix at your peril, sir. *The Corseted Domme* is built for pleasure… my pleasure, and I will not have her used for any other purpose, certainly not to propagate any pointless war. I bid you good day, sir. This is a busy airship station so I expect somebody will be along soon to release you."

At that, Lady Sally left her unfortunate victim tied to the mooring tower, and headed off for her airship.

She burst into the control room. The engines were already thrumming, and the propellers whirring. Captain Wyndham was ready for launch and Clarissa had her brass hand clutched on the tiller ready to operate the elevators.

"Set off now, captain. We need to get away as soon as possible."

The captain gave the order to release the cable from the mooring tower. In an instance the giant dirigible reversed, turning around in one sweeping movement, and accelerated up into the air.

"Where's the man from the Ministry?" asked Captain Wyndham.

"He's a little tied up at the moment."

The captain laughed. He knew Lady Sally was planning something, "How did you manage that?"

"As a strict dominatrix, I always carry rope in my undergarments, one never knows when one might require some. Oh, and I kneed him in the balls too."

Wyndham was in hysterics. She was amazing.

Victoria was more concerned for her mistress, "But the Ministry will be after you now. You could end up in prison."

Lady Sally was still fuming, "Don't be such a fuss-pot, Victoria. I will not have them take *The Corseted Domme* away. She is built for pleasure, and no other purpose. They can do what they like, but this airship is an English woman's property, and I will protect my rights. In the meantime, I will continue with my travels.

"Full-speed ahead, captain."

10

Lady Sally's airship powered away from Essen. It was the first occasion Captain Wyndham had tested her acceleration, and he was not disappointed. She easily reached a cruising speed of 80 mph and sped away, leaving the smoke and grime coated Ruhr receding in the distance.

They were many miles away before the embarrassed man from the Ministry was discovered and untied from the mast.

"I must take my frustrations out on my slaves," announced Lady Sally. "I fear I've rather neglected them today. Set the course for Vienna, my next stop."

Captain Wyndham looked anxious, "Have you seen the weather forecast, your ladyship? Thunderstorms and lightning are forecast!"

Victoria looked terrified, "Please madam don't go through lightning."

"Really, just because you had an unfortunate experience with lightning." Lady Sally explained to the captain, "I tied her onto a tree with iron chains once, and whilst I retired to the summer house for a cup of tea, there was a freak storm, so the poor dear got struck by lightning. She got a bit of a shock."

"It singed my pubic hairs off," added Victoria.

"Madam, I would strongly advise against taking *The Corseted Domme* through a thunderstorm. It's very risky."

Captain Wyndham recalled recent history of airship travel, and the cases of dirigibles brought down by lightning strikes with no survivors: the German Zeppelin, *von Cockenberg*, crashed into the North Sea in '02; the *USS General Dick*, crashed into the Golden Gate Bridge in San Francisco in '04; the British *R-101*, exploded during a test flight above Windsor in '05, and the Italian airship, *Il Phallusini*, caught fire in mid-flight in '07 after being struck by lightning, with all crew and passengers burnt to a frazzle.

To be honest, the captain had to admit airship travel was not particularly safe; in fact, with the hydrogen bags on board, they were pretty much floating explosions. Although the duralumin frame of *The Corseted Domme* didn't conduct electricity, and was safer than other metal-framed airships, it was nevertheless a hazardous business taking an airship through a storm.

But Lady Sally was having none of it, "Don't be such a wimp, captain. Besides, I have an appointment for tea in Vienna. Let it not be said Lady Sally Rudston-Chichester would ever be late for tea!"

With that she left the control room to go and punish her submissive gentlemen, taking Victoria with her. Talk of lightning had given her an inspired idea, and she went via her private quarters to get changed and pick up one of the devices from the chest secreted there.

Lady Sally had the men assembled in her playroom. She had changed into one of her corsets, a fetching, turquoise, satin one with whale bone stays, which left her breasts exposed. She decided to give the men a treat as she had spent much of the day occupied with her business in the Ruhr, and the unfortunate incident with the man from the Ministry of War.

She carried a teak wooden box with brass fittings. This was the first of the devices she had brought on her travels from the Rudston Hall workshop. She would test it on Victoria first; as her maid was used to being the guinea pig for any new toys she acquired.

The group of men gathered around the object, gazing upon it with curiosity, which on Lady Sally opening the lid and pulling down its drop-sided front, turned to alarm. The box contained an object like a metal rattle with wires attaching it to a battery cell contained within the box. It was an electro-vibrator. Devices of this kind had been on the market for a while, ostensibly as a cure for female 'hysteria' but, in reality, to give women a rip-roaring orgasm. Lady Sally's ingenuity in developing the basic model was in the variety of attachments she had made for it. These were designed to stroke or probe different parts of the male anatomy and inflict a new and exciting style of discomfort on them.

Lady Sally turned a brass handle to charge the battery and send the current to the hand-held device in which the various attachments could be inserted. She charged the battery for several minutes before pausing. A humming noise emanated from the box. She couldn't have the current wane in the middle of her play so she wound the handle furiously to charge it more. The hum turned into a buzz. She hesitated. Best be on the safe side, she thought, as she cranked the handle again. The volume of the buzzing increased so that it now sounded like a swarm of wasps.

"There, that should do it," she announced. "Now Victoria, pull up your petticoats and pull down your underwear. I want to give this toy a test run."

Victoria looked apprehensive. He had been on the receiving end of Lady Sally's experiments in male torment before, sometimes with disastrous results. Nonetheless, he did as he was told. He gathered up the layers of petticoats with one hand and pulled down his lacy, frilled knickers with the other. His cock dangled invitingly. He was too anxious to get an erection.

Lady Sally selected an attachment; it consisted of long copper wires. The box buzzed expectantly. As she held the device in front of Victoria's eyes the thin wires vibrated and throbbed.

"You could perhaps test it on the back of your hand, madam," suggested Victoria tentatively.

Lady Sally gave him a hard stare, "Certainly not. Besides, I want to test the effect of the current on a penis."

She lowered the device and brushed it against Victoria's cock. When it made contact, blue sparks shot out form the copper threads. The effect was instantaneous, and dramatic. With a loud yelp, Victoria was propelled across the room by the force of the current. When he eventually sat up, he had a glazed look in his eyes and his hair, formerly tied into a tight bun, had sprung out of its binding and stood on end. The other men looked on in alarm.

"Oh. I think I may have the current just a tad on the high side. But, other than that, the effect appears to be most agreeable," said Lady Sally in a tone exhibiting complete indifference to Victoria being electrocuted.

"Is it safe?" asked the judge, demonstrating a concern for the legalities of knowingly using a dangerous machine, and momentarily forgetting he was there to submit to his mistress.

"But, of course. After all, I only gave my maid the tiniest shock, I didn't actually kill her. Besides, there's no damage done. It's even aroused her; she's got a hard-on." And remarkably it was true, Victoria had a massive erection as a result of the experience. "And for questioning my judgement, I will try it out on you first."

She ordered him to stand underneath two brass rings hanging from the ceiling and proceeded to tie his wrists to them with rope. She secured his ankles to a corresponding set of rings set in the floor. As a result was left suspended with every part of his body exposed to Lady Sally's ministrations.

Having worked out the charging mechanism, she did reduce the current by winding the handle in an anti-clockwise direction. She was pleased she could control the flow of the electricity as this would make the wielding of the electro-vibrator far more interesting.

She decided to keep the same attachment on. She brushed the copper wires against the judge's cock. Blue sparks shot out from the tips of the wires. The judge squealed in response to the sharp pain, like pins being pressed into his sensitive flesh. Lady Sally turned the current up. The wires touched the swollen tip of his prick, and this time the shock waves caused him to writhe against his restraints.

"Well, here is a curious thing," said Lady Sally, taking his cock in her hand, "this device appears to have a stimulating effect on the male member. I wonder if it will get harder if I increase the current?"

The motor in the hand-held device whirred as the current flowed and the vibrating mechanism throbbed. Lady Sally held it against the judge's cock. A shower of blue sparks spurted against his member.

"Aargh," screamed the judge his body flailing against the sharp pain… though his cock remained hard.

Lady Sally wrapped her fingers around the throbbing penis, squeezing it hard.

"How remarkable. The stimulating effect is not reduced… or maybe the pain just turns you on? How does that feel, slave?" she taunted as the copper wires brushed along the length of his hard cock.

"Aargh." After recovering his breath, the judge continued, "It's a sharp, spiky pain, like my cock's being penetrated by sharp needles, mistress."

"Excellent."

Lady Sally turned her attention to one of her other submissive men. She soon had the bishop strapped onto the whipping bench, his bare backside raised invitingly up for her, but this time for treatment more devilishly fiendish than a whipping. She knew which attachment she was aiming for, pushing a long-bullet-like fitting into the device. It was made of brass, with less conductivity than the copper wires, but that was not the property she wanted to test; she wanted to try out the electro-vibrators vibrating qualities.

The brass fitting was long and sleek and felt deliciously smooth. Because the bishop had not been warmed up she, rather considerately, coated the shiny brass with lubricant-not engine-oil, though she was tempted by that.

"So, bishop, you have taken a vow of celibacy?"

"Yes mistress. I am wedded to God and, therefore, cannot take a wife or indulge in the sexual act because sex out of wedlock is a sin," he explained, sweat dripping from his brow as he watched Lady Sally handle the brass object.

"Do the scriptures say anything about anal penetration?"

"No mistress, provided it's not sodomy by another man, I don't believe they do."

"Ah, so your faith allows you to be abused in such a way?"

"Yes mistress, I suppose so," he replied nervously. "I can see no Biblical impediment to that, just as I can find none that prohibits mistress from whipping me."

"How splendid that the scriptures can be so accommodating to the needs of a dominatrix!"

Lady Sally stepped around the bench. She parted the bishop's smooth bum cheeks and inserted the brass bullet into his hole, gradually working it inside him. The bishop strained and gasped, but could do nothing, indeed revelling in the feeling of being filled by the shiny object as it penetrated deep inside him.

Once inserted and nestled snugly in his backside, Lady Sally switched the device on. The electrical current was mild, and she was disappointed at not deciding on a similar attachment in copper, but it did vibrate. Using the crank on the hand unit, she was able to change the pace of vibration. The bishop was already groaning in pain... or pleasure; it was hard to tell which.

The bishop moaned whilst the motor in the device hummed loudly as the vibrations increased in intensity.

"Oh please, mistress. It feels like my arse is being stretched and pounded at the same time."

Lady Sally laughed. She was enjoying her new toy. Her only disappointment was there was only one and she could only inflict her torment on one gentleman at a time... but that would soon change when she opened the crate and introduced her accomplice in punishment. That would mean double the fun.

She ratcheted up the vibrations and delighted in seeing the bishop wriggle and squirm on the bench.

Lady Sally was so preoccupied with administering the punishment she didn't notice the darkening sky or the build-up of heavy clouds as the airship headed south.

She left the vibrating object inside the bishop as she tied the duke onto the wall board, tightening the leather straps around his torso so he couldn't move.

"Damn," she cursed, "I should have bought two of these electro-massagers with me, then I could leave one vibrating in a slave's arse. Never mind. Victoria, make a note to pack two... no, three, of these on my next trip."

"Yes, madam," her maid concurred.

There was nothing for it but to remove the object from the bishop's arse. She peered into the box, pondering which attachment to use next. She chose one with a comb fitting, in copper.

Out of the slaves she invited, it was the duke who had the sexiest body. He was well-toned and muscular, with a well-formed abdomen and a tight backside. He had a shock of unruly dark brown hair that gave him a jaunty, self-confident look. She would soon change that expression.

Lady Sally directed her attention to his torso, pulling the comb over his abdomen and chest. Blue sparks cascaded from the teeth of the comb.

He withstood the treatment stoically, but she soon got a reaction when she dragged the comb across his sensitive nipples. The squeals, and the tightening of his fists with each stroke, indicated to Lady Sally she'd hit the right spot.

She suddenly became aware of how dark it was. In fact, she could barely see what she was doing, and was using the light from the sparks to illuminate the duke's body. It was a combination of the approaching dusk and the thickening, dark cloud. Also, she noted, the airship was gradually ascending. Lady Sally didn't think to question why, she was confident Captain Wyndham knew what he was doing. She didn't want to switch on lights for fear of ruining the dungeon-like atmosphere generated by the shadowy pieces of equipment lit up only by the sparks from the electro-vibrator.

She turned her attention to the duke's cock. She raked the comb across it, making it spark and vibrate at the same time. There was the same fascinating effect. His prick twitched with the shock and vibrations, and then immediately rose to an erection. She pulled the comb along the duke's shaft. He certainly had the best-looking cock. It was beautifully proportioned with a long smooth shaft, not marred with thick blue veins like the judge's. She must have that inside her soon... she was getting quite damp at the sight of it, though that didn't stop her from tormenting it further, digging the teeth into his glans.

The sound of rumbling thunder rolled in the distance. The airship was still ascending. The captain appeared to be heading into the clouds, and the centre of the on-coming storm. Lady Sally stepped over to the viewing window and saw why. In the distance, and in the last glowing embers of sunlight, she saw mountains... the Alps. *How exciting!*

She returned to the duke, flaunting her bare breasts. She had his beautiful, long cock in her hands, and started to rub. Then she had an inspired idea. She turned the electrical current right down and the vibrations right up and ran the comb along the shaft. His erect cock twitched with arousal and delight.

"Oh mistress, please mistress," he gasped.

"You're not going to come, are you? You know you mustn't come," she teased.

"Oh, please mistress, I can't stop."

The little teeth were throbbing against his hard flesh. Lady Sally turned the vibrations up one more notch, which proved too much for the duke as his come spurted out over the floor, thick and sticky.

"Oh dear, Well, you didn't show much restraint there did you," she scolded, secretly wishing that spunk was inside her.

She was disturbed by the hysterical voice of her maid.

"Madam, there's lightning ahead. The captain is driving us straight into the storm!"

"Well, of course he is. After all, that was my instruction."

11

Unperturbed by the impending storm, and the first signs of turbulence as the wind whipped up, Lady Sally tied the banker onto her rack with rope, and selected another attachment from the wooden box. If the earlier one resembled a comb, this one was more like a hair brush with clusters of copper wire sticking out from a moulded brass oval.

She examined it carefully, running her fingers across the prickly wires, "This is rather like my little hedgehog flogger, but with added electricity."

She adjusted the current to her satisfaction and brushed the wiry hairs against the banker's nipples to test it. She was delighted with the results as the spiky pain made him squeal, and squirm against the ropes. She tested the prickles against his penis and, as the blue sparks flew, the playroom was lit up by a flash of lightning.

Victoria, having a phobia of lightning following her unfortunate experience of singed pubes, dived under the rack, and covered her eyes.

Lady Sally rolled her eyes in disgust at the maid whimpering at her feet, "Really, what use is a maid who runs off at the first sign of a little storm."

The thunder rumbled and cracked around *The Corseted Domme*.

She switched the attachments around. This next one consisted of a glass tube, which when the current was turned up, gave out a purple, unearthly glow in the darkness, it now being night, and the airship enveloped in black storm clouds.

There was another flash of brilliant white. It lit up Lady Sally as she stood there with her breasts bursting out of the turquoise corset, holding a purple glowing stick like a demon from a sexy version of hell.

She got to work with the glass tube, which sprayed purple sparks when it touched sensitive flesh. Lady Sally didn't know where to turn next as she turned from rack to wall board to whipping bench wielding the purple stick with relish. The moans, squeals and screams from her slaves could not drown out the cracks of thunder as the airship drove into the epicentre of the storm.

Another flash of lightning filled the viewing window with a blinding white light.

"Oh, how exciting. This storm is quite turning me on!" she exclaimed, ripping off the glass tube attachment and replacing it with a bullet-like brass fitting.

She turned the current down and the vibration up… right up high. She wriggled out of her satin knickers, plonking herself on her upholstered throne, desperate for release. The thunder rumbled… the lightning flashed… the brass object buzzed, as Lady Sally pressed it against her sex.

She rolled it over her cunt lips, then onto her clit, sending shock waves of erotic pleasure shooting through her.

The giant airship rolled and rollicked against the gale, tilting dangerously as it forced its way onwards, its tip penetrating the dark folds of cloud.

"Oh my god, madam. We're going to crash!" wailed Victoria from under the rack.

Oblivious to the storm, indeed, in tandem with the storm, Lady Sally pushed the whirring, vibrating object up her crack. The pleasure of using her new device along with the wild excitement of the storm meant she was sopping. She moaned in pleasure in time to the rumbling thunder, and thrust the throbbing object deeper inside her with each lightning strike until she could hold back no longer, breaking into a long, satisfying orgasm.

"God, that was good!" she exclaimed after she'd recovered.

She stood up, unsteady on her feet both from the exertions of her climax and the airship which was listing from side to side.

It was at this point cook appeared. She was confronted with Lady Sally, crotch sopping with juices, breasts hanging out, dishevelled black hair, wild-eyed, and precariously balanced on stiletto ankle-boots, holding a vibrating brass bullet.

"I can't go on like this your ladyship," she grumbled. "I can't do any baking with this 'ere airship thing rolling from side to side. And me jelly moulds have fallen on the floor; I'm telling you milady, they'll all be dinted now."

Cook, being considerably shorter than her employer, was eye-level with Lady Sally's bare tits.

"But it's supper time, cook. I could murder a smoked salmon and cucumber sandwich."

Cook crossed her arms and pulled a face, "A sandwich. You expect me to make sandwiches in these conditions."

"Well yes, and a pot of tea as well, of course."

There was another crack of thunder, followed at once by a flash of lightning. The airship listed sharply. Lady Sally tottered one way on her high heels but managed to keep her balance. The airship rolled to the other side. She teetered for a moment, then collapsed on top of cook, whose face became smothered in Lady Sally's breasts.

She lay there for several minutes, cook crushed under her corset-clad body. The airship was still rolling from side to side with turbulence. Lady Sally had great difficulty pulling herself up, not being able to receive any assistance from her maid who was still a gibbering wreck underneath the rack. Eventually she heaved herself off the floor.

Cook gulped in a deep breath, "Oh my lord," she exclaimed, "I've been suffocated by a pair of boobies!"

"Yes, as I was saying cook – that will be pot of tea. And bring the sugar bowl and silver tongs as I feel in need of sugar to boost my energy levels... and a plate of salmon sandwiches... and whilst you're at it, make some for the captain. I expect he'll need nourishment, flying in these conditions."

"This ain't proper, milady," cook complained as she stormed back to the kitchens.

"I'll take tea in the control cabin, cook," she replied, ignoring the grumbles of her employee.

Being tied down in various ways, Lady Sally's slaves were safe from the rolling airship. So she headed for the cockpit to see how the captain was faring and how the storm looked from the front of the gondola.

She opened the door to see Captain Wyndham, with his brass goggles on, staring into the gloom, a look of concentration etched on his face. Clarissa's nipples were flashing red lights, the automaton's indicators for hazardous conditions.

The captain was oblivious to Lady Sally's presence. His focus was on flying *The Corseted Domme*, getting her through the storm and over the mountains in one piece. His hand gripped the steering wheel whilst Clarissa held onto the tiller operating the elevators. The brass dials on the control panel set in her body were going wild, their needles swinging back and forth.

Captain Wyndham was enjoying himself if truth be told. If you wanted a safe life, you did not enter the world of aviation and airship piloting. He revelled in the risks. He enjoyed the challenge of driving the dirigible through such extreme conditions. He had the ability to blot out the dangers and concentrate on the task at hand. He'd come close to death numerous times flying bi-planes and lived to tell the tale, so why wouldn't he survive this?

A bright shot of lightning illuminated the whole scene outside the control room. Peering down, Lady Sally could see the snowy crags of the mountain tops directly below her, almost within touching distance. One slight loss of control and the airship would crash into the peaks, plunging them to an icy and fiery death.

Captain Wyndham didn't flinch. Lady Sally was most impressed with the conduct of her airship pilot.

"You're dealing with this very calmly, captain," she commented.

Wyndham looked around in surprise, not realising Lady Sally had been stood behind him for the last few minutes.

"Well, there's no point getting in a panic, Lady Sally. There's a job to be done, and it requires complete concentration."

Thunder crashed. Lightning flashed.

"It's rather beautiful and exhilarating, this display of unfettered natural forces, is it not?"

"Yes, Lady Sally, it's awesome. You get the closest view of it up here at the front of the gondola. We have to stay near to the mountains; we won't go any further into the storm than necessary, and I can follow the line of the peaks so we don't get blown off course."

"Will we make it through do you think, captain?"

"Yes, we should. I think we're through the worst of the storm now."

"And will we be in Vienna in time for tea?"

The captain laughed, "I know, madam can't miss tea time. Provided we survive; we've had a tail wind for the whole journey, so time's not the problem."

The airship rolled back and forth with turbulence. Lady Sally, just at the side of the captain's chair, teetered on her heels, collapsing tits-up into his lap with her legs draped over the edge of the chair.

Captain Wyndham's heart jumped a beat. He'd never been so close to Lady Sally before. He gazed at her naked breasts, their dark areola and distinctive phoenix tattoo visible. His flying goggles had the effect of magnifying everything, so her tits looked exaggeratedly enormous through their lenses. He could smell her, a mixture of sweet perfume and wanton sexual need. She looked incredible; both wild and unflappable at the same time.

"Well, you certainly got an eyeful there, captain," she said, smiling up at him with a wicked glint in her eye.

His heart was throbbing with arousal, but he tried to compose himself, "Indeed, Lady Sally. Here let me help you up."

He took hold of her hands and pulled her up from his groin. She was soon on her feet again.

"Oh look, bless cook, she's made us the tea," said Lady Sally as one of the rigger-men came in with a tray.

Lady Sally perched on the arm rest on the pilot's seat next to the captain, "I will take tea here, and look on as we complete our passage over the mountains."

It was a stunning, exhilarating sight. Fork lightning crackled over the snowy peaks as *The Corseted Domme* began her descent into the Austro-Hungarian Empire.

Lady Sally held out a china plate, "Take a sandwich, captain."

12

Lady Sally spent most of the night in the gondola watching the descent of the airship through the storm, taking time out only to release the slaves from their bondage and send them back to their quarters. It wasn't until the early hours of the morning, after they had left the storm behind, that she retired.

Thanks to Captain Wyndham's skill and determination, they'd survived the ordeal. Once they were safely into Austria, he caught up with much-needed sleep, allowing his automaton co-pilot to take the controls until they neared their next destination, the palace of Schloss Schmegmabaum on the outskirts of Vienna. Lady Sally was visiting the Princess Maria Labiastein, the consort of the Crown Prince to the Austrian Emperor, and an old friend of her deceased mother.

Lady Sally's maid was still traumatised by the fresh encounter with lightning.

"Really Victoria, pay attention," she scolded. "I need help with my wardrobe. The Princess was a friend of my mother. We've never met before, and I want to make a good impression. She lives in one of the most splendid palaces in the whole of Austria."

Lady Sally gazed into her wardrobes, at the section dedicated to extravagant ball gowns. She was undecided on whether simple and elegant or flowery and flamboyant would be proper for tea with the Princess.

"One would like to make an impression," she commented on choosing the most outrageous dress she could find in her wardrobe. It was pure silk, the material decorated with large roses, with a huge bustle and a bow at the back, accompanied with a massive bonnet.

After the airship docked at the mooring mast, Lady Sally disembarked with her slaves as her attendants, dressed in silk knickerbockers and extravagant wigs. Her transvestite maid, dressed in her French maid's uniform, was also in attendance. The captain was relieved to be left behind to supervise the crew who were checking that no damage had been caused to *The Corseted Domme* by the storm.

Lady Sally was met at the tower by a horse drawn carriage. It would be unfair to describe the Austro-Hungarian Empire of the time as backward, though it certainly wasn't as technologically or industrially advanced as her neighbours, the Prussian Empire or the British Empire. That the Princess still used a horse and carriage, rather than a steam-powered one, or motorised charabanc, like Lady Sally's, was clear evidence of this.

The Empire possessed an airship fleet, but it mainly consisted of discarded Zeppelin class dirigibles not required by their more advanced northern neighbours. They would certainly not have seen anything as spectacular as *The Corseted Domme*, which was, of course, at the vanguard of airship technology. This was where Lady Sally wanted to place herself in this meeting, as the young, technologically aware lady of devices, to impress her older, aristocratic rival.

The park was exceedingly grand, Lady Sally had to admit, though she did not care for the formality of the gardens compared to the more naturalistic aspect of Rudston Hall. The palace was huge, and magnificent, a product of centuries of building work by the Crown Prince's ancestors. The entrance hall was in the grand baroque style with richly decorated gold carvings and embellishments. Victoria gasped in amazement at its dazzling richness, commenting to Lady Sally on how magnificent it was. But then, as she noted, her maid was easily dazzled by a bit of 'bling', that and large, latex coated breasts of course. Lady Sally's tastes were more delicate, and she considered the palace over the top, too lacking in the taste and refinement of an English country house like Rudston Hall, for her liking.

They were met in the grand entrance foyer by the Princess Maria Labiastein. She was a tall and thin, middle-aged woman with a haughty look. She was also dressed in magnificent gown and was accompanied by a coterie of attendants.

The footman introduced the party, "Princess, let me introduce The Right Honourable Lady Sally Rudston-Chichester of Rudston Hall, England."

The two women faced one another. There was an embarrassing silence. The two women still faced one another, the Princess obviously waiting for her younger visitor to curtsey. Lady Sally was having none of this. She was Lady Sally Rudston-Chichester, English gentlewoman, businesswoman extraordinaire, mistress of devices and premier dominatrix of the age. She expected everybody to submit to her, and she was not about to defer to anybody, even an Austrian Princess. They stared at one another, and Lady Sally was an expert at staring people down, as her piercing, blue eyes had an uncanny ability to bore through those of an adversary.

In the end, it was Princess Maria who relented, saying grudgingly, "Velcome to Schloss Schmegmabaum, Lady Sally."

"It's a pleasure, Princess Maria."

"Vot a delight it is to meet you at last. Your mother used to write such amusing letters to me, saying what a wild, wanton and disobedient little girl you were, and now look at you…"

Victoria rolled her eyes. This had not started well.

"Let me introduce you to my submissive gentlemen," said Lady Sally, deliberately intending to provoke, as she introduced the duke, bishop, judge and banker, "and finally, my transvestite maid, Victoria."

"Ah yes, ze English and their strange vays, ya."

They were led through several ante rooms, the ballroom, the dining room, the library, the yellow drawing room, the blue drawing room, and the pink drawing room, before ending up in the red drawing room.

"Schloss Schmegabaum is ze most magnificent palace in Vienna, if not the whole of Europe," boasted the princess.

Lady Sally turned her nose up, "Yes, indeed it is moderately opulent, but not to my taste. Do you have any steam-powered water pumping systems like Rudston Hall?"

"*Nein*,"

"Or aether-driven electrical lighting systems?"

"*Nein*, we prefer the old vays here in Vienna. Ve don't have any of these new technologies. Besides, I have an army of domestic staff to snuff the candles out at night."

Princess Maria invited them to sit at a table whilst one of the footmen set out a tall pot, cups and saucers and a cake stand plied with slices of apple strudel. One of them poured out a dark, brown liquid from the pot.

"What's this?" exclaimed Lady Sally.

"Vy, it is coffee," replied the princess.

"Coffee! But have you no tea?"

"*Nein*, but ve alvays have coffee with our *apfelstrudel*."

"Oh dear, I'm terribly sorry, but I'm feeling faint."

Victoria bustled around her mistress, and started fanning her, "Oh dear, she's hyperventilating."

"I'm fine, Victoria, stop fussing. But, it's three-thirty in the afternoon, it's *tea* time!"

"*Ya*, in England maybe, but here in Austria ve take coffee."

"I will partake of a piece of apple strudel, but will pass on the coffee, Princess Maria. It tends to upset my stomach."

Lady Sally took a pastry; it was indeed a fine slice of apple strudel. If relations between the two women had developed in a more cordial manner, Lady Sally may well have asked for the recipe for cook.

She fished around for a subject on which they might converse, "Do you ride, Princess Maria?"

"*Ya*, ve have the finest horses in the world here in Vienna. Lipizzaner horses are bred and trained here at Schloss Schmegmabaum for the Spanish Riding School in Vienna."

"How intriguing. I breed the purest, sleekest, black Arabic stallions. I ride them myself of course, and race them too. My horses have won the Derby on many occasions and the Ebor Shield at York races six out of the last seven years though I was cheated out of victory on that one other occasion."

"How very interesting, Lady Sally, though I prefer the elegance, refinement and control of the Lipizzaner."

"On the contrary, I find riding a fine stallion terribly invigorating, indeed, I have to confess it makes me rather horny. Does riding make you horny, princess?"

"*Nein*, certainly not."

Princess Maria Labiastein switched the conversation to the ladies' respective domestic arrangements.

"Do you have only the one maid, Lady Sally? He, or is it she?" she added disdainfully. "He could do with more discipline. Look, his petticoats are somewhat untidy."

Lady Sally was fuming, Victoria hadn't dressed herself to an acceptedly high standard. She didn't consider the trauma of last night's storm adequate excuse for such slap-dash standards which reflected badly on her mistress, but she was not about to concede that point to the princess.

"We had rather an adventure travelling through the storm, and she has not quite recovered from the experience yet. She is extremely loyal and will do anything for me, won't you, my maid?"

"Yes, absolutely anything, madam."

"Here in the palace I believe in total discipline and obedience for the household staff."

"I couldn't agree with you more, princess. I too am strict on my servants. I believe corporal punishment is essential for the control of the male species. Consequently, my servants carry out any task I need from them. Perhaps princess is willing to enter into a little wager to see how far her servants are prepared to go for her," Lady Sally suggested with a mischievous twinkle in her eye.

"I don't understand what you mean, Lady Sally," replied the princess, suspicious of what she was plotting, and reluctant to fall into a trap.

"Well, let me see, I can get any of my male slaves to suck cock for me at my command. Would your servants do the same for you? Let me demonstrate. Victoria roll up your petticoats and pull down your knickers for me."

Princess Maria's servants looked on in horror. *Was their mistress about to ask them to do the same?*

"Such is the discipline and control I wield over my servants, I can make a duke suck a maid's cock," exclaimed Lady Sally triumphantly as she took Victoria's penis between her fingers, manipulating it into an erection.

The duke, fully aware of what was required of him, and in the full knowledge his place was to serve Lady Sally in every particular, was already on his knees. Once she had massaged her maid's member to its full hardness, she offered it to the duke.

She threaded Victoria's cock into his mouth, and the duke started sucking.

Princess Maria looked upon the spectacle in disgust. Her footmen gasped both in shock and concern that their mistress might require them to do the same.

The duke entered into the spirit of the task with gusto, grasping the erect penis in his fists and running his lips along its shaft energetically to the sound of Victoria's moans of pleasure. He sucked hard and fast until the maid approached her climax and, anticipating when she was about to come, withdrew his lips and finished her off with several hard pulls with his fist. Victoria came over the thick-piled carpet woven with the Labiastein family coat-of-arms.

The princess was indignant with rage.

"I have never seen such a disgusting display... and from a fellow member of the European aristocracy! I'm speechless. You and your entourage are not welcome in Schloss Schmegabaum, Lady Sally. I'm afraid I must ask you to leave immediately."

Lady Sally did not appear overly distressed at her ejection from the palace. Indeed, she took a certain pride in demonstrating the depths of submissive behaviour her servants were prepared to plunge to for her.

Captain Wyndham was surprised at how quickly the party returned, expecting they would be moored for at least a night before setting off for their next destination.

Victoria rolled her eyes, "We've been thrown out of the palace!"

"But what happened?" the captain asked.

"Don't ask," she replied. "Madam had one of her moods."

Lady Sally followed, greeting the captain with a tirade of indignation.

"She had no tea! Well, I've never been so insulted. The apple strudel was good though... but, honestly, not to serve any tea. And it was tea time! How uncivilized. I'm appalled. I shall never visit Vienna again."

Having got that off her chest, Lady Sally turned to Captain Wyndham. "Is all well with *The Corseted Domme?*"

"Yes, madam. The crew have done a thorough check. They've examined every inch of her external coating and the hydrogen bags, and I've checked the engine rooms. There's no damage. She's ready to fly."

"Well, in the circumstances it's best if we set off straight away. I can't possibly stay in Austria another minute without a decent cup of tea!"

13

Captain Wyndham soon had the engines fired up and the airship on its way. The enforced early departure from Vienna meant a leisurely stroll up through eastern Europe to their next destination, Potsdam. The captain had reservations about returning to the Prussian Empire so soon in case word of Lady Sally's treatment of the representative from the Ministry of War had spread to the British Consulate in Berlin. Perhaps they could keep a low profile on the visit to one of Lady Sally's uncles, the Archduke Karl August von Hardonberg, though he realised that wasn't exactly her style.

Lady Sally, following the disappointment of her altercation with Princess Maria Labiastein, sought some amusement to cheer her up. She had just the thing. It was time to unleash her new toy into the world.

Secreted in her bed chamber, away from Victoria's prying eyes, was the crate she'd collected from the workshop of Ernst von Siemen containing another automaton. Her maid got very excited when she summoned her to drag the crate into her living quarters in preparation for its opening. She extracted the instruction manual, but this was written in German so she didn't understand a word. Not that this mattered to her, after all, manuals were tedious, and she'd be able to work it out for herself. It would be more fun that way.

Lady Sally slid the wooden lid off the crate. Her maid was eager with anticipation at the revealing of the contents of the box and thrilled when she saw it was another brass automaton. She lay quietly in the box in all her shiny, brassy glory.

"She's called Borghild. I rather like the name, so I shall keep it," said Lady Sally.

Staring out at them from the crate with glass eyes, she was an object of beauty. Where Clarissa was designed for the functionality of airship piloting, Borghild, with her curvaceous, brassy breasts, was constructed as a sex-toy. There was another significant difference, which was that the new automaton was not moulded entirely in brass, rubber was used in strategic parts of her anatomy. Thus, Borghild's lips had rubber in their brass moulding, and at her crotch there were rubber folds and a pliable rubber vagina.

"Oh, she's lovely can I touch her, madam," crowed Victoria, running his fingers along her smooth, brass tits before even getting permission from her mistress.

"Take your hands off. Look what you've done now, you've got grubby fingerprints over her shiny, brass boobs now," scolded Lady Sally.

She opened a panel in her side to access the controls. It looked pretty straightforward to Lady Sally as she pressed what was obviously the 'on' button. These controls operated her movements whilst other switches and dials worked her rubber mouth and vagina. On flicking the 'on' switch, she stood up and stepped out of the crate.

Clarissa and Borghild both used the most advanced automaton-technology developed at the Siemen workshops, but they had entirely different functions. Clarissa was designed to sit in one place, only requiring arm and hand movements to grip the steering wheel and joy-stick of the airship., Her sophistication was in the wiring connecting her to the airship controls, and the brass dials that measured temperature, wind speed, direction, velocity, elevation, hydrogen bag capacity, and other features required for the navigation of a modern airship.

Borghild was a fully functioning automaton. She had complete use of legs, arms, wrists, hands, not to mention lips and cunt lips, and was designed to deliver pleasure, or indeed frustration, depending on how her owner decided to use her. Her brass fingers were programmed to recognise how imminent a man's ejaculation was, or indeed how near to orgasm a woman's vagina was. Lady Sally was thrilled. Borghild represented the finest advances in automaton-technology, and she was all hers to torment her submissive gentlemen with.

"Can I dress her, madam?"

"I expect I'll get no peace until I let you, and I intend to introduce her tonight. Put the blonde wig on her, and dress her up in a nice rubber outfit, after all she is a fetish sex-toy."

"Yes, of course, madam."

Victoria was thrilled at the prospect of handling the new automaton. She couldn't resist the temptation to fondle the shiny metal, plant kisses on her brass boobs and finger the fake, rubber vagina, at least until Lady Sally noticed and reprimanded her.

She found a blonde wig, arranging it on her bald head, and brushed the hair until it was smooth and sleek. Borghild's eyes were remarkably realistic; Victoria could swear she was being watched as she went through the (extraordinary large) fetish clothing section of Lady Sally's wardrobe to pick out a suitable outfit. She had big, brass breasts, though she still wasn't as busty or voluptuous in shape as her mistress. Victoria sought a tight dress to show off her shape and found a red latex one that clung tightly to the brass. She also found the matching red, rubber stockings and gloves.

"That's perfect," proclaimed Lady Sally. "You can see just enough of her shiny thighs, whilst keeping the secret of the rubber vagina hidden."

Lady Sally decided to change into red rubber as well so the two figures, the mistress and her gleaming, brass accomplice, looked like twins in shimmering latex.

"Now, Herr von Siemen, described how the automaton works. She's incredibly ingenious. She's programmed to follow the behaviour of a designated master, I mean mistress, which is me, naturally. The photographic cells in her eyes record actions of her mistress and mimic them. I must give it a try."

Lady Sally picked up a riding crop. She did tend to leave them lying around-*as one never knew when one might be needed.*

"Lift your petticoats up and bend over, maid," she commanded. "Let me try an experiment."

Victoria did just that. Lady Sally delivered ten sharp cracks across her backside. She handed the crop over to Borghild. The mechanical brass fingers wrapped around the crop, her movements remarkably smooth for a machine. Her arm clicked and whirred as it was pulled back to shoulder height. There was a pinging sound as the shoulder's mechanism released to bring arm and crop swishing onto Victoria's backside with a crack.

"Ow. That bloody hurt. She's hits harder than you, madam."

"Well, I certainly can't be having that. When she's finished, I'll just give you one of my hardest strokes, then we shall see."

Meanwhile the automaton continued smacking the crop against Victoria's arse.

"Oh dear, there's just one problem," Lady Sally pondered, "I don't know how to stop her."

"What!. Ow. You can't. Ow. Stop her. Ow."

"Perhaps I ought to read the manual, but it's all gobbledegook to me."

"Please, madam. Ow. Do something. Ow. Quickly. Ow."

Lady Sally sat nonchalantly flicking through pages of unintelligible German, hoping the illustrations might inspire her.

"Ow. Please, madam. Ow. Find how to… Ow. Switch her off. Ow."

Lady Sally sauntered over to the automaton.

"Of course, I knew how to switch her off all along," she smiled, as she fiddled with settings to bring the mechanical arm to a gradual halt.

She took the riding crop from Borghild's hand and, raising it high above her head, slashed it across her maid's arse, now marked with a row of red stripes.

"Ow!"

"So, tell me now Victoria, whose are the hardest strokes?

"Yours, of course, madam," he mumbled.

"Excellent. How very amusing. Now let's introduce Borghild to my guests."

14

Borghild's movements were a tad mechanical, which was only to be expected. Indeed, she marched in a military style goose-step, which contributed strangely to her kinkiness.

Lady Sally asked Victoria to summon the captain to the playroom, on the grounds he would be fascinated by the technological advances manifested in her new automaton.

Her slaves gazed upon the pair in awe at the gleaming, scarlet rubber in matching outfits. Lady Sally's elegant and shapely legs were on full show in the short dress alongside the shiny, brass ones of the automaton.

Lady Sally proceeded to introduce her, "This is Borghild. She has been especially designed for me by Ernst von Siemen, the renowned automation manufacturer. I made the diversion into the industrial wastelands of the Ruhr to pick her up from the manufactory. She will be my accomplice in punishment for the rest of my travels and has been designed specifically with my needs for sadistic domination in mind. I expect she will play a full part in assisting me. Remember, though, there will be no point pleading for mercy from her, as she'll take no notice. This will mean more fun for me and double the pain for you!"

The springs and sockets behind Borghild's eyes clicked and whirred, swivelling her sockets from side to side with a gaze of disconcerting perspicacity as her photographic cells took recognition of the images of the four men.

Captain Wyndham made an appearance before this announcement.

"Ah, there you are captain. I trust things are quiet in the control room."

"For a change, madam, yes."

"I hope my adventures are not too exacting for you, captain?"

"No, not at all Lady Sally; it was intended as a compliment not a complaint."

"Excellent. There's no point asking the opinion of this bunch of miscreants: bankers don't know about anything useful, bishops have no appreciation for technological achievements, judges are hopeless, except for contesting an argument..."

"I say, that's unfair," interrupted the judge, "I believe I can make a strong case for arguing for the intellectual capacity of a judge. The evidence is very strong…"

Lady Sally gave him a withering stare.

"And as for dukes, well they are useless."

"Fair comment mistress," acknowledged the duke with a nod of his foppish lock of hair.

"But I know you, captain, will appreciate the technological marvel of Borghild."

Captain Wyndham inspected the automaton with considered curiosity. He looked into her eyes to examine the photographic cells, he examined the construction of her joints, and studied the control panel that operated the automaton.

"Truly remarkable," Lady Sally. "She's a work of art. I've worked with Clarissa and she's marvellous, but the quality of the brass moulding and engineering of the limbs are more sophisticated in this model. And her eyes… it's as if she's alive. Can she talk? Has Herr Siemen mastered that technology?"

"No, regrettably not captain, though that's just as well. I couldn't put up with anyone who contradicts me, not even an automaton."

"No, indeed not, I can see that," the captain concurred.

"You must stay and watch her in action. Right, let's get to work. I doubt if Borghild is ready to master knots and buckles yet but, if she observes me closely, she will learn."

Lady Sally set to work putting her submissive gentlemen into bondage. She mentally divided the protagonists into those who would receive pain, and those who would receive pleasure. The bishop and judge were chosen for the former, strapped face forward onto the wall boards with their arses exposed, the latter selected for interrupting her earlier. The banker and duke were tied on their backs, the former on the bench, the latter on the rack. It was important Borghild learn the essentials of delivering corporal punishment first.

Lady Sally selected two identical floggers, each with a piece of leather in the shape of the ace of spades at its end. She placed one in the hand of the automation. Her photographic eye cells registered how Lady Sally gripped it, and mimicked her by wrapping her brass knuckles around the black, leather handle.

Lady Sally set about flogging the bishop with the implement, leaving the judge to Borghild. The automaton's mechanical eyes swivelled around to watch Lady Sally deliver a dozen or so strokes to the bishop's backside, starting gently but blossoming into a crescendo of ferocity. Borghild recorded the behaviour in the photographic cells, goose-stepped over to the judge and began to flog him. Her actions were staccato as she could not mimic the graceful, fluid movements of Lady Sally; after all she was an automaton. Nonetheless, Lady Sally was most satisfied with the results. Being an automaton, her actions were hard and unforgiving. Borghild soon had the judge whooping in pain.

Lady Sally went through several implements, a whip, a leather strap, a wooden paddle and a cane so the automaton gained experience of handling different objects. Whether she could ever develop the instinctive affinity with them a skilful and experienced dominatrix like Lady Sally had was doubtful; sadistic punishment was an art form in which she excelled. Nevertheless, the results were evident in the glowing, red backside of the judge.

Lady Sally was in a dilemma. She wanted to put Borghild to full use, and that meant bringing her rubber lips and vagina into play. This meant the automaton had to learn the right behaviour... from herself. It was an extraordinarily lucky slave who got to have sexual contact with her. But when the mood took her she was not averse to getting pleasure from her slaves, especially loyal and obedient ones who understood she was using them to satisfy *her* needs. There was nothing for it. If Lady Sally wanted Borghild to put her rubber labia into action, she needed to show her how. Luckily, she was feeling horny herself. She'd experienced a couple of stunning orgasms from masturbation already, but *sometimes one just needed a cock in one's cunt*. It simply could not be avoided.

In any case, she had singled-out the duke's elegantly curved, hard cock for such attention, and there was no time like the present. She stepped across to the rack where he was strapped by wrist and ankle cuffs, deliciously helpless.

When Lady Sally's lips touched his, he was surprised. He was able to raise his head slightly to meet her sensuous mouth. She was a woman of extreme passions, and when it took her fancy to have sexual contact with one of her submissive men, she did so without restraint.

Captain Wyndham was an observer on the activities. He admired the flawless moulded construction and technical wizardry of the automaton, but this latest development had an unsettling effect on him. Of course, he was acquainted with Lady Sally's nature by now and was not shocked by anything she said, or did, anymore. But the captain always considered her relationship with her slaves to be one purely of domination. To see her kissing one of them, and with passion and pleasure, aroused strange feelings. He could not help it, but he was jealous. How he would like to be the recipient of such a kiss. This unsettling feeling was about to get worse.

Having broken away from the kiss, Lady Sally ran the rubber gloves along the duke's body until they came to nestle his balls. This attention was unexpected though very welcome. She wrapped her fist around his cock, which sprang to a taut erection the moment Lady Sally's lips had touched his. Lady Sally liked to handle a nice cock, and the duke possessed a most pleasing one. When erect it had a nice curve to it, and it was smooth and firm. She pulled at it making him gasp with pleasure.

The automaton monitored Lady Sally's actions closely, her eyes whirring and clicking as she studied what the mistress was doing.

Still gripping the base of his cock in her gloved hand, Lady Sally leant over him, and placed her lips over the tip of his aroused member, much to his astonishment.

"Oh, mistress," he groaned.

Although he suspected there might be a penance to pay later, the duke considered the unexpected pleasure of having Lady Sally's red lips around his cock to be well worth it. And for her part, Lady Sally enjoyed sucking a nice cock, loved wrapping her tongue around its tip and running her lips along its shaft. She felt the thing twitching in her mouth, and the paroxysms of pleasure shooting through him as he wriggled and squirmed against his restraints in erotic delight. She loved the feeling of his relief being entirely in her control.

She took a break from sucking the cock before moving on. By now Borghild was pressing her rubber lips against the banker's, the sensation being most peculiar, and the antiseptic taste of the rubber lips as they pressed against his was decidedly strange. She was soon stroking his body, the brass hands pushing against his flabby flesh, the automaton not being able to reach the subtlety of teasing-touch Lady Sally possessed.

The automaton mimicked her by massaging the banker's hairy sac with her brass fingers and squeezing his erect cock with an iron grip which made him squeal. When Borghild copied Lady Sally by putting her rubber lips around his cock, the mechanical jaw clicked, locking into place around his member. The grip was incredibly tight as the banker felt the rubber squeeze on his cock. It was oral sex like he'd never experienced before. The brass head bobbed up and down, pulling relentlessly at his cock. A sensation that should have been sensuous and arousing was, in reality, unpleasant. The rubber mouth worked on his cock with the single-mindedness of a machine, and without the lubricant of saliva, thus making his cock turn red raw with the squeezing and rocking motions.

Lady Sally didn't waste any more time getting down to action. She released the buckles on the wrist cuffs to free the duke's hands, and pulled off her rubber knickers, tossing them to the floor. Victoria was there in a flash to pick up the scrunched-up ball of rubber, seemingly to tidy up, but really to sniff the aromas of her mistress's juices mixed with the rubber.

The duke's eyes widened in expectation, as Lady Sally crouched over his face, inviting him to reach out with his tongue and lick her crack, which he did with relish. Lady Sally moaned with pleasure as her juices gushed over his mouth. She allowed him to give her oral sex for a considerable length of time, the intensity of the pleasure and need building up in her until she couldn't hold out any more. She was desperate for that cock inside her.

She lowered herself onto him, grabbing his hands, and guiding them onto her tits where they could knead and fondle the soft flesh of her breasts enclosed tightly in the shimmering, red latex whilst she rode him. Lady Sally was close to her climax, and after grinding his groin energetically she soon reached her orgasm.

"Yes, yes!" she panted, as the waves of her climax shuddered over her.

She lifted herself off the duke's cock, noting with satisfaction that, although its tip glistened with pre-cum and her juices, he had not come. Yes, she appreciated a submissive who could satisfy her desires whilst restraining his own. She was impressed by the control he had shown.

Captain Wyndham watched the spectacle with a mixture of unease and arousal. Who could not fail to be turned on by Lady Sally's abundant sexuality? And in this excited state with her dark waves of hair flailing around her as she fucked the duke, her flushed cheeks and wicked smile, she looked more exciting and alluring than ever. He could not hide the fact of the growing erection underneath his trousers, and neither did it escape Lady Sally's attention.

Lady Sally climbed off the rack to watch as Borghild mounted the bench. Having watched his mistress's exhibition on the adjacent rack, the banker was apprehensive at how the automaton might set about reproducing it.

First, she revealed the rubber lips of her false vagina. The folds of rubber were an excellent reproduction of the real thing. It was forced down on him with such pressure he could barely breathe. The rubber was coated with talcum powder and smelt sweet and sickly. Whilst struggling for breath, he did his best to lick Borghild's rubber cunt.

Being fucked by the automaton was an even more disconcerting experience. The rubber cunt gripped his cock like an iron fist. It then pounded him at a relentless pace. The rubber squeezed him too hard to allow him release, yet the rapid fucking motions made him desperate for one.

"Mistress, please, I can't take any more."

Lady Sally was highly amused, but was just about to step over to the automaton's control panel when there was a grinding noise. Borghild's brass frame collapsed onto the banker's fat body, whilst the rubber vagina still held his erect cock in a tight grip.

"Help. I'm stuck. I can't move. And it's still squeezing my cock."

"Oh dear, I wonder what's happened? Well, I suppose there's the instruction manual. Does anyone know any German?" asked Lady Sally.

The duke knew Greek because he studied classics at Brasenose College. The judge knew Latin because of his legal training. The bishop had a smattering of Hebrew. The banker knew Chinese because of the associations of his bank. Captain Wyndham had a smidgen of Swahili following his time in the Zulu Wars, whilst Lady Sally was fluent in French and Italian and knew a modicum of Russian, Arabic and Hindi. None of them knew any German.

"Oh dear, how unfortunate. It looks as though you'll have to stay like that until we arrive in Potsdam and get help."

The captain, whilst sharing Lady Sally's amusement at the banker's predicament, offered to intervene.

"Madam, it looks to me as though Borghild's power source has either run down or failed. How is she powered?"

"From what I can remember from Herr Siemen, I believe there's a combination of both clockwork mechanism and battery."

Wyndham pointed to Borghild's backside, "Look, her arse has a key hole set in it."

"How observant of you, captain. Victoria, go back to the crate. I recall seeing a key of some kind."

Said key was inserted into the automaton's backside and several turns were enough to re-set the spring and coil mechanism again, release the grip of the rubber vagina, and restore enough movement to the automaton to move her. This was much to the banker's relief, as he was crushed by the weight of the brass body, and his penis was red raw from being squeezed.

The captain suggested the battery cells needed charging too and offered to examine them.

"I think poor Borghild has over-done it. She's done splendidly for a first outing, but I'd better give her a rest."

The whole party looked overwhelmed by the exertions of the night, and it was late by the time they'd finally prised the automaton off the banker. Lady Sally declared it was time to retire, leaving her maid to tidy up after them.

She turned to Captain Wyndham, "You look flustered, captain. Are you alright?" she enquired.

Captain Wyndham shuffled uncomfortably, "Yes, I'm fine Lady Sally. I've just been admiring the technological marvel of the automaton."

He daren't say what he was really thinking; that he was admiring the flesh and blood marvel of Lady Sally Rudston-Chichester.

15

The flight north across central Europe was an opportunity to test *The Corseted Domme*, Captain Wyndham pushing her to speeds of over 100mph to see how she handled. He was brought up on speed trials of bi-planes and got a visceral thrill out of flying fast. Besides, the race was on to get to Potsdam, the next destination, in time for afternoon tea.

After the excitement of the previous night, Lady Sally decided to give Borghild a rest and have a late breakfast, though brunch Lady Sally style was an interesting experience. Much to cook's disgust, she insisted on eating her fried eggs off a slave's backside instead of from a plate. She had the bishop on all fours whilst cook flipped the egg, fresh from the sizzling oil, onto his arse. He had the least hairy backside after the duke and had been told to wash it thoroughly. The hot fat certainly made him jump, and Lady Sally had fun with the knife and fork, digging into the flesh as she cut into the yoke. The runny yellow dribbled over the bishop's bum cheek.

"Congratulations cook. That's the perfect fried egg. The white cooked to perfection and a satisfyingly runny yoke."

"I dunno why you can't use a plate like normal people, milady. The things I 'av to put up with," she grumbled.

"Just fry me another egg, cook. And Victoria, will you pour me another cup of tea," Lady Sally ordered, reaching out with a china cup in her hand.

After brunch, she buckled down to some serious boot worship, always a good exercise for instilling a proper sense of obedience and reverence for mistress. She reclined in a comfortable chair with her legs stretched out on a footstool as the four submissive gentlemen took it in turns to lick her boots.

She possessed the largest collection of kinky boots in the country, having a particular fondness for Italian leather because it was undoubtedly the softest. She employed the services of a high-class shoemaker who made footwear to her own specifications, which was where the particular pair of boots she was wearing today came from.

Her maid helped her choose, assisting Lady Sally into the knee-length boots with long spiky heels and a line of silver eyelets where the laces fastened. There was plenty for a slave to get his tongue around; every so often she pointed out a tiny patch of leather or an inch of shiny, metallic heel a slave missed.

Yes, she reflected, this was certainly a satisfactory way to pass an afternoon. She was conscious the captain was pressing ahead at speed and, looking out of the viewing window watching the fields, rivers, roads and railway lines below flash by, made her queasy.

The airship slowed as she began her descent. Lady Sally was dropping in on one of her uncles, the Archduke Karl August von Hardonberg, who resided at Schloss Charlottenhoff in the outskirts of Potsdam. If the Ruhr was the industrial heartland of the Prussian Empire, then Potsdam was its aristocratic and military centre. Lady Sally had not seen her uncle since she was a child, when relations between the British and Prussian Empires were more amicable, though Lady Sally was not going to let the discord between their two nations stand in the way of a good cup of tea.

The airship flew over the houses of Potsdam as the captain sought out the mooring station at the palace. *The Corseted Domme* certainly caused a stir. As her giant frame floated over the town her engines thrumming quietly, everybody looked up to watch. But the captain noted a different response from their flight over London; their people were excited and waving whereas the reaction from the inhabitants of Potsdam was more one of suspicion… even envy.

The dirigible moored at the docking station and they disembarked, on this occasion, Lady Sally deciding to take only her maid and the captain with her.

"I know what these military types are like," she said. "My slaves are for my exclusive use. I don't want them buggered by some Prussian officer!"

"Madam, is this a good idea?" questioned her maid.

"What do you mean, Victoria?"

"Will we get into any trouble?" she asked.

"Trouble? I never get into trouble Victoria. Well, only if somebody offends me…"

"But everybody offends you, madam."

"Oh, don't be so ridiculous. Look, my uncle has even laid on a welcoming party for us."

It was, indeed, an impressive reception. There was a whole regiment of Prussian infantrymen in golden, pointed helmets and smart, grey uniforms with polished buttons. There was a great deal of military hardware on display; a row of howitzers and a cadre of steam-powered armoured-vehicles.

At the head of this entourage was an aristocratic Prussian gentleman in military uniform with an enormous grey, handle-bar moustache. This was Lady Sally's uncle, the Archduke Karl August von Hardonberg, a general in the Prussian army, as well as one of the principal families of the Empire.

But Lady Sally was prepared, and not to be outdone. Being patroness of the Rutshire Fusiliers, she was herself in full military dress and her regiment's colours. She was dressed in a royal blue uniform, which hugged her figure perfectly, a peaked cap with the regiment's crest and the shiniest, thigh-length leather boots. When she emerged in her uniform, the heads of the Prussian infantry turned with military precision. She was, undoubtedly, the sexiest thing in military uniform they'd ever seen.

The archduke gave Lady Sally a warm welcome, "Greetings my niece. It is such a pleasure to see you, and your airship. You've grown up into a... well into a..."

"Splendid specimen of womankind. Yes, I know Uncle Hardonberg, I have blossomed since I stayed at Schloss Charlottesburg as a child many years ago. It's quite a welcoming party you've laid on for me."

"Thank you. The regiment of the Prussian army I command is presently stationed at the palace, along with a squadron of Zeppelin. Your airship is most impressive, Lady Sally. I should be grateful for a tour. I'm anxious to hear every detail about her."

"Yes, she is a marvel of the age, uncle."

"I'm delighted to have your airship... I mean, your ladyship, here in Potsdam."

Captain Wyndham listened into this conversation with interest, bemused at how, faced with Lady Sally looking incredibly sexy in her military uniform, the archduke's attention was focused on her airship.

Archduke Hardonberg and Lady Sally led the way, followed by her maid and the captain. The troops formed a guard of honour, wheeling around to march behind them with military precision, their boots crunching on the gravel.

The captain studied everything, observing the battle readiness of the troops, seeking out where the airships were moored and noting the vast warehouse of armaments. This was stuffed full of crates containing the latest model of blunderbuss from the Krapp munitions factory.

To Lady Sally, the palace was the same over the top, somewhat tasteless, baroque grandeur of Schloss Schmegabaum. At least she was offered tea, which was a vast improvement on her Austrian host.

Once they had settled into comfortable armchairs, tea was served. It was a much- needed cup of Assam. Lady Sally recognized its flavour at once.

Her nose for tea was so finely tuned that, merely from smelling its aroma, she could tell it was a leaf from her own plantation.

"Would you like a bratwurst, Lady Sally?" said the archduke, offering her a plate of long sausages in bread rolls.

Lady Sally looked askance at them but, not wanting to appear an ungrateful guest to her uncle, took one from the plate.

"How intriguing. Why, they are enormous. The German sausage is so much longer than the English one though ours is much thicker. I'll try a little mustard on it."

Lady Sally spooned a dollop of mustard on the tip of the sausage where it protruded from the bun. She put the sausage to her red lips and bit its end off.

"Mm," she said. "Quite pleasing, though I doubt I'd persuade my cook to use them. She's very set in her ways."

"You must tell me about your airship. It's a remarkable machine, and I'd be fascinated to hear more about it."

Lady Sally was not easily taken in though flattery was the best means of getting her to lower her guard.

"How many people can it carry?"

"Principally one... me, of course. And such entourage as I care to have travel with."

"No, I think you misunderstand me, my dear. If you were to fill the airship with a large number of people, how many do you think it will carry?"

"Oh, I've no idea. You'd have to ask the captain."

Captain Wyndham gave a guarded response, "As Lady Sally says, the airship was designed solely for her personal use, I couldn't begin to estimate how many passengers she could carry."

"Very well. And how big are your air bags, Lady Sally?"

"Bloody enormous," muttered Victoria under her breath.

Archduke Hardonberg looked indignant at the intervention, so the captain stepped in to smooth things over.

"There are twelve hydrogen bags, each with a capacity of 200 cubic feet."

"That's huge. She must be an unwieldy vehicle?"

The captain shrugged his shoulders enigmatically.

"So, what is her top speed?"

The captain was rescued from giving a straight answer by the arrival of a group of men in the drawing room. The captain recognised from the long, grey greatcoats and brass goggles around their necks that they were a cadre of airship pilots. Captain Wyndham looked curious. The Archduke was giving orders to launch his airship fleet. *But why?*

Whilst Archduke Hardonberg was deep in muffled conversation, the captain caught Lady Sally's attention. She had just taken a bite of the bratwurst and had the final portion of sausage sticking out from her lips.

"Your ladyship, there's something wrong. I think he wants to capture your airship."

"Really captain, what makes you think that?"

"His line of questioning, and the orders he's giving to his airship pilots. This whole place is gearing up for war. It's only an instinct but I believe he's after *The Corseted Domme*."

"But he's my uncle."

Captain Wyndham shrugged, "Families. My cousins argued so much, you'd think they'd start a world war!"

"Oh, how ghastly! Well, I can't allow him to get my airship. What do you suggest we do?"

"I think we make our excuses and get back to the airship as soon as we can. Does madam have any weapons on board?"

"Weapons, no. Why do I need weapons?"

"You've got your bazookas, madam. They're a deadly weapon," interjected Victoria.

"Don't be so impertinent maid! You're in for some serious punishment when we get back."

"There's a warehouse full of munitions near the mooring mast."

"What, you are thinking of stealing guns? How jolly daring, captain. Yes, you simply must do it!"

Archduke Hardonberg had finished his conversation with the airship pilots and was returning to his guests.

It was Victoria, surprisingly quick-witted, who came up with a feasible excuse. He caught the Archduke before he sat down.

"Her ladyship's very sorry, but she has to return to her airship."

"How disappointing. What's the problem?"

"It's a lady's thing," whispered Victoria. "It's a sartorial disaster, I'm afraid. You see, her ladyship's corset has split, and she needs to change into a new one."

Lady Sally added, "I'm very sorry. I shall only be a few minutes. It's a desperate situation. You see, the whale bone stays are digging into my ribs, and it's most incommodious."

Archduke Hardonberg looked bemused, but could only graciously accede to his guest's request.

Lady Sally, Captain Wyndham and Victoria hurried out of the palace and back along the gravel drive towards the mooring tower.

The captain was right; the palace and its grounds was a hive of military activity. Lady Sally had to agree with him, the best course of action was another hasty departure.

16

They headed back to the gigantic airship, the captain rushing ahead, his hand pressing onto his fedora hat to prevent it flying off in the breeze and his long, canvas coat flowing behind him. Lady Sally and Victoria followed, trying to keep up with his pace. These hurried escapes were getting to be a habit.

They approached the shed where the munitions were stored.

"Damn," cursed the captain. "They've put a guard on the door."

"That is not an insurmountable problem," said Lady Sally. "Leave this one to me."

She marched up to the Prussian soldier in his grey uniform with a brass blunderbuss slung around his shoulder.

"Oh, hello there," she smiled sweetly, fluttering her eyelashes at him, "I wonder if you could provide me with a little help. You see, the lace on my boot has come untied, and my corset is so tight I can't bend down to tie it up."

The soldier noted Lady Sally's cascade of black hair tumbling out of the cap, her jacket tailored smartly to follow the line of every voluptuous curve and her leather boots with silver eyelets along their front. One of the boot laces was loose.

"Of course, madam," he said, dropping the blunderbuss onto the ground, and kneeling at her feet.

For one delicious moment his face was eye-level with Lady Sally's crotch, and the crisply ironed seam of her trousers where they tucked into the boots. But the moment was fleeting

Lady Sally's knee flew straight into his balls with all force she could muster. The soldier collapsed straight onto the ground grasping his groin in agony. She swept into action, pulling a line of cord from her pocket and tying his ankles together. The captain leapt forward to take up the blunderbuss, aiming it at the unfortunate infantryman. Within seconds he was fully trussed up in rope bondage.

"We could do with a gag for him so he can't alert anyone," said the captain.

"Victoria! Take your knickers off will you."

Tied up and gagged, the soldier was dragged into the warehouse out of view.

"We'll take a crate of blunderbusses," said the captain. "There'll be one for you, Lady Sally, one for me and enough to arm most of the crew if it's needed. Besides, we can't carry any more."

The captain and Victoria grabbed a crate, etched with the company name, *Krapp Munitionshersteller,* dragging it out of the shed towards the mooring tower. The captain heaved it up within his muscular arms and staggered forward. They still hadn't been discovered, Archduke Hardonberg having been taken in by the ploy of the broken corset, at least for the moment.

When they got back to the airship, they dashed to the control room to make a fast getaway. Captain Wyndham fired up *The Corseted Domme's* engines, set the propellers whirring, and adjusted dials on Clarissa.

From the front of the gondola they had a full view back to the grounds. They watched as the whole regiment of the Prussian Army sprang into action, dashing towards the airship to reach it before it took off. They had been found out. Not only that, but a fleet of Zeppelins had already taken to the air.

One of the rigger-men came into the control room to receive instructions.

"We're setting off straight away," barked Captain Wyndham.

"But we haven't released the guy lines yet, captain."

"There's no time for that."

The captain put the airship into full throttle. The giant dirigible strained against the lines. There was a succession of pings as the wires snapped, whip lashing the ground and causing mayhem by scattering the approaching infantrymen.

The Zeppelin fleet was in pursuit.

The Corseted Domme, released from its mooring lines, span around full circle to pull away from the mooring tower. She began her ascent up through the layer of low-lying clouds into the dazzling brightness of the sky.

Lady Sally turned around to see what was happening behind them.

"They're gaining on us, captain," exclaimed Lady Sally.

But if the pilots of the smaller Prussian Zeppelins thought Lady Sally's giant airship might be slow and unwieldy, Captain Wyndham was about to prove them wrong. Despite being three times the length of the other airships *The Corseted Domme's* light, duralumin frame and her geodesic design meant she could exceed the speed of any airship in the sky. She had accelerated up to 80 mph and was soon touching 100 mph. The captain was going to push her to the limit.

"Oh no, we're in trouble now, madam!" exclaimed Victoria.

She had seen, far away in the distance, another fleet of six Zeppelins blocking their path, and heading towards them. They were trapped between the two fleets.

"We're going down," shouted the captain.

"Oh no! Should I warn cook? She's making trifles for dinner!" called Victoria.

"No time for that," replied Lady Sally.

Clarrisa rammed the elevator's joystick backwards. At a speed of over 100 mph, the airship tipped to an angle of 45 degrees, and shot back towards the clouds.

Lady Sally and Victoria went flying to the front of the cockpit in a tangle of arms, legs, petticoats and boobs. Lady Sally ended up with her face in the captain's crotch, whilst Victoria ended up wrapped around Clarissa's brass body.

"Really, captain, you should be more careful," Lady Sally scolded.

"Madam, I hardly think stiletto heeled boots are the best footwear for the control room."

"You don't understand captain. As a lady, one does not bother with practicalities, one should endeavour to look fabulous at all times."

The captain gave a grim laugh whilst trying to concentrate on flying the airship with Lady Sally's breasts wedged in the steering wheel.

The airship hurtled through the clouds at 120 mph.

"What's your plan captain?"

"We are travelling under cover of the cloud, madam. Then I'm going to give the Prussian airships a surprise."

"Jolly good. How exciting. Today has exceeded all expectations for my adventures."

The captain was about to embark on a hazardous manoeuvre. He had to rely on the sheer speed and bulk of *The Corseted Domme* to intimidate the Zeppelins, whilst praying they would be no match for the strength of her duralumin frame if there were a collision. He daren't tell Victoria what he was going to do in case she wet her knickers... but then he remembered they'd been used as a gag for the Prussian guard.

He spotted an opening. He could see the Zeppelins through a gash in the puffy cloud ahead. He was going to thrust the airship through the crack and penetrate the fleet of airships.

"Hold on tight!" he shouted.

Clarissa jammed the elevator control forward, the tip of the airship shot upwards, pushing the puffy clouds to one side. What a sight it must have looked to the Prussian airship pilots. They had seen the gigantic airship disappear only to push through the upper level of the clouds a few hundred feet in front of them. There she emerged, her huge, bulbous shape penetrating the sky.

They attempted to avert a collision, the fleet scattering before the awesome length and girth of Lady Sally's dirigible. But airships not being the most manoeuvrable of vehicles, there was one unable to spin away in time.

There was an almighty crash above them as the duralumin tip of *The Corseted Domme* rammed into one of the Prussian airships, piercing its sheath and penetrating into its hydrogen bag. Then there was an explosion. An enormous explosion. They watched from the relative safety of the gondola to see fireballs and the debris from a smashed Zeppelin float past through the sky.

"Jolly good show, captain," shouted Lady Sally. "That showed them!"

"Oh," groaned Victoria, "I think I'm going to throw up."

"That'll teach them not to mess with Lady Sally Rudston-Chichester," Lady Sally proclaimed, triumphant at their daring escape. "And to think all my uncle wanted was to lure me to Potsdam to capture my airship. We showed him, didn't we captain?"

"We certainly did, madam," replied the captain, exhausted now the adrenalin rush from the high-speed flight had passed.

The airship zoomed ahead at top speed. They had avoided any imminent risk of capture, but would not be safe from reprisals from the Prussian military until they crossed the border into the Russian Empire, which was always intended as Lady Sally's next destination.

She prised open the crate of weaponry they'd stolen from under the nose of Archduke Hardonberg. Inside, the box was full of the latest model of blunderbuss from the Krapp manufactory, the foremost munitions factory of the age.

The butt of the weapon was polished wood, but the barrel, muzzle, trigger, and eyesight were moulded in brass. Lady Sally admired the ingenuity of the springs and sprockets of its mechanism and was curious about the brass dials on its barrel.

"Where are the chambers for the bullets?" she enquired of the captain.

"There are none. It's a lightning gun. It uses lumiferous aether to project an electric current. See, it has various settings from stun to kill, right up to explosion," he replied pointing to the dial on its barrel.

"Oh no, not more lightning," groaned Victoria.

Captain Wyndham and Lady Sally peered into the wide, conical muzzle of the rifle at the circuits and wires of its inner workings.

"It's the latest technology, and quite deadly," the captain explained. "The Prussian Empire's army will be a formidable force if it's armed with these."

"Well, in my opinion it's a splendid weapon, and beautifully designed," said Lady Sally, raising the shiny barrel to line the sight up to her eye, taking aim at an imaginary target outside.

When she slung the blunderbuss's leather strap over her shoulder, along with the uniform of the Rutshire Fusiliers, she felt quite the infantry-woman. Lady Sally was delighted with her new acquisition and, given how her adventures were developing, it looked as though the blunderbusses might prove useful.

She made a mental note to telegraph Rudston Hall to block any further export of brass from her Zanzibar mine to the Prussian Empire.

In the excitement, she had forgotten about the other crew and passengers who must have wondered what on earth was happening.

Lady Sally was reminded of this by the appearance of cook in the control room, with a face like thunder, her apron covered in strawberry jelly and a bowl of whipped cream on top of her head.

"This is the last straw, milady. I'm trying to make mi trifles, and we shoot off like the wind, then I get turned this way and that. Now look at me!"

The captain and Victoria spluttered, trying, unsuccessfully, to restrain from laughing, though Lady Sally was the picture of calmness and restraint.

"I'm terribly sorry cook, but we simply had to make a quick getaway. I will make sure we stock up on fresh supplies of jelly when we make our next stop. In the meantime, I'd love a nice cup of tea."

"Tea. I'll give you tea," she grumbled, as she stomped back to the kitchen.

"I must say, the afternoon's excitement has made me horny," she announced. "I could do with some playtime before dinner. Come with me Victoria."

Her four submissive gentlemen were wowed when they saw her dressed in military uniform with the blunderbuss slung over her shoulder. They did look somewhat shaken following the roller coaster ride. Lady Sally gave a brief outline of the circumstances of their enforced and hasty escape from Potsdam.

"Bloody traitorous relatives. How satisfying it is to be back in the company of loyal and devoted submissive men. Now, I have another toy I wish to try out."

Of course, the new-fangled technologies of things driven by clockwork, electricity or ether were all very well, but a sound, steam-driven sex-toy was hard to beat, as Lady Sally was about to show. Her maid retrieved this particular object from the box in her rooms.

It was a pumping mechanism powered by steam. There was a small copper boiler with a pressure gauge mounted on it, copper pipes connecting to a system of belts, wheels and pulleys which operated a piston; all mounted on a wooden board. Straightforward steam-driven technology, which everybody was familiar with by now. Lady Sally's twist was the phallus shaped rubber tube fitted over the piston.

Lady Sally wondered who to try it out on first. The banker's arse was so fat the thing would likely get lost in it. Anal toys were good to try out on the bishop, given his belief that sperm should only be used for the purposes of procreation. A good fucking up the arse was a means of generating a unique combination of sexual pleasure and pain without spilling any seed.

She strapped the bishop onto the whipping bench with his backside sticking invitingly out ready to receive the rubber phallus. The machine was placed on a weighty, cast-iron stool and screwed into place. Lady Sally was insistent on that because, once the machine got going, it vibrated, and she didn't want the thing jumping onto the floor in the midst of its operation.

Lady Sally whipped her men whilst the pressure in the little copper boiler built up. Once the needle on the gauge reached flickered up to a high level and the machine began hissing, she knew it was ready. She lined the rubber phallus up with the bishop's hole. It was a splendid object, made of purple rubber from Lady Sally's rubber tree farm, naturally, with a large knob at the end and a ridged shaft. In fact, it was satisfyingly realistic.

The velocity of the device was controlled by the volume of steam generated as the boiler burned off the water. Lady Sally twisted the brass dial that operated it. The copper pipes thrummed and vibrated as the steam coursed through to the piston and set off its pumping motion. The whole machine throbbed on its wooden base as, starting slowly, the piston gradually built up its motion. It was fiddly at first, but once Lady Sally got the knob of the rubber phallus nestled inside the bishop's arse, it worked like a dream. The false cock eased itself into him with slow, pulsing strokes. The bishop expelled a groan with each thrust of the piston as the phallus was driven deeper into him.

Satisfied it was not at risk of slipping out, Lady Sally was in a position to concentrate on her own pleasure. After the excitement of the day, she was desperate for release, but the military uniform was so sexy and empowering she was reluctant to take it off, and besides the brass buttons were so damned fiddly. She fingered her crotch with one hand whilst whipping the duke's cock and balls with the other.

In the background the hissing and thumping sound of the machine built up as its tempo increased.

There was nothing for it, she needed relief. She chose the judge for this next task because he had the longest tongue. She ordered him to kneel before her. He looked up adoringly at the domineering figure, stunning and sexy in the smart military jacket with its brass buttons and golden, brocaded cuffs and collar. He was eye-level with her crotch. He could see the dark, damp patch on the military breeches.

"You look magnificent, mistress," he gasped.

The throbbing sound of the fucking machine got louder as the piston pumped harder and harder into the bishop's arse. His groans and pleas got correspondingly louder as the rubber phallus drove up into his arse and filled him.

"Now, I have a task for you," explained Lady Sally to the judge, her legs set apart as she stood over him issuing instructions. "You have permission to touch my crotch, and then I want you to unbutton my breeches, pull my knickers to one side and use your tongue to bring me to climax. Do you understand?"

"Yes mistress. Thank you, mistress," said the judge, thrilled at being offered the opportunity to pleasure his mistress.

He ran his hand over the crisp, cotton material of her breeches.

"Mm, that feels good," purred Lady Sally, as his fingers pressed against her sex.

Meanwhile the steam was building up, and the piston pushing relentlessly into the bishop's arse.

There were five shiny, brass buttons in Lady Sally's breeches. The judge lingered over each one. Although desperate to come, this was rather tantalising and only built up her anticipation. He took each button in his fingers, pushing and twisting against Lady Sally's crotch until it popped out of its button-hole. Five times, he played with each button in this way, the pressing of the hard brass against her cunt lips, making her more and more aroused.

When the buttons were undone and the royal blue material parted, the judge buried his face into Lady Sally's damp, satin underwear. She smelt glorious; the mineral aroma of her juices mingled with her perfume. He kissed the dampness on her knickers.

The bishop's grunts and groans turned into squeals of pain and delicious pleasure as the steam-powered cock continued to thrust inside him.

"Oh, please mistress," he pleaded, but to no avail, Lady Sally's attention being focused on her own pleasure.

The judge pushed the satin of his mistress's knickers to one side to uncover her sopping folds. He relished this task. He ran his tongue across her cunt lips seeking out her nub of pleasure for special attention. His tongue rolled around her clit, flicking it and licking it as Lady Sally gasped with pleasure. He kissed her lips, then pushed the tongue deep into her sopping slit.

The pressure in the fucking machine built up so much it started whistling, jets of steam shooting out from the copper boiler. The needle on its gauge was creeping up to the part of the dial coloured red... for danger. The piston pumped at a frenetic pace, driving the rubber phallus deep into the bishop's arse.

"Madam," said Victoria, tentatively, wary of interrupting her mistress,

"I think the machine might be over-heating."

"Shut up, Victoria," she snapped in between gasps and moans as the judge's tongue explored her cunt.

Her climax was imminent now. She grasped the edge of the rack to steady herself in anticipation of her release.

The judge turned his attention back to her clit, sensing Lady Sally was on the point of climax. He flicked it with fast, hard licks, finally sending her over the top. Her whole body tensed and then shuddered with waves of pleasure.

"Oh yes, yes! Yes, that's good."

Boom!

There was a huge explosion. Thick clouds of steam filled the room. Shards of red-hot copper hurtled through the air.

Victoria, and the three gentlemen instinctively dived to the ground. The bishop, of course, was still bound to the bench and, being in the front line, was hit by several fragments of scorching copper. The rubber phallus came to a standstill, lodged into his arsehole.

Captain Wyndham rushed to the playroom to investigate the explosion. "What the...!"

Lady Sally, leaning nonchalantly against the rack with a glazed expression, peered back at him through the clouds of steam, "Oh my, well that was quite an orgasm."

18

Victoria was left to tidy up the damage whilst Lady Sally retired for a relaxing bath. The bishop, despite one or two burn marks from fragments of hot copper had, more or less, survived his ordeal at the hands of the steam-driven rubber phallus.

After Lady Sally had bathed and changed, it was time for dinner. Despite cook's protestations, she managed to present a palatable meal. The whole party, famished by adventures and explosions, wolfed down their food heartily. Admittedly the trifle was a jumble, resembling an Eton mess, but then no-one was going to argue with any combination of jelly, custard and cream, however presented.

"We've entered into the airspace of the Russian Empire," explained Captain Wyndham over dinner. "That means we're safe from any reprisals from the Prussian military. In the current climate, to send an airship fleet into Russia to pursue you might provoke a war."

"Oh really. How amazing to have a war fought over one," commented Lady Sally.

"What's our next destination, madam?"

"We are going to the forests in the environs of St Petersburg to visit another of my uncles, Count Clitovsky."

Victoria rolled her eyes, "Not another mad uncle?"

"No certainly not. Count Clitovsky is a most welcoming and jovial fellow; he's my favourite uncle. If you recall, you met him when I visited in '07 on my way to Samarkand."

"Oh yes, I remember," Victoria acknowledged, then turning to the captain continued, "did you know that madam is descended from a Samarkand courtesan?"

"It's not your place to divulge such information, maid," she scolded. "But, yes that's true. I should add I'm proud of my ancestry. She seduced the third Earl of Rudston and ended up marrying him. I see no shame in having such roots. Indeed, I believe her exotic, silk route blood runs in my veins."

Having had an explosive day, Lady Sally decided they should retire to bed.

The Corseted Domme, was left in the control of her automaton co-pilot for the night, along with one of the rigger-men, who was on watch in case the captain was needed. Fortunately, it was an uneventful night as the huge dirigible ploughed over the Russian Steppes, and then in a north-easterly direction.

The next morning, Lady Sally brought Borghild out to play again. The captain had recharged her battery cells with lumiferous aether and wound her clockwork mechanisms up so she was now in full working order.

Lady Sally conducted the morning as a training session for her automaton sex-toy. She demonstrated how to secure buckles and tie knots so Borghild could assist with putting her slaves into bondage. It was hard work at first as the complex movements were not easy to transfer from the photographic cells in her eyes to the mechanical parts of the automaton. But, with practise, the skill of Borghild at even deft and difficult actions was remarkable.

Using her submissive gentlemen as guinea pigs, the automation was able to refine the movements of her rubber mouth and vagina. The men enjoyed the experience far more than was good for them, but Lady Sally decided to indulge them for the sake of her automaton. By the end of the session, much spunk had been spilled in the interests of training her assistant. The result was double the trouble, double the punishment and, therefore, double the fun and sadistic satisfaction for Lady Sally.

By the time they were descending over the dense forests on the outskirts of St Petersburg, it was tea time, which was perfect. Lady Sally, being familiar with the terrain, went to the front of the gondola to help the captain guide the airship. She pointed out a clearing in the woods where a mooring mast stood out.

It was a tricky landing, as the captain had to navigate the airship low over the trees without touching them, and then manoeuvre her into a space not designed for an airship on the scale of *The Corseted Domme*.

They had arrived at Glansnikov, the summer residence of Lady Sally's uncle, Count Clitovsky. This was his country estate, a seasonal residence or *dacha* as it was known locally. The count's palace was in Moscow, but he resorted here in the summer to get away from the court life of the Russian Empire. Although called a palace, the residence was a summer hunting lodge, and nothing like as grand as Shloss Schmegabaum or Schloss Charlottenberg.

Once they'd disembarked, they were greeted warmly by Count Clitovsky and his Siberian husky dogs. He gave his niece an enormous and heartfelt hug.

Count Clitovsky was a short, round man with a bushy black beard dressed in a peasant style tunic with an enormous bear-skin hat on his head, even though it was far too warm for a fur hat.

"It's wonderful to see you again, my dear. Hopefully, now you have your new airship you'll be able to visit your uncle more regularly."

"Yes, I hope so, uncle. The captain's been flying at 120 mph to get here on time."

He pulled a fob watch from his pocket and checked the time.

"Ah yes, 3.30 pm exactly. I know my niece. She's arrived just in time for tea. Don't worry, my dear, the samovar has been boiled up for you."

"Thank you, uncle. I'm ready for a good brew."

"Are you enjoying your travels?"

"Oh yes, uncle. Mostly it's been wonderful, though I've had one or two horrid experiences. I got served coffee in Vienna. Can you believe it, uncle? Coffee!" she exclaimed in disgust.

"Oh, those Viennese are just not cultured."

"I will give you an account of my adventures over tea," said Lady Sally as they strolled along a forest path to Count Clitovsky's wooden lodge.

There are many countries where partaking of afternoon tea is not merely the consumption of a drink, but a ritual. Lady Sally had instilled her own peculiarly English tea-time traditions at Rudston Hall, but Russia was another place where tea was taken very seriously. Indeed, the count had a whole room in the lodge devoted to it, and it was to this place they resorted.

The room's centrepiece was the samovar. This was a giant cylindrical boiler in silver engraved with the Clitovsky coat-of-arms, which consisted principally of an upright black bear with a cup in its paw, drinking tea. The samovar had an elaborate base, cylinder, steam vent, cover and tap, in silver. The coals had been heated in anticipation of Lady Sally's arrival, and the samovar was bubbling with boiling water.

Count Clitovsky filled a silver tea pot with black leaves and poured boiling water into it from the samovar. Although Lady Sally was gasping, she appreciated these matters could not be rushed, and that patience was required for the perfect cup.

"What blend of tea are you using, uncle?" she enquired.

"Ah, it's a blend of Keemun and Yunnan, as well as Lapsang Souchong from my favourite niece's own tea plantation."

She waited patiently for the tea to brew for precisely the right time before the count poured the dark fluid in each cup. The guests, which on this occasion included her maid, the captain and the four gentlemen, were invited to top up the tea with boiling water from the tap in the samovar according to their tastes.

"Absolutely delicious," enthused Lady Sally. "One must never rush the preparation of tea. It is Russian Caravan tea, is it not?"

"What's that, madam?" enquired the captain, feeling more at ease in Count Clitovsky's lodge than the grand palaces.

"It's called Russian Caravan Tea because it's been transported along the silk route, and on their journey the leaves acquire the flavour of the camp fires. This is why it has a smoked flavour.

"Yes, that's absolutely right," confirmed the count.

"Ah, this is wonderful," Lady Sally sighed. "It's good to be in the company of friends. But my word, uncle, we've had such alarms and excitement over the last days."

She proceeded to tell her uncle about her adventures in great detail, culminating in the dramatic escape from the Prussian Empire.

"It's terrible," the count reacted after Lady Sally completed her account. "I'm disgusted by the behaviour of Archduke Hardonberg, but then I've not been on good terms with my brother for many years. It's not helped by the state of the world. We're aware here in Russia that the Prussian Empire has been arming itself, and your account has confirmed the state of things. I fear war is afoot, niece, and I don't know how it can be stopped."

"And how will the Russian Empire fare if it came to that?"

"We're ill-prepared. We are backward in technological advances; we have no electrical devices, we have not mastered the use of aether, we have no foundries, no munitions works, and no airship fleet to speak of. Look at your magnificent flying machine. That technology is beyond us."

"But *The Corseted Domme* is a vehicle built entirely for pleasure, uncle," Lady Sally pointed out forcefully.

"There is political discord everywhere in the Russian Empire. I know there's talk of revolution and, as you know, niece, despite my standing, I have sympathies with them. Indeed, I secretly harbour anarchists here at Glansnikov."

"You have anarchists here? How intriguing."

19

Lady Sally was eager to give her Uncle Clitovsky a tour of *The Corseted Domme*, and to demonstrate her two automatons. So, after tea the group returned to the airship.

The count was impressed The airship was magnificent, its silver coating gleaming in the sun as it lay secured to the mooring tower. It was vast, taking them twenty minutes to walk around the whole airship to admire the sleek, bullet-like shape of her fuselage. The interior was just as impressive, with its teak and brass fittings everywhere, especially Lady Sally's private quarters, which were the most sumptuous.

Lady Sally let the captain take her uncle on a tour of the engine rooms and the internal frame of the airship He returned to the control room amazed at the gleaming duralumin structure and the massive air bags that kept the airship afloat.

"She is incredible, dear," he remarked, once the tour had been completed. He sighed, "you see the Russian Empire does not have technology as sophisticated as yours or the Prussians. I don't know how we will fare if war should come as we have nothing to defend ourselves against these superior machines."

He was even more amazed by the demonstration of the automaton co-pilot, Clarissa.

Lady Sally extolled her virtues, "the skill of her brass moulding, the sophistication of her gadgetry, and the precision of her gauges are remarkable. But, she's only designed to sit here in one place and pilot. You must come and see my other automaton, Borghild, in action if you want to appreciate an automaton with full working parts."

They returned to the dungeon playroom to see her guests stripped naked and the automaton, in her blonde wig and still dressed in gleaming red latex, stood there holding a whip. Count Clitovsky, being familiar with Lady Sally's particular predilections was not in the least phased by his niece's behaviour.

"I've been training her. Watch this." She pointed to the banker. "Hog-tie," she commanded.

Borghild's photo-sensitive cells had been programmed to lip-read. She had no auditory function but, as long as she was looking at Lady Sally, she could interpret any spoken instruction.

She set to work. Her eyes clicked, whirred and swivelled around to the banker. She put the whip down and picked up a coil of rope. She began by securing his wrists, coiling several loops of the rope around them before pulling the cord through the loops and tightening them with a knot. Taking up more rope, she wrapped it around his upper arms above his elbow and across his chest before tightening with a knot. Lady Sally noted how the rope dug deep into his flesh. Pushing the banker in the back, she forced him onto his knees and left him in that position, allowing him to gaze up adoringly into her unforgiving brass features. Then she pushed him face down on the floor. She rested her ankle-boots on his back, digging their sharp heels into him. She completed the hog-tie by winding more rope around his ankles, securing it with a knot and then bending his legs back for the remaining loose rope to be tied to his wrists.

"Her rope work is a little untidy, and does not have the elegance or symmetry of mine," commented Lady Sally, "but that will improve with time. How much she has learnt to mimic in such a short time is amazing."

"The complexity of actions she can perform with those brass fingers is incredible," added the count.

The banker's two bum cheeks, either side of the threads of rope tying his ankles to his wrists, were left accessible. Borghild dug her metal-tipped heels deep into the flabby flesh of his arse, making him squeak in pain.

"This one is a squealer. I think I should put a stop to that," Lady Sally said, retrieving a ball-gag from the row of brass hooks.

Lady Sally lifted his head, thrusting the rubber ball in his mouth before tightening the buckle behind the back of his head. She was pleased with this. The balls were made at the manufactory at the rubber plantation and shipped to Rudston Hall where her own craftsmen attached them to the leather straps to create the ball-gags. Lady Sally loved them and had several in different sizes and colours because her slaves had big mouths and often needed silencing.

The automaton drilled her heels into the banker's arse even harder, leaving deep, red impressions in his flesh. She stood astride his bound legs, where his cock and balls had been left exposed, squashed against the floor. Borghild pushed the metal tip into his balls, digging sharply into them, pushing them against the flooring. There was a muffled gasp through the gag from the banker. She ran the heel along the shaft of his cock before pressing hard, squeezing his glans against the floor. When she lifted her foot, it was clear how throbbing and sore his penis was.

"She's learning behaviour from me," commented Lady Sally. "You see how she torments him. She has seen me do that. Her development is such she can make choices from actions stored in her photo-sensitive eyes."

"Quite incredible," exclaimed Count Clitovsky, fascinated by Lady Sally's demonstration.

Borghild picked up the whip again. She slashed it against one bum check, and then against the other, and continued to do so with successive hits. The tendrils of leather slapped against the banker's backside. Her strokes still had a staccato, robotic quality about them, lacking the fluid movements of Lady Sally, but it was, nonetheless, an incredible achievement for the limbs of an automaton to achieve such flexibility.

"Harder," said Lady Sally. The robotic head clicked and swivelled around to face her, her strangely knowing, glass eyes staring at her mistress. "Harder, Borghild."

Sure enough, she followed Lady Sally's instruction by setting upon the banker, tied up and helpless on the floor, with stronger stokes. She raised the whip high above her head and, with one swooping movement, brought the thongs of the whip slashing against the banker's flesh. His pain was evident from his muffled squeaks and his attempts to wriggle against his restraints, though the automaton's rope bondage was far too tight to allow any freedom of movement, let alone escape

"What a remarkable demonstration, my dear. I can see that in between your adventures you've had fun, in the indomitable manner of Lady Sally Rudston-Chichester."

Lady Sally laughed, "Oh yes, I've definitely been having fun."

"And you say the Prussians have this technology? It's frightening what uses it could be put to in the wrong hands."

"Yes, indeed uncle. Herr Siemen is a great inventor but, when I collected this automaton, his manufactory was being taken over by the military. He has invented such a remarkable toy for sexual pleasure, but I fear no more automatons with Borghild's special skills will be manufactured now."

"Yes, it's a shame when you consider what uses she could be put to. Automatons like her could be used to release us from all manner of manual tasks."

"Oh no, uncle, I have another vision for her; that she can enhance our sexual pleasure and take it to new heights."

Count Clitovsky shrugged, "Well yes, I know that is your particular interest, niece."

"You must stay and have dinner on *The Corseted Domme*, and then we can make plans for tomorrow."

"I was thinking of a bear hunt in the forest."

"Oo! I should love that. I've never been on a bear hunt."

20

The next day the party gathered outside the summer lodge to be met by Count Clitovsky. They were greeted with a morning toast of blueberry infused vodka; the shot, of what was practically pure alcohol, certainly woke them up.

Naturally, Lady Sally was dressed for the occasion.

"You see, isn't it lucky I insisted on packing my hunting gear? Didn't I tell you I should be prepared for every possibility," she said to her maid, looking the picture of a young country mistress, dressed in tweeds, a deer stalker hat with a pheasant feather, and sturdy, brown walking boots.

"Yes, madam, of course you were right… you're always right."

She brought one of the electro-magnetic blunderbusses stolen from the Prussian military. Lady Sally insisted this was an ideal opportunity to try them out, and that she had hit upon the perfect thing for testing it. The count and captain carried normal hunting rifles. Victoria was armed with a parasol, to protect her mistress from the sun.

"Do you hunt, captain?" asked Lady Sally.

"I don't hunt, madam, but I can shoot. When I was in the army, I fought in the Zulu Wars, before I left to pursue my interest in aviation."

"Oh, how terribly exciting. You must be a jolly good shot then?"

The captain shrugged, feigning modesty, but conveying the message he was indeed a crack-shot.

The party went hunting on foot because the density of the pine forest and its undergrowth precluded riding horses, which was why Lady Sally had chosen not to wear her scarlet jacket and black jodhpurs.

Lady Sally turned to her four submissive gentlemen, "I have a proposal for making this hunt more challenging for you, and interesting for me. I want you stripped naked. Then I'll give you a half-hour head start whilst I partake of another couple of shots of my uncle's delicious vodka before I set off in pursuit with my lightning blunderbuss."

The four men looked concerned.

It was the judge who was the one most prepared to incur his mistress's wrath, who spoke out, "But aren't there bears in these woods, mistress?"

"Well, yes. This is a bear hunt, isn't it?"

"Isn't it dangerous, mistress?" he queried.

"Don't be so disputatious; those hours in the court room have done you no favours. I'm hoping to bag one as I should love to have a black bear-skin rug for the entrance hall of Rudston Hall. You'll simply have to trust to my judgement. Now, at least if we find no bears, I'm guaranteed entertainment. Who knows, there may be a reward for the last one to be captured."

Tentatively the four men undressed. Apart from the duke, they were hardly brilliant specimens of the male species. The banker was too fat and the bishop too thin and weedy. Though the judge at one time had a tolerably athletic frame, over the years he'd spent far too many hours with his nose in law manuals to keep it.

When they were ready, and completely naked, she was ready to send them into the forest to be hunted.

"At the count of three. One... two... three."

She struck them each three times with her riding crop before sending them out in turn towards the forest. They looked comical as they ran off into the woods, their arms and legs flailing around in an ungainly fashion. It was only the duke, an Oxford blue for the hundred-yard dash, who might present a challenge.

The count's Siberian huskies, though not specialised hunting dogs, were sniffing at the discarded clothes to pick up a scent for the chase.

In the meantime, whilst allowing time to put distance between herself and her quarry, Lady Sally had another slug of vodka, whilst Count Clitovsky and Captain Wyndham took shots at pheasants. The men heard the blast of the rifles in the distance and wondered if the hunting party had started its pursuit. The captain bagged the most birds, gaining appreciative comments from the count.

It wasn't so long before Lady Sally got bored, "Come on, let's go."

She marched on ahead, her enormous bustle of Harris tweed leading the way.

On the count's command, the huskies scampered ahead, leaping and barking excitedly.

Once they'd penetrated the forest they proceeded carefully, treading through the undergrowth. Lady Sally led the way, the eye-piece of the blunderbuss fixed to her eye, not wishing to miss the opportunity to take a pot shot at one of her gentlemen.

It wasn't too long before the dogs started barking, and she spotted a flash of skinny, white flesh through the trees. She took aim and fired.

A stream of blue light burst through the air and struck a bush which, on impact, burst into flame.

The force of the shot propelled Lady Sally backwards straight into Captain Wyndham, who was directly behind her, forcing them both to crash into the undergrowth. She fell right on top of him, her huge bustle pinning him to the ground.

"Bugger, I missed him."

The captain, despite being winded both by the impact and weight of Lady Sally on top of him, was able to mumble, "It's just as well or the bishop might have met his maker. I think, madam, you may not have the settings correct. You were meant to shock a little not frazzle."

Captain Wyndham was happy to lie there for a while, the warmth of Lady Sally's body pressing on him, strands of her pine-scented, dark hair covering his face. His heart was pounding at the proximity of her sensuous curves to his body.

It was Victoria who leapt forward to aid her, taking her hand and pulling her off the captain.

She turned to him, an enigmatic smile on her lips, "Well, captain, this is starting to become a habit. Maybe I should punish you for these enforced indiscretions."

"Madam, madam, are you ok?"

"Yes, I'm perfectly fine, Victoria. There's no need to fuss."

The captain picked the blunderbuss up from the forest floor and adjusted the settings of the dial on the barrel.

"That should work if you want to deliver a tiny electric shock."

"Thank you, captain," she said taking the rifle from him. "I'll test it out on my maid first."

"What! But madam."

"Stand over there Victoria. Pull your petticoats up, and your knickers down."

Her maid obediently did as she was directed. Lady Sally pulled the eyesight up to her face and trained it at a spot on her maid's backside. She pulled the trigger. A line of purple light shout out from the barrel and hit Victoria with a sizzling zing.

"Ow! Madam, that stings."

"Excellent. Just turn it up a tiny notch for me captain and that will be fine."

After this interlude, they set off in pursuit of the bishop again. It was not long before the huskies sniffed him out. On being spotted he attempted to run off, but Lady Sally had the blunderbuss at her eyes and was ready with a direct hit on his arse as he was trying to escape. There was a yelp in the distance as the bishop crashed to the ground.

They ran through the undergrowth to catch up with him, and capture him. Lady Sally produced a leather collar with metal studs from one of the many pockets in her tweed dress and secured it around his neck. She threaded rope around a brass ring in it so she could pull her hunted quarry behind her.

It wasn't long before they caught up with the banker and the judge. Lady Sally was an excellent shot, and she was delighted to get direct hits on their backsides. The purple sparks of electricity delivered a sharp sting to the flesh and, Lady Sally noted, left a little red mark, which she told them they should treat as a mark of honour.

Not surprisingly, it took them more time to hunt the duke who was more athletic. They were climbing up an incline when they spotted him on the brow of a hill, his back to a tree. The dogs were strangely subdued. They soon saw why. Before the duke was a bear. A huge black bear, and it was snarling and roaring at the terrified gentleman.

The captain hurriedly adjusted Lady Sally's blunderbuss to a current that could kill. She lifted the sight up to her eye. The count and captain took aim, in case she should miss.

"Help!" came a plaintive moan from the top of the hill.

Lady Sally lowered her blunderbuss.

"What a magnificent creature. Having seen one in the flesh, so to speak, I couldn't possibly shoot a black bear."

The other two lowered their rifles.

"What do you want us to do, my dear?" asked the count.

"Well, I suppose I could let the bear eat him."

"That's a tad harsh, even for you, my niece."

"Give me cover and, when I get close, fire a shot to distract the bear," said the captain as he plunged up the slope to rescue the duke.

As he got nearer he approached more carefully, crouching to take cover in the undergrowth. When the captain was just behind him, the count shot his rifle into the air to distract the beast. The bear's head swivelled around, growling, slaver dripping from its jaws. The captain grabbed hold of the duke, terrified to the point of not being able to react, and bodily dragged him down the slope behind him. They stumbled into the others, the captain's momentum sending him crashing into Lady Sally's arms.

"Really captain, two encounters in the space of a few minutes. I'm beginning to wonder if they are not accidental at all."

"I'm sorry, Lady Sally," panted the captain. "I couldn't stop myself."

"Good show. I believe you have saved the day."

They were not out of the woods yet. The black bear stood up on its hind feet at the top of the hill, snarling, weighing up whether to charge at them. Victoria had wet her knickers again. This was just too much for her; explosions, daring escapes, collisions, and now wild bears.

The black bear got down onto all fours again, growled contemptuously at them, and proceeded to slope off in the opposite direction.

"That was a lucky escape," said the count.

The duke was effusive in his thanks for the captain, and the daring rescue.

Lady Sally was wistful, "What a magnificent beast. I simply could not pull the trigger. Seeing the creature in its natural habitat I can see how wrong it would be for me to have a bear rug in Rudston Hall."

They marched off back to the lodge, the four slaves, collared and linked with a line of rope, were led by Lady Sally.

On their return, it was tea time of course, so they retired to the tea room for a cup of char from the steaming samovar. When it was dusk Count Clitovsky lit a bonfire, and they sat outside the lodge, the gentlemen warming their still-naked bodies by the flames.

Lady Sally, having discovered her uncle kept a whole range of flavoured vodkas, began sampling every one of them.

There was a rustling in the trees and Lady Sally made out the outline of black figures in the shadows.

The count called out, "It's alright, you can join us."

Lady Sally's eyes flashed with interest, "Are these your anarchist friends?"

21

Three shadowy figures, two men and a woman, emerged from the trees. Count Clitovsky introduced them as Dimitri Bollokov, Sophia Testlikova and Peter Krapotkin. They were formerly students from St Petersburg, radicalised during the revolution of 1905, now in their twenties, thin and poorly fed, and dressed in black. They cast their eyes over the visitors with surly suspicion.

"This is my niece, Lady Sally Rudston-Chichester from Rudston Hall in England," said Count Clitovsky, introducing his guests.

Lady Sally rose to her feet, teetering on her boots, worse for wear for the many shots of vodka. It was lucky that, unusually for her, she was wearing practical footwear as, if she had her trademark heels on, she must surely have toppled into them.

She thrust her breasts out and gave them a lopsided grin. She wielded her formidable powers of charm and sexual allure to engage them and win them over. That was easy for the male members of the band as, however radical their beliefs, Lady Sally usually found her dominatrix persona, not to mention her huge breasts, projected a powerful argument.

"How intriguing. I've always maintained an interest in radical ideas. You must tell me what you believe in."

They were wary at first, given her obvious wealth and aristocratic voice, but she encouraged them with attentive nods and alert eyes.

The one called Dimitri Bollokov argued that the peasantry could become a revolutionary vanguard, by organising themselves into communes and sharing redistributed land to become autonomous collectives.

"How fascinating," said Lady Sally.

The one introduced as Sofia Testlikova talked of the need for free education for peasants and workers as a means of providing everybody with the tools to both understand and put into action revolutionary ideas. She argued passionately for the equality of women.

"Well yes, I'm all for that," agreed Lady Sally. "Indeed, I propose you go further. I extol the virtues of female supremacy and male submission of course and, as you can see, I put those principles into practise."

The last radical, a young man called Peter Krapotkin offered a critique of Darwin's theory of evolution. He argued that man's achievements were a result of co-operation not struggle, and that this communism of people would transform the development of mankind.

Lady Sally nodded enthusiastically as she listened to the young people's arguments.

"Do you have any bombs?"

There was silence.

Victoria rolled her eyes in alarm. She didn't like where this conversation was heading.

Lady Sally was capricious at the best of times but after a toxic combination of blueberry, damson, raspberry and bilberry vodkas, she had the potential to be positively dangerous.

"Well, we believe in taking action," offered Dimitri Bollokov.

"Perhaps I'm under a misapprehension, but I understood anarchists had bombs."

The three shifted uncomfortably.

"There's nothing wrong with a good explosion," added Lady Sally. "Why, I've experienced many explosions in my time; there's been several on my travels so far."

"And still counting," muttered Victoria under her breath.

"You need to take action. Is that not a creed of anarchism?" pursued Lady Sally.

"Well yes, but..."

"Any action will do. It will be a statement," she said, taking another slug of vodka.

"Well, actually we do have a bomb," offered Sophia Testlikova.

"Oh, do let me take a look."

The young anarchist pulled a large, cast-iron ball with a fuse sticking out of it from her bag. It looked satisfyingly like bombs drawn in cartoons.

"What an impressive looking bomb. Have you decided what to do with it?"

"Not yet. We want to strike against something symbolic to show people what we're capable of."

"Well, you don't want to kill anybody, after all, even I think that would be rather beastly. Ah, I have it," she exclaimed, "the perfect target."

The three young radicals looked on open-mouthed, surprised at having found an unusual supporter in the form of this aristocratic English dominatrix, but nonetheless feeling compelled to listen to her suggestion.

"The Alexander Column in Palace Square," she offered triumphantly.

There was a moment's silence as the anarchists mulled the idea over until it met with universal acclaim as a potential target. A monument erected in honour of Tsar Alexander I; it would be the perfect act to destroy this symbol of the Russian Empire and, furthermore, prove they could strike at the very centre of Russia's capital.

"But how are we going to get into the centre of St Petersburg with a bomb?" Kropotkin asked.

"It's perfectly simple. You can hitch a ride in my airship and sneak into St Petersburg..."

"Sneak into St Petersburg!" exclaimed the captain, "In the largest dirigible that's ever been built."

"It's perfectly feasible. I have every faith in you, captain. We fly in under cover of the dark. We lower a couple of our young friends here into Palace Square. They plant the bomb at the plinth of the column, and light the fuse. We pull them back up into the airship and make our getaway as it explodes in the square. It can't possibly fail."

Although they were agreed the column was a perfect target, the band of anarchists were divided on the proposition of actually blowing it up. Krapotkin voiced reservations about the use of violence. Dimitri Bollokov debated if this was the opportune moment. The most vocal supporter was the young, female student, Sophia Testlikova, who had fallen in love with Lady Sally, seeing in her a model of feminine dominance she aspired to. After a long and detailed debate, any misgivings of the other two were overcome. So, as an autonomous collective, they agreed to Lady Sally's drunken proposition

Her maid looked alarmed. Victoria had experienced enough explosions as it was.

Count Clitovsky shrugged his shoulders. He knew his niece too well to try to persuade her from a course of action she'd decided on, however mad-cap. But he was beginning to regret giving Lady Sally a free-reign in his vodka cellar.

He explained to the three young radicals, "You must understand I have to disassociate myself from you. I won't be able to harbour any of you after this, it will be too incriminating for me. Does this mean you are on my way, my dear?" he added turning to Lady Sally.

"I'm afraid so, uncle. As you know I was planning on departing first thing tomorrow in any case. We'll drop our young friends off somewhere and speed on our way."

The scheme having been put forward and agreed upon by the band of anarchists, Lady Sally did not hesitate in putting it into effect.

She said goodbye to her Uncle Clitovsky, who gave her a big hug, "You are incorrigible, my dear, but I would not have it any other way!"

They boarded the airship, along with the young radicals.

For the captain this was a hazardous expedition. They had to switch off the lighting in *The Corseted Domme* and travel under cover of complete darkness. They floated low over the sky, the captain peering through the gloom to navigate the airship over the streets of St Petersburg. Fortunately, Palace Square was an instantly recognisable landmark, and one that he could pick out even in the pitch black of night.

The airship hovered directly over the column, the captain and Clarissa holding her steady. Lines were lowered from the gondola, and Dimitri and Sofia lowered themselves on the metal guy line until they were near enough to jump onto the ground.

Lady Sally watched as Dimitri unwrapped the bomb, placed it by the plinth of the column as Sophia lit the fuse. They grabbed onto the wire again and were hauled up into the airship. They had no more than three or four minutes to get clear before the bomb blew up. The captain eased the airship forward to make sure it was out of the range of any explosion or threat of being damaged by flying shards of granite.

They waited expectantly. There was a flash of red, and then… boom!

The bomb went off with a massive explosion. At first it didn't appear that the column had been damaged but, its base having been fractured, it started to wobble, and then topple over. There was an almighty crash as the column thundered onto the square, the angel statue on its pinnacle being thrown against the stone and shattering into tiny shards. Fragments of broken, red granite flew through the air. Dust and debris circled in the night air.

"How satisfying. You can't beat a good explosion."

Lady Sally's maid shook her head in despair. *Whatever next.*

22

The next morning Lady Sally lay slumped in an armchair in her Chinese, silk dressing gown embroidered with dragons, somewhat worse for wear. Her uncle's vodka had left her with a throbbing head, yet her maid insisted on clumping around in a huff. She couldn't imagine why.

"Did we really blow up the monument?"

"You certainly did," confirmed Victoria in a tone of reproof.

Lady Sally smiled as her memory of the event returned through the vodka induced haze.

"Well, Victoria, there's no point one being a *Mistress of the Air* if one cannot have adventures, and besides, it was a daring escapade and a magnificent explosion... one of my finest, I think."

"Yes, madam, of course, madam," replied her maid, not terribly convincingly.

"And where are our anarchist comrades now?"

"The captain dropped them in a village in the forests where their comrades are living in a commune. If you recall, you invited them to join the airship's party, but they said you were far too dangerous for them... and they are anarchists, madam."

"I don't know what they're fussing over. It was just a little explosion... and nobody got hurt."

As if her maid's grumblings weren't enough whilst in this fragile state, Lady Sally now had cook on the warpath.

"Milady, I can't put up with this no more."

"What, the explosions?"

"No milady. Your explosions is your business. I mean the food going missing. The kitchens, that's my business."

"Can't this wait cook. As you can see I'm not at my best this morning."

"Not when cold chicken legs goes missing, milady... and currant scones... and bottles of ale. I tell you there's a thief on board. Now, I don't want to cast no aspersions, milady, but there's some strange characters on this airship."

"'T was ever thus, cook, as you well know. But why would anyone want to steal food? Everybody's fed perfectly adequately, even if my gentlemen are made to eat off the floor as humiliation, they're hardly left to starve."

"I'm just saying what I've seen, milady. I know where every ounce of sugar is in that kitchen, and I knows when things go missing."

"Well, just keep an eye on the situation cook, maybe one of the rigger-men wanted a snack in the middle of the night. Now, to more pressing matters, do you have a good remedy for a hangover?"

"Ah, so now you needs mi advice."

"Yes cook, but I'd rather not have it served with recriminations."

"You needs raw eggs... raw eggs and Worcester sauce, that'll do the trick. I'll get you some."

Cook stormed off triumphantly.

Lady Sally was restless. She fancied some amusement but with the minimum input from herself. She could set the automation sex doll off and see what havoc she could cause, but there was another option... one of her dastardly devices.

She summoned up the effort to put her make up on and get dressed. She put on one of her many corsets, this particular one with scarlet panels and black ribbons, over a black silk blouse, and matching-coloured skirt. She enlisted Victoria's help in lacing up the corset to cheer her up. Lady Sally knew her maid too well, knew she loved to handle her wardrobe and help her get dressed. There was many a time Lady Sally had caught her maid trying on her undergarments, for which she had to be reprimanded. Helping her get dressed might take Victoria out of her reproachful frame of mind following the business with the anarchists.

Just getting out of her dressing gown and putting something sexy and empowering on improved her mood.

She got Victoria to retrieve the device she wanted to test and summon her slaves to the playroom. She intended to activate Borghild to demonstrate the art of sensual tease for her as the device she was about to use required the availability of four hard cocks.

She had her four submissive gentlemen lined against the wood-panelled wall, deciding not to put them into bondage on this occasion. They were issued with the instruction they were to stand with their hands behind their backs, and the stricture that they were not permitted an erection. She saw the effort of will this took for them. Dressed relatively demurely as she was (at least for her) the curves of her breasts were visible under the silk blouse, along with a peek of hard nipples pressing against the sleek material.

She marched back and forth before them with, a leather whip in her hand, so they could admire the curve of her shapely backside in the tight skirt, as she inspected them. Borghild followed behind her with her goose-step mechanical march.

"Hmm, let me see how long you can withstand my ministrations without getting an erection."

She ran the thongs of the whip teasingly along the duke's chest, across his abdomen, over his balls and, finally, along the length of his cock, teasing him into arousal with the soft leather thongs. His breath deepened and the muscles around his neck tightened as he tried to resist both the touch of the leather tendrils on his penis, and the anticipation of what might follow.

"Hmm, very good. I'm glad to see you can exercise some control."

She went along the line, repeating the same teasing acts on the other gentlemen. They all, with different quirks and mannerisms, tried to resist the tantalisingly teasing strokes of the leather whip. Their cocks twitched with arousal, but they were able to control themselves. Lady Sally needed to use other means to break them.

She went back along the line to face the duke. She fixed her blue eyes on his. Her cleavage, with the distinct phoenix tattoo on one of her breasts, swelled in front of him. Whilst still fixing his gaze, her hand strayed to his cock and balls. She brushed her fingernails across the tip of his cock, and he expelled a gasp. Nobody could resist Lady Sally's touch when she was minded to induce a hard-on. The red painted nail ran along his shaft, and at once the flaccid flesh responded, throbbing as it was with need and desire. She wrapped her fist around it and squeezed. She felt the object hardening within her fingers. When she released it, the cock sprang up, it's shaft now hard with blue veins standing out.

"You have such a pleasing cock, duke. It's just such a shame you cannot exercise adequate control over it."

"I'm sorry, mistress," he mumbled.

The automaton mimicked Lady Sally's actions, running her smooth, brassy finger along his cock. Borghild's touch was cold and firm. She closed her brass fist around the duke's member. The gears whirred, and the fingers tightened… and tightened, around it.

Meanwhile, Lady Sally moved along the line, replicating the same acts, and exactly the same sensitivity of touch with each of her slaves, so she could set a fair test for each of them.

Borghild's fist was closing tighter and tighter around the duke's cock, its glans squeezing out from her brass fingers.

"Ouch. Mistress, the automaton won't let go," called the duke to attract Lady Sally's attention.

She was focused on arousing the cock of the bishop who was proving the most resistant to her attention. Besides, she considered it would serve the duke right for succumbing to his carnal needs so quickly, to have the automaton squeeze the lust out of him.

She teased and stroked the bishop's pencil-thin penis with the tips of her fingers, allowing the painted nails to drag along his flesh until he too had surrendered to Lady Sally, his hard cock sticking out.

She turned back along the line to admire the tension of the automaton's gears and springs as the brass fingers squeezed ever tighter around the duke's cock. His face was red with the effort of controlling the pain. Lady Sally felt he'd suffered enough and, besides, she did not want him to lose his erection; it was necessary for the next phase of her torment.

She looked Borghild in the eyes, and said firmly, "Release."

On her command, the automaton's fingers uncurled, pulling away from the duke's raw, pulsating, but still hard, cock.

"Ah, I see that none of you can resist your mistress's touch."

"No mistress," they muttered.

"Now for another test."

Victoria brought forward the next of Lady Sally's devices... an electrically powered masturbating machine.

The instrument in question looked like a rubber octopus. It consisted of a control panel fashioned in brass with a gauge and lever with several notches. Attached to it was a set of four rubber tubes, with an open-ended rubber sheath at the end of each tube.

Lady Sally pulled the rubber sheaths over the four erect cocks on display in front of her. They did not fit tightly as there was a sealed air pocket around them. The four men looked worried, recalling how the last of Lady Sally's devices caused an explosion; the bishop in particular, still having the scars caused by the red-hot shards of copper.

"Don't worry, I promise this machine won't explode," assured Lady Sally, though none of them seemed especially convinced.

"Let me explain how it works. The rubber tubes are filled with aether, which transmits electro-magnetic waves. When I move the lever forward, the electro waves pulse through the tube into the sheaths, causing the rubber to pulsate and ripple. No doubt you can imagine the erotic effects that might have on your cocks. Here, let me show you."

Lady Sally flicked the lever up one notch, the needle on the dial flickered up. The machine emitted a low buzzing noise. It was possible to see the current travel along the tube as it caused the rubber to expand and contract. As the device warmed up, the pulses came through at a regular pace.

The effect within the sheaths was remarkable. The sensation was like an invisible hand running up and down the shafts of their cocks. At the lower power range of the device, the feeling was, initially, one of considerable pleasure though counter to this was a sensation of being milked without being allowed an emission.

Lady Sally was highly amused, "At this level, I can keep you in a state of suspended animation, making your cocks throb with need, whilst ensuring they stay unfulfilled. On the other hand, when you increase the current," Lady Sally flipped the lever up two notches, "it works as a masturbating machine, and will bring you to an inevitable climax. Of course, I can alternate levels of current and keep you on the edge of release before reducing it."

The demonstration had the desired effect as the pulse of the rippling sheath increased and the electro-magnetic current pulled the rubber back and forth at speed.

There was a collective sound of gasps, groans and moans as the device did its work until the current subsided again.

"What happens at top speed, mistress, if I may be so bold as to ask," enquired the judge.

"It's the first time I've used the device, so this is an experiment. I've had it specially designed, and the ingenuity of it is that the four sheaths will throb at precisely the same rhythm. So, I propose a little competition. Whoever comes last is the victor, and whoever comes first is the loser."

Lady Sally stretched and yawned, "Of course the wonder of the device is that I can sit here and admire its effects. I can even have a cup of tea. Victoria, go and fetch me a cuppa, I'm gagging for one."

Her maid set off to fetch the tea. Lady Sally kept the device thrumming on the second notch. The exertions of the previous day, not to mention the vodka, were taking effect again. She yawned. Her eyes were heavy. In seconds she was sound asleep.

Meanwhile, Victoria got delayed in the kitchens. She got caught by cook and felt compelled to act as a sounding board for her complaints about stolen food. She then went via the control room to take a cup of tea for the captain, only to have to listen to his praise for the amazing Lady Sally, and how much fun her rip-roaring adventures were. Victoria agreed with much of what the captain said, but merely had reservations about the explosions… the lightning… and the electrocutions.

When she returned to the playroom with a silver tray, a lovely pot of Darjeeling and a plate of fancies, he spotted Lady Sally fast asleep on her throne. The four men were dancing in paroxysms of equal measures of stimulation and frustration. The dastardly device had throbbed on for the last half an hour with the effect of driving the men to distraction bordering on madness.

Victoria gave Lady Sally a gentle nudge, "Your tea is here, madam."

Her eyes flickered open. She was confronted with the sight of the men, rubber tubes attached to their cocks, twisting and twitching as the device held them on the brink of climax.

"How amusing," she laughed. "See how effective the toy is. A couple of minutes and they're reduced to dancing puppets."

"Actually, it's been half an hour, madam. You fell asleep."

"Half an hour. Why that's appalling, Victoria. Why did it take so long to get my tea?"

She turned the lever on the control back to its first notch whilst she took tea, which gave the men a modicum of relief. It was only a temporary respite as, after tea, she decided to explore the higher currents of the device.

She pushed the brass lever straight up to its third notch, making the needle on the pressure gauge swing wildly. Once the electro-magnetic waves had pulsed into the tubes, it made the men jump with surprise. Lady Sally was now exploring the full masturbatory potential of the device. She saw the rubber ripple at greater speed as it pulled against the flesh of the four hard cocks.

"Do you fancy a wager, maid? Which one will come first?"

"I reckon the banker, madam" said Victoria, noting how his ruddy, rounded face look set to burst.

"Hmm. Yet he has the fattest cock, which might afford him greater protection from the device. I think I will go for the judge. Do you think any of them will survive the fifth level?" said Lady Sally as she slid the lever forward to the fourth notch.

"No, madam, I wouldn't give odds on that."

The rubber pulsed faster and faster. The sensation was strange, wholly different from being masturbated by hand as there was no hardness of grip, only a pulsating throb which bounced along the shafts of their cocks at enormous speed. The four men were groaning, clearly approaching the point of no return.

Lady Sally might have watched as they reached there, now inevitable, climaxes, but she could not resist trying out the highest level. It was all part of experimenting with the devices to use them to their fullest extent.

As the pulses raced through the tubes, the effect as soon as they reached the open-ended rubber sheaths was instantaneous. They screamed at the shock and intensity of the waves throbbing along their shafts. They lasted seconds and soon shot their loads over the floor; the judge first, much to Lady Sally's satisfaction, then the banker, then the duke, and finally, the bishop. Dribbles of cum trailed from the four cocks, and there were blobs of sticky, white spunk splattered on the ground, the machine having projected it a long way. Lady Sally turned the device down to one as they collapsed to the floor in exhausted pleasure at having been allowed release.

"I think I should make them lick their disgusting messes from the floor," commented Lady Sally looking at the globs of spunk. Well that was an excellent experiment. What a splendid device. My humour is much improved now."

23

The last couple of days had been peaceful, apart from the noises of pain and pleasure from Lady Sally's playroom, which could even be heard in the cockpit. Captain Wyndham set *The Corseted Domme* in the direction of her next destination, Istanbul. They flew due south over the Russian Empire at high altitude, mindful that the Russian secret police would be investigating the bombing in St Petersburg, and sightings of the mysterious airship over the capital. He was also aware the Russian fleet did not have an airship capable of attaining the altitude of *The Corseted Domme*, so he knew they were safe from being intercepted.

She was travelling at speed. The captain looked down at the patchy clouds rushing past below him. Beyond that, two thousand feet to the ground, he watched the Russian Steppes roll pass. There was wheat... fields and fields of wheat, with only the occasional farmstead or village to break it up. This was the longest stretch of the journey. When they reached the mooring station in Istanbul, he needed to take on more hydrogen as the air bags were becoming deflated. Up to now this part of the trip had been uneventful.

He had not seen much of Lady Sally since the escape from St Petersburg. He could leave much of the flying to Clarissa, as this stretch was undemanding, but he was content to sit in the control cabin whilst she dealt with her submissive slaves as she wished, which was exactly what she was doing now.

In fact, Lady Sally was putting Borghild to new uses. The automaton was permanently dressed in the red latex outfit Victoria had dressed her in on the first day. On this occasion Lady Sally had put on a purple, rubber cat-suit. It was one of her favourites. The quality of the rubber sheets produced on her plantation was remarkable. The manufactory used brass rollers (using the brass from her mine, naturally) to produce the thinnest possible material, which created the tightest fitting clothes. The purple latex suit, which needed Victoria's help and lots of talcum powder to squeeze into, clung to her, accentuating every curve of her voluptuous body. Her arse looked magnificent in it; a beautiful globe of purple, whilst the top of the cat-suit was low-cut, and showed off her formidable cleavage perfectly.

For this session, Lady Sally and the automaton were encumbered with another accessory. They each had a leather belt around their waists, which supported huge strap-on phalluses. The adaptability of the rubber from her plantation was remarkable. These objects had been moulded in the workshops in Malaysia. Unlike the pliable, tight-fitting, latex material, these were made from hardened rubber. They looked amazingly authentic too. They had large rounded knobs and ridged shafts. Lady Sally had sent photographs of her favourite cocks for them to model the massive dildos on.

Borghild looked scary in her strap-on, the black rubber making a stark contrast with the shiny yellow of her brass hips. The object of this afternoon was to teach the automaton the art of anal penetration. To this end, the four gentlemen had been put into bondage, leaving their backsides exposed. Lady Sally and Borghild warmed them up with some flagellation before they went away to put the leather belts on. When they returned with the strap-on dildos secured to their waists, the men looked on in fearsome trepidation, seeing what their mistress had in store for them.

Lady Sally started by getting to work on the banker who having the fattest arse, was the best one to be singled-out as the first victim. Her stiletto ankle-boots clicked on the wooden flooring as she stepped over to where the banker's shoulders were secured in rope bondage. It was an awesome view for him. Lady Sally's shimmering, purple outfit clung to the curves of her waist, and protruding from that glorious shininess was the thick rubber phallus. Lady Sally threaded it between his lips.

"Suck on it, slave," she commanded.

The banker pushed his mouth as far as he could stretch whilst in bondage but only reached far enough to take the bulbous head of the false phallus.

"That's not good enough. You can take more than that."

Lady Sally took matters into her own hands, gripping the banker's bushy whiskers and pushing the rubber cock deeper into his mouth to the back of his throat. He gagged, and she withdrew slightly, before pushing in further. She slid the black object, now glistening with spittle, out of his mouth.

Lady Sally moved around to the rear end of the bench where the banker's arse was strapped, his flabby flesh invitingly exposed for her. The automaton took the position in front of him. As Lady Sally was parting his bum cheeks, readying to penetrate him with the rubber cock, so Borghild, mimicking the mistress, pushed herself into the banker's mouth. With him gagged by a mouthful of rubber dick at one end, she eased the dildo into his hole, pushing it until it was firmly nestled in. Such moans of pain, humiliation and pleasure he could make were muffled by a mouth full of rubber cock.

The two mistresses went to work on him. Lady Sally rammed her strap-on deep inside him, filling his back-passage. Meanwhile, Borghild's gears whirred as she thrust herself into his mouth with a relentless mechanical action. The other three looked on, anxious, yet strangely excited at the same time, knowing it would soon be their turn for such attention.

Lady Sally gripped the ropes that bound the banker to the bondage bench to gain greater purchase to push her latex clad hips further into him. She fucked him hard and unrelentingly, the rubber cock going deeper and deeper with every stroke. Satisfied he'd been given a good fucking, she withdrew the rubber cock. The automaton pulled her strap-on out. His mouth having been full of rubber, the banker now drew in deep drafts of air.

"Thank you, mistress," he said, not realising his ordeal wasn't over.

The automaton moved to take up Lady Sally's position over the banker's backside. She did not stand on ceremony, and it was lucky he had been warmed up and his hole stretched because Borghild's hips clicked as she drove the rubber cock straight into him. Lady Sally was a cruel mistress, but she was subtle in the delivery of her particular style of punishments. Of course, the automaton had no such skills. Her photographic cells had seen how the hard object had been used to penetrate the hole, and she set about her task with determination. Even Lady Sally could get tired, but the only thing capable of stopping the automaton was a mechanical fault… or Lady Sally telling her to stop, or switching her off.

Lady Sally enjoyed seeing the banker's fat arse get such a fucking, but even she acknowledged there had to be a limit, knowing the automaton was capable of carrying into the night without any break. Besides, she had three more slaves waiting for the same treatment.

Whilst Lady Sally turned her attention to the duke, bishop and judge, Captain Wyndham was racing the airship through the sky. He was just taking time to marvel at how beautifully the airship handled when he heard a splutter from outside the control room window. He craned his neck around to look at the engines. The propellers had stopped whirring. The airship was descending to the ground at 100 mph. They were going into free fall!

24

Captain Wyndham sprang into action. He had no idea what caused such a catastrophic engine failure, but he knew what had to be done. The next minutes were critical because *The Corseted Domme* was hurtling to the ground, and an explosion bigger than any Lady Sally had experienced, not to mention a fiery death.

He picked up the speaker funnel and barked instructions to the rigger-men, who were already on their feet, alarmed at the rapid descent. Clarissa jammed the elevators as hard as she could to level the airship's trajectory. If they could halt the descent even for a few moments, there might be hope for them.

The airship stabilised, hitting a more level trajectory. The captain stared anxiously outside the windows, praying the rigger-men had got to their stations in good time. At the rear end of the airship, beyond the tail on the upper side of its frame, he saw what he hoped; a series of parachutes billowing in the wind. This was the airship's emergency braking system in the event of such a catastrophe. Captain Wyndham gave a wry smile, all the new technology; steam, aether and electricity, but what might save them were big pieces of material and rope.

They weren't safe yet. It was a dangerous operation to bring an airship of these dimensions down in a controlled way with no engines. The parachutes slowed them, and the airship had levelled off, but they still had to undertake the tricky manoeuvre of landing safely without a mooring mast. It was every airship pilot's nightmare. The situation was at least stable, and he could spare a few minutes to explain to Lady Sally what was happening. He put Clarissa in charge of the controls, leaving her with one of the rigger-men, who was under instruction to fetch him at the first sign of any changes in their flight pattern. He headed back along the gondola.

The sight that confronted him was chaotic. The positioning of the whipping bench was such that the unfortunate protagonist tied to it, which was the duke, was facing the rear of the airship. So, when it veered sharply downwards, the angle of trajectory pinned the rubber phallus on the automaton deep into his arse, and there it was well and truly stuck. Lady Sally, who had been at the other end of the bench having her strap-on sucked, went flying. She was now slumped in a heap against the viewing window, a massive black cock sticking out from her waist. Victoria was reduced to jelly, wailing that they were all about to die.

"Well, I hope you have an explanation for your poor steering, captain," scolded Lady Sally.

A faint smile came across his lips. Given her undignified predicament, he was hardly expecting praise.

"The engines have cut out, madam. All of them, which is exceptional. You might expect one engine to develop a fault but not four, and for all of them to fail is strange."

The captain stepped over to Lady Sally and offered a hand, pulling her onto her feet.

"What does that mean, captain?" she asked.

"We have to make a forced landing, with no engines, and no mooring mast."

"Is it dangerous?"

"About as dangerous as it gets for an airship."

"Oh, how exciting," she exclaimed.

"Oh, madam!" groaned her maid, who had wet her knickers again.

"It's a tricky manoeuvre, I'm not going to deny it."

"And if it doesn't work?"

The captain shrugged, "A thousand cubic feet of hydrogen combined with fire – the biggest explosion you're ever likely to witness."

Caught in a gust of wind, the airship lurched to one side. Lady Sally, teetering on high heels and thrown off balance by the sudden movement, toppled forward. The captain leapt forward to catch her. Instinctively his arms wrapped around her shoulders and pulled her towards him to prevent her from falling. Her breasts pressed against his jumper, his body becoming enveloped in the shiny, latex cat-suit, whilst the stiff rubber cock dug into his midriff. She looked up at him with an enigmatic smile, those piercing blue eyes burning right through him. Their lips were close. He only needed to lean forward slightly for them to touch, and for him to kiss those sensuous, red lips. He longed to, but did he dare take such a liberty with a strict dominatrix?

The airship lurched again and the fleeting moment passed. Captain Wyndham was thrown back to the desperate reality of their situation.

"I'm sorry, Lady Sally, but I have to go back to the control room. I can't wait any longer, we have to try to make our landing."

"I'll accompany you to the bridge. If I'm going to meet a fiery doom, I shall want a front row seat," she said in a nonchalant tone of voice.

They rushed across the length of the gondola. Clarissa was holding the airship steady. *The Corseted Domme* was making a long, slow descent, the billowing parachutes behind her, controlling her speed. The captain took up his seat, with Lady Sally between him and the automaton with a grandstand view of the wheat fields looming closer and closer as they gradually lost altitude.

The captain put the mouthpiece of the speaker funnel to his lips, pulling it away to explain to Lady Sally what was happening, "The rigger-men are waiting to throw out the anchors. The timing is crucial, and then we have to hope that at least a few of them hook into the earth and bring us to a stop. The anchors suspend the airship in the air. If they don't hold, then the gondola will hit the ground."

The airship glided over the wheat fields. The terrain was perfect for this landing, the captain would have encountered enormous difficulties if they were still flying over the forests. He held on. Judging the altitude and timing were crucial. Concentration was etched over his face. He held his nerve until the last possible moment, shouting through the mouthpiece, "Now."

He leapt from his seat and craned his neck around to look towards the rear of the airship. He saw the cables flying through the air with the heavy, iron grappling-hooks at their ends. He saw one hit the ground and bounce off. "Damn," he said. He watched as another scraped through the ears of wheat without gaining any purchase in the soil. "Bugger," he swore. He saw the next grappling-hook disappear into the wheat. It tore through the ears before locking into the ground. "Yes," he shouted triumphantly. The fourth and fifth anchors dug into the soil.

The anchors pulled them to a sudden halt, lurching the airship sharply backwards and then forwards. Lady Sally was thrown by the velocity of the movement across the cockpit against the captain, the rubber cock ramming into his posterior and pinning him against the viewing window, Lady Sally's body pressed against him. Her face was alongside his.

"Wonderful captain. Jolly good show!" she shouted.

And then she planted a kiss on his cheek.

The captain was overwhelmed. His heart was pumping. Was it the adrenaline from surviving such dangers, or was it the kiss from Lady Sally? He saw his reflection in the glass, the pursed outline of her red lipstick on his cheek.

The airship was suspended in the air by the anchors. The bottom of the gondola was no more than ten feet from the wheat field, you could jump to the ground from it. However shaken the crew and passengers might be, they were alive. And *The Corseted Domme* suffered no further damage, the gondola never touched the ground and the duralumin frame had withstood the stress of the impact.

Lady Sally turned to him, "Truthfully captain, how dangerous was that?"

"Bloody dangerous. When I realised the engines had cut out, I'd have given our chances as 1 in 100. We're lucky."

"It's not luck captain; it's skill and bravery. I told you I was a good judge of character when I chose my airship captain."

Captain Wyndham blushed with pride.

"Oh look, it's exactly three-thirty. Just in time for tea. I think we could do with a brew."

25

The Corseted Domme was suspended over the wheat fields. The rigger-men secured more guy lines to secure her into position. By the time they'd finished the task it was turning dark and, given the airship was perfectly safe, the captain left investigation of the causes of the engines cutting out until the next morning.

They had landed on a huge estate in the Russian Steppes, pretty much in the middle of nowhere. There was no house or village in sight, just miles and miles of wheat, though it was hard to imagine nobody had noticed the plight of the giant airship as it made its enforced descent and landing.

In the morning, Captain Wyndham went to the engine room to discover the fault and what work might be needed, if indeed it was going to be possible to repair *The Corseted Domme* in situ. They were supplied with tools and spare parts, but there was a limit depending on the extent of the damage he found.

Meanwhile, Lady Sally was left with a leisurely playtime with her slaves whilst the airship was safely moored by the anchors and wires.

The engine room was eerily silent. Normally, this was the hub that drove the airship, powered the huge propeller blades, distributed the gas around the air bags and circulated the dimethyl aether that propelled the engine. It was a labyrinth of shiny copper pipes, pressure gauges and steam engines. It was usually a throbbing, steaming mass of activity, full of deafening noise: the hissing of steam, a constant thud of pistons, and the whirring of propeller blades. Captain Wyndham stood amidst this complex maze of pipes and machinery.

At the heart of the engine room were two giant cylindrical boilers. These were huge orbs of shining brass with gaskets at the top and two outlet valves at the front. Captain Wyndham ran his hand along the smooth, beautifully rounded surface of the brass. They were magnificent, two wonderfully rounded objects without a single blemish. He caressed the shiny brass. He gripped one of the valves between his fingers and tweaked it to see if it expressed any residue of steam or water.

He was trained and knew enough about the design of the engine to investigate the cause of the crash. His eyes were drawn to a pipe hanging loosely from one of the engines with drips of oil falling from it. He went over to take a closer look. He knelt down and dipped his finger into the pool of thick, slimy engine-oil which had accumulated on the floor.

He examined the pipe carrying the oil more closely. It powered the flow of aether to the engines and to cut off this supply would cause the airship to lose altitude dramatically. It was strange. He might have expected a split like this to occur at a joint where the metal had been welded or where there was a point of stress, but what he saw was a clean break. This was unusual, after all *The Corseted Domme* was a brand-new airship, and he had supervised the fitting of the engine room himself. In fact, the break was suspiciously clean.

When he investigated further, he found that the pipes servicing each of the airship's four engines were split in the same manner.

Captain Wyndham could reach only one inescapable conclusion. The fractures couldn't have been caused by wear or stress; they must have been made deliberately. He examined them carefully, noting the edges of the pipes had serrated marks where they had split as if they had been sawn through. This only confirmed Wyndham's suspicions and left him in no doubt somebody had deliberately tried to sabotage the airship. He was shocked–*who would want to do that?* Having discovered the cause, it was an easy job to weld the pipes and fix them. That was surely the least of his problems. The crucial question was who had perpetrated this dangerous act of sabotage.

He had to find the mistress and tell her at once.

Lady Sally was in her playroom punishing her submissive gentlemen, and there were various activities taking place. She had produced another one of her dastardly devices, this one a steam-powered spanking machine. She was aware her previous experiment with a steam-powered device had ended in disaster and explosion. This time she resolved to keep a closer eye on the boiler and not to get distracted by her own enjoyment.

The implement consisted of a wooden base which the protagonist bent over and a hand rail to which his wrists were secured by cuffs. The active part of the device was at the other end of the base where there was a brass rod to which various attachments could be fixed. The rod was powered by a boiler and steam engine, which powered a piston which in turn caused the rod to swing to and fro.

The lucky, or was it unfortunate, person attached to this device was the judge. The attachment at the end of the rod consisted of a leather hand. The device allowed Lady Sally to deliver an entirely hands free spanking whilst she could direct her attention elsewhere. Naturally, the machine could be adjusted to allow more steam to the piston and give both harder and faster whacks.

Lady Sally was satisfied with the performance of this device as it delivered consistent hard slaps against the gentleman's backside.

Elsewhere, Borghild had been let loose on the duke and the banker. She had been given free-reign to put into practise everything her photo-memory cells had learnt over the travels. But Lady Sally was somewhat concerned the automaton appeared to have developed her own libido. The activity she appeared to select was to lay on the rack, her feet supported by the wooden bar at its end, whilst she allowed the two men to penetrate her rubber vagina. The duke was at this very moment giving her a good fucking, whilst she gave oral sex to the banker with her rubber lips. From the expression in her glass eyes she appeared to be enjoying the experience.

Watching her automaton get screwed made Lady Sally horny. Indeed, she had not had an orgasm for a while which was not good enough. Confronted with the bishop, she felt compelled to force him to overcome his objections to penetrative sex in order to satisfy her.

To that end she followed her automaton's example and had laid herself on the whipping bench, her ankles lifted up, and resting on a wooden bar. In this position her cunt was at just the right height to be penetrated.

The bishop offered his protestations, "But, mistress, sex is a sin, and against my vows of chastity."

"Then you will have to choose between your God and your mistress, because I need to be fucked, now!"

It was in this state the captain found Lady Sally when he burst in excitedly.

"Really, captain, this is most inconvenient. You know I don't want to be interrupted when I'm having fun."

Realising Lady Sally's state of undress, and seeing the bishop's cock ready to enter her, he was embarrassed.

"I'm sorry, Lady Sally, but I wouldn't do so unless it was important. I think I've found the cause of the airship crash. It's imperative I speak to you in private."

Lady Sally picked up on the tone of urgency in Captain Wyndham's voice. She brought her fearsome temper under control, acknowledging he wouldn't have interrupted her unless it was something important. She climbed off the bench and put her knickers back on.

"Very well, captain, these slaves will be quite happy for a while. I'm sure Borghild can look after them."

Lady Sally and her maid followed Captain Wyndham out of the dungeon.

"So, what is it you've discovered?" she asked.

"Madam, I believe *The Corseted Domme* has been sabotaged!"

26

"Sabotaged! How very shocking. What do you mean captain?"

"It's probably easier if I show you," replied Captain Wyndham beckoning her and Victoria to follow him into the engine room.

When the captain opened the engine room door, Lady Sally gasped in amazement. Her living and dungeon quarters were designed and fitted to her personal and precise specification, but she left the detailed, technical aspects of her airship to Barnes-Wallis, Captain Wyndham and their team of artificers.

As she stepped tentatively into the room, she looked around in wonder at the intricate network of polished copper around her. She was struck, not so much by the technical complexity of the inner workings of the airship, remarkable though these were, but more by the enormous potential it offered for unusual punishments for her slaves.

"Why, Captain Wyndham, this is quite incredible. I had no idea. Would I be right in thinking these pipes get very hot, uncomfortably hot?"

"Why, yes Lady Sally, but…"

"So, would I be right in thinking this lets out a burst of hot steam?" she asked, examining a nozzle on one of the boilers.

"Well, yes Lady Sally, but…"

"And would these pipes be strong enough to suspend someone from if you chained them tightly enough?" asked Lady Sally, her imagination running away with her.

"Yes, possibly Lady Sally, but there's something I have to show you."

"Oh yes, of course, I'm terribly sorry. It's just I had no idea the engine room might offer such intriguing possibilities for erotic and corrective pleasure. But yes, do go on captain."

Captain Wyndham showed her the copper pipes, and pointed out how cleanly they had been sliced, and the tell-tale serrated markings which showed the pipes had been attacked with a hack-saw.

"The supplies to the four engines have been cut. That was what was so strange. It's not surprising to have an engine failure, but not to all four at the same time. I'm sorry Lady Sally, the only conclusion I can come to is that this was done deliberately."

"How shocking," gasped Lady Sally, "who could possibly want to do such a thing? Could it have been one of my slaves do you think, Victoria?"

"Madam, I doubt it, after all they're usually a bit tied up."

"Well yes, I suppose there is that."

"It's not impossible," Victoria continued, "one could have sneaked away in a moment when he wasn't in bondage but, to be honest, there's not much opportunity for that when you're around."

"Do you have any enemies?" asked Captain Wyndham.

Victoria rolled her eyes, "Well, where do you start?"

"Really Victoria, that's very naughty of you and quite unfair. Of course, a lady of my temperament and predilection will, how should I say, encounter people who disagree with one and occasionally some unsolicited corrective therapy is required. But no, I can't think of anybody in particular."

"How about Lord Melchiot?"

"Oh well yes, there was him. But he was most tiresome, and he treated his horses so abominably. You have to admit he deserved to be tied naked to his horse and sent galloping around in front of a full grandstand at Epsom Downs. Besides it was highly amusing. I seem to remember you laughed so much you dropped the sugar tongs in my tea. I was not best pleased as I'm sure you will recall."

"And then there was the suffragette you chained to the railings," continued Victoria.

"Oh, but Victoria you know that was merely a misunderstanding. Besides it turned out splendidly in the end. The news coverage was such good publicity for her cause and, once the little confusion had been sorted out, we ended up best of friends."

"How about UKSOLD?"

"UKSOLD, what's that?" queried Captain Wyndham.

"The UK Society of Lesbian Dwarves," replied Victoria.

"What?" exclaimed Wyndham. "Blimey, Lady Sally, what circles do you mix in?"

"Very varied ones, I can assure you captain. Well, yes it's true. I'm always having altercations with them. But they are so irritating and self-righteous. They just need putting in their place every so often."

"And then there was the whole of the winning Oxford crew of the 1908 boat race who you paddled with their own oars...

"Well, yes Victoria, if you are counting, there may be one or two whom one might have upset along the way. But I assure you that any correction I've administered was totally deserved."

Captain Wyndham had to add, "As well as those, there's the British Empire's Ministry of War, the Prussian Empire's army and airship fleet, and the Russian Empire's secret police."

"Well, when you put it like that, I suppose I do have a few enemies. It's quite an achievement for a lady to be pursued across Europe by as many as three empires."

They stood in silence for a few moments reflecting on the implications of the captain's revelations.

"What do we do next?" asked Lady Sally.

"Well, repairing the airship is not a serious problem. I've got the tools to do that and, once the pipes have been soldered, there's no reason why she can't be restored to full power. The trickier question is who did it?-And are they still on the airship?"

"You mean we have a stowaway?"

"I think that's likely, though it was a suicidal act to try to bring down the airship. We have to be vigilant. I'll tell the crew to watch for anything unusual. The inside of the airship is vast, it's a maze of gangways and steps to access the hydrogen bags. It could be hard to find anybody hiding there."

"Oh, my god!" exclaimed Lady Sally as a thought struck her. "Cook's reports of thefts from the kitchens. That could be our stowaway. We must put a guard on the kitchen door. Cook won't like it, but we have to catch the perpetrator of this heinous act of sabotage."

"You're right. I suggest we make a sweep of the airship frame too. Whoever it is could strike again."

Lady Sally and Victoria returned to the playroom whilst the captain donned his protective helmet, gathered up the blow torch and soldering irons, and set about repairing the damage. It wasn't a difficult task, and wouldn't take him more than an afternoon.

The blow torch shot out a tongue of blue flame and, using spare copper kept in the tool box for just such a purpose, the captain repaired the pipes. He built a new ring of copper around where they had been cut. They should be strong enough now to circulate the diethyl aether, which was the fuel that fired up the engines.

The captain returned to the control room to test everything was in working ordered. He adjusted settings and gauges, then started the engines. At first nothing happened, but that was no concern. It took a while for the aether to circulate around the system and as it did, sure enough, the engines fired up. He checked. All four of them were fully functioning. He pulled a lever, and the propellers began to start up, he left them rotating until they built up to full-speed.

The Corseted Domme was fit to take to the air again, which was just as well because approaching across the wheat fields was a troop of the Russian Empire's army led by a steam-driven armoured vehicle, which hissed and rattled towards them. It appeared word must have got out they'd crash landed here.

Once again, the captain was forced to take urgent action. He called the crew to pull in the guy ropes and get ready to release the anchors. The engines were repaired in the nick of time as they were forced into making another speedy exit. He told one of the men to fetch Lady Sally to the bridge.

"What alarums are there now, captain?" she asked on her arrival.

The captain merely pointed across the fields to the approaching platoon of Russian soldiers.

"Don't worry captain, I believe I have the means to delay them. I have to be honest, I've got fed up of looking at wheat."

She picked up a lightning blunderbuss from the stolen crate of weapons left in the control room. She turned the dial up to the highest possible setting, opened a window in the cabin, and leaned out. She raised the sight to her eye and aimed... aimed at the fields of wheat, dried out by the summer sun on the Russian Steppes, at a point in the path of the approaching enemy.

She fired. A purple light fizzed through the air. It struck the parched ears of wheat, which exploded with blue flame, and then caught light. It being summer, and the wheat so dry, the flames spread like wild-fire.

The captain turned towards Lady Sally with a look of unabashed admiration, "Genius! That should buy us enough time to escape."

The rigger-men on the ground, alert to the threat of the approaching soldiers, were toiling as fast as they could to pull the great iron grappling-hooks out of the ground. When the last one was released, both anchors and men were pulled up into the gondola of the airship.

The Russian military were thrown into a state of alarm and confusion at the sight of the balls of fire rolling across the steppes. There was no way they could get anywhere near the airship. They looked on, powerless, as the mighty dirigible soared into the air, swung around 180 degrees, and accelerated into the sky.

27

"Hurrah. Lady Sally Rudston-Chichester makes another dashing escape. We're getting good at this, aren't we, captain?" Lady Sally called, jumping in the air excitedly.

"We certainly are, madam. Though I expect your maid will be traumatised."

"She'll get over it. Besides, she's been my maid for years, she knows what to expect. I think she feigns her alarms most of the time, you know. Full-speed ahead, captain."

"I'll have to take her up to top speed to get out of Russian Empire's air space, but we've still a long way to go. Are we still headed for Istanbul?"

"Yes, my next destination is the Ottoman Empire. But don't panic, captain, I've no intention of getting into more trouble. I want to go shopping in the bazaars. I've arranged to meet Mustafa Shagazade, my agent there, a merchant who purchases supplies for me from the silk route traders. After all, one can't possibly go travelling without a shopping trip somewhere, can one?"

"Indeed not, madam."

"God, this excitement has made me horny again. As you saw, I'd just persuaded the bishop to overcome his theological objections and give me a good fucking. It's so frustrating, I simply must have another orgasm. But I'm not going to fuss around waiting for my slaves to get an erection, I know exactly how I'm going to get my pleasure. You must come and join the fun later captain when you can leave the controls. And then you must join us for dinner to celebrate another intrepid escape."

The captain daren't hazard how Lady Sally intended to pleasure herself, and wasn't going to enquire, "Maybe I will later."

"Jolly good," said Lady Sally before returning to her playroom to see how Victoria and her guests had coped.

When she returned, the steam-powered spanking machine was still whacking the judge's backside with its leather hand. In the excitement, she had completely forgotten about it. Luckily, it wasn't turned up high enough for the boiler to explode, and its whacks, although delivered at a steady pace, were not overly hard. The judge's arse was throbbing red though, but it was nothing he couldn't take. The automaton, left to her own devices, delivered all manner of sexual pleasures to the other three men. In fact, they were forced into fucking her so many times they looked totally exhausted, Borghild's needs being pretty much incapable of being satisfied.

Lady Sally's crotch was sopping, and her need desperate. Her intention was to put the automaton to work on *her* pleasure. Grabbing the strap-on belt from one of the hooks on the wall, she set about strapping it around Borghild's waist. As Lady Sally ran her hands over the automaton's brass hips expecting to appreciate her smooth, shiny finish, she felt a completely different sensation.

"Ugh, that's disgusting."

The automation was wet and sticky, being covered in the sweat of the three men who had been lying on top of her thrusting their cocks into her rubber vagina. Although she was desperate, she couldn't possibly have the automaton pleasure her in that state, and have her flawless, white skin sullied by their smelly sweat.

"Victoria, get the brass cleaner and rags and clean these bodily fluids off Borghild. And give her a good polish while you're at it."

"Yes, madam," her maid sighed, but with the hint of a twinkle in her eye, polishing the automaton being one of her favourite tasks.

She stripped Borghild of her latex outfit until she stood there in her brassy nakedness. She dipped a rag in a tub of *Brasso,* a relatively new cleaning product, in which Lady Sally had bought shares. She started with the automaton's brass breasts, spreading the oily substance across them with the rag, and then rubbing thoroughly. There was a pungent, metallic smell, which, though initially overpowering, after a short while became intoxicating. The smell combined with the brisk rubbing movements against the smooth brass tits were giving her a hard-on.

"Victoria, I can see what's happening, there's a bulge in your apron. Get on with the job, I haven't got all day!"

Following the reprimand, the maid got on with the task at hand without compromising the thoroughness of her cleaning. By the end the automaton was gleaming.

"Yes, that's not bad Victoria. But I think you ought to clean out the rubber vagina too."

"The rubber vagina, madam, but…"

Her mistress gave her a hard stare.

"Yes of course, madam, but I'll put rubber gloves on for this job."

Victoria fetched hot soapy water. Of course, when she inserted her hand through the rubber gash, there was a large, sticky pool of cum accumulated inside it. She had done numerous foul tasks in service to mistress over the years but this one had to be the most disgusting.

"She's finished, madam," said Victoria, tossing the spunk soaked cloth into the bowl.

"Oo, she looks new and sparkly now," said Lady Sally as she ran her hands admiringly across the automaton's firm, brass breasts. "I've got warm myself up again now but I couldn't have put up with that sticky sweat against my skin."

Lady Sally stretched the leather belt around the shimmering, yellow waist, pulled the strap and tightened the buckle so the strap-on was secured fast. The black, rubber phallus stood out proud. She wanted that thing inside her. She ran her fingers along its ribbed hardness. Handling the object and feeling it's unyielding stiffness was enough to get her juices flowing again.

She fixed Borghild in the eye and ordered, "Pleasure me!"

Was she imagining it or was there a little light in the automaton's eyes, and a barely discernible twitch in her rubber lips expressing excitement.

Lady Sally stripped off and got onto the rack, lifting her legs up in the air and resting her ankles on the wooden frame. She felt her sex oozing with juice. The automaton's gears clicked into action.

Borghild had been trained in the art of sensuous domination by her mistress well. She had learnt how to tease, she had been shown how to bring her human controllers to a point of sexual arousal and hold them there before tipping them over the edge. She exercised these newly honed skills on Lady Sally. After all, the instruction had been to pleasure her.

Consequently, the automaton did not immediately climb on the rack and thrust the strap-on inside her. The tiny springs and cogs in her mechanical hand clicked and whirred. She reached out to run her smooth brass fingers, still cool from the *Brasso* cleaner, along her torso. Lady Sally arched her body in surprise and pleasure as the hands stroked her large breasts, circling them around her dark areola before clasping a nipple between two brass fingers and squeezing hard.

Lady Sally was perfectly aware of the delicious combination of pain and pleasure such an action aroused, having observed it in many slaves, Though she rarely allowed a slave to touch her tits, and none dare take the liberty of squeezing her nipple. Borghild had no such reservations, and the effect was both surprising and pleasant. She felt her crotch get moist with every squeeze and rub of her sore nipple.

The automaton turned her attentions to her mistress's crotch. Her hand unrolled and her fingers clicked straight as she inserted a digit up her cunt. Lady Sally gasped as the brass object circled inside her. A second finger found her clit in the folds of flesh around her cunt and began to rub. The sensations from the rubbing and twisting were exquisite, and Lady Sally was rapidly approaching her climax, though she still wanted the rubber cock insider her.

"Inside me. Fuck me!" she screamed.

Borghild's head twisted around, the hair of the blonde wig flying through the air as she recorded her mistress's wishes. The limbs clicked into action as she climbed up onto the rack where she knelt, positioning herself between Lady Sally's upraised legs, the rubber phallus poised to enter her.

When penetration came, it was sudden. The automaton's hips clicked and, with a piston-like action, drove straight into her cunt. There was no holding back, this was a full-on fuck. Lady Sally reached her arms out to grip the wooden frame of the rack and arched her back to take the rubber deeper inside her. Borghild lowered her metal frame over Lady Sally so the weight of her brass body pressed on Lady Sally's breasts, making her gasp and pant even harder.

The automaton was relentless, pushing the hard rubber phallus inside her with forceful strokes. The sensation of being fucked by the automaton was strange, somewhat akin to being on a bizarre fairground ride. Lady Sally couldn't argue with the results though as she was rapidly brought to the brink of climax. With only a bit more pounding from the pistons in the automaton's mechanical hips she was brought to the point of ecstasy, bucking and twisting against the heavy brass pressing on her body as she screamed out in pleasure.

It was at this point Captain Wyndham entered the playroom to see Lady Sally in mid-orgasm and the automaton still pushing the black, rubber cock into her. Her submissive gentlemen and Victoria were gathered around the rack, watching as their mistress got a good fucking from the automaton.

He had experienced too much of Lady Sally's lifestyle to be shocked by the vision, though he couldn't deny it was erotic seeing her naked body squeezed between the wooden rack and the brass automaton. It wasn't jealousy, after all, it was hard to be envious of a machine, yet he fought to suppress the feeling that he would love to be in the position of the automaton.

"Stop! Stop!" gasped Lady Sally, knowing that, without her command, Borghild would continue until her batteries went flat.

"Phew, that was something else. What a marvellous little sex-toy you've proved to be."

28

Following the discovery that *The Corseted Domme* had been sabotaged, the captain implemented a new regime of security measures. He and his men did a thorough sweep of the engine room, the area containing many hazards and opportunities for further sabotage. A huge padlock was put on the engine room door for which only he and Lady Sally possessed a key. They found nobody, but they did find gnawed chicken bones, confirming the suspicion the stowaway was the culprit for the thefts from the kitchen.

Consequently, he put a surreptitious watch on the door to the kitchen, thinking that if the interloper didn't have food, he might be tempted to raid them again, and be discovered. He didn't get away without an ear-lashing from cook though.

"I told yer didn't I. I said there was someone stealing food from me kitchen. Did anyone take any notice of me? No, 'Milady High and Mighty' just carried on till we's been sabotaged. Look at the state of mi kitchen now. No sooner have I got tidied up after one alarum and we have a crash, no less!"

"Yes, I'm very sorry cook, but we've got guards all over the airship now," the captain reassured her.

It was the frame of the airship that presented the greatest problem. The body of the airship containing the bags of hydrogen was a vast complex of walkways and steps amongst the vast air bags. It would be easy to hide there and stay undiscovered. The captain and his men did a systematic sweep, taking care to examine every hidden corner in the duralumin structure. They found nothing.

This was the space that caused the captain the greatest concern, it being easier to restrict access to the engine room. He placed guards on the entrances, but if somebody was inside, or managed to get inside, there were so many nooks and crannies to hide. In addition to which the hydrogen bags were, in many respects, more hazardous than the engine room. If the stowaway was reckless enough to cause an engine failure, then splitting an air bag and igniting the hydrogen didn't bear thinking about. It would be suicidal though, causing an explosion to end all explosions.

The captain armed the crew with the blunderbusses stolen from the Prussian military arms store though they were under strict instructions not to use them anywhere near the hydrogen bags.

Lady Sally, having been inspired by what she saw in the engine room, decided to transfer her activities there once the captain had completed his searches. She checked with the captain what could be safely used and was now set on exploiting what the engine might offer in terms of corrective pleasures.

It was a different environment to her sumptuous panelled playroom with its sophisticated mahogany and brass equipment. This was a labyrinth of pipes, conduits, valves, pumps and boilers. Whilst the airship was in flight it was also a cacophony of noise. Hissing, throbbing and pumping echoed around the engine. Above it was the constant and deafening roar of the propellers as they whizzed around driving the airship along at a speed of 100 mph.

"Victoria, help me chain these slaves up."

"Pardon, madam."

"Help me chain these slaves up," she shouted at the top of her voice.

"PARDON, MADAM!"

"Bloody hell, I'll do it myself," she said grabbing the chains and getting to work.

She soon had wrists and ankles chained or handcuffed onto copper pipes. The four men looked distinctly worried. Lady Sally's health and safety record on the trip so far had not been great, and here she was in an area that thrummed with moving objects, and numerous hazards. One false move and a dangling cock could easily get sliced off. The banker used his actuarial skills to calculate the odds of serious injury, the judge worked out the legal basis for any compensation claims, whilst the bishop merely prayed to his god they would get out alive.

Lady Sally's attention was directed at the massive cylindrical boilers at the heart of the engine room, directly facing where she had secured her submissive gentlemen. They were great orbs of gleaming brass with a valve on the front of each one. They were designed to allow steam to escape should the boilers overheat. By tweaking the little nubs of metal on their smooth, rounded surfaces it was possible to adjust both the direction and velocity at which the steam escaped. Lady Sally considered that watching the slaves jump and hearing them squeal as jets of hot steam hit them would be amusing.

The engine room hummed and throbbed with the sound of mechanical devices.

Lady Sally ran a hand along the surface of one of the boilers. Its curves were beautifully smooth. The surface was warm to touch but not so hot as to prevent handling.

"Aren't they magnificent objects, my maid?"

"Pardon, madam."

"AREN'T THEY… oh never mind."

Her hand strayed to the little valves sticking out from the rounded surface of the brass boiler. She gripped it between her fingers and twisted. There was a hissing sound, and a tiny jet of steam squirted out. The valves were mounted on ball bearings so that, by pulling them, Lady Sally could adjust the direction of the steam. Turning the valves narrowed the hole from which the steam expelled, and consequently its force and distance.

Now to test the object out. Her first experiment was to see if the jets of steam could reach to where her slaves were chained. She twisted the valve. A spray of steam shot out into the air and covered them in a hot, moist haze. That was enough for Lady Sally to understand the principle. It was just like the hose her gardener used on the flower beds at Rudston Hall. She turned the valve and, gradually, the stream of steam became narrower and more concentrated until it was a single jet. This steam shot across the engine room and hit the duke in the chest, right on a nipple.

He howled with shock and pain, the combination of velocity and heat causing a distinct sensation on the nipple. The duke twisted against his chains to avoid it, but was trapped as the jet of hot steam drove against him.

Lady Sally was most amused at seeing the effects of steam, which was clearly delivering an exquisite form of corrective punishment.

She pulled on the valve, rolling it downwards so the steam struck his groin in a sharp jet that pounded his cock and balls. Lady Sally was reminded of a hydro-vibrator she once used which propelled jets of water to massage muscles or, indeed, induce sexual excitement when directed against the crotch. She remembered it as being a most pleasurable experience. The difference here was the steam was red-hot, and the density of its impact more akin to spiky needles than a massage.

She kept one boiler trained on the duke's genitals whilst twisting the valve on the other to open up another jet of stream. This one she used to shock the other men, shooting it at random so none of them could anticipate where the next jet was going to land. She aimed mainly for nipples and cock and balls as this certainly had the most impact. She soon had the four of the men jiggling in an impossible dance to avoid the jets of stream striking their tender flesh. The sounds of hissing, thudding and whirring were now joined by howls and squeals of surprise and pain. It was most satisfying, and Lady Sally was having enormous fun with this newly discovered instrument of torment.

There was one problem though. The men were sweating both with the background heat of the engine room, and the more specific heat of the steam. Victoria, in her maid's uniform, looked especially uncomfortable, her round, red face streaming with sweat.

Lady Sally was starting to regret wearing one of her rubber outfits. The steam got everywhere, even in the narrowest gaps between tight latex and flesh, and once the heat penetrated under the rubber there was nowhere for it to go. Lady Sally was getting hot and though, being a gentlewoman, she did not perspire much, she found being in proximity to the valves and sprayed by the hot steam caused her to sweat profusely. The engine room assumed the qualities of a steam room.

There was nothing for it. Lady Sally peeled off her rubber cat-suit and left it, dripping with steam and sweat, on the floor of the engine room. Now naked, she instantly felt better. Indeed, the sensation for her was much like being in a stream room. There was an exceedingly sensuous pleasure to the heat. Little rivulets of hot water dripped along her skin, running across her breasts and trickling from her abdomen to her crotch.

A haze of hot vapour filled the engine room. She had to peer intensely to aim the jets of steam. She now had them trained on the banker and the judge, giving their balls an intense treatment. It was great fun watching the impact of the jets on their most sensitive parts and hearing them yelp.

However, the heat of the steam had become so intense as to become unbearable. In addition to which the thumping noise of the propeller in particular was giving her a headache. She shouted in Victoria's ear to tell her to fetch towels and, after several attempts, the message got through. Her maid, still fully dressed, was relieved to escape. When she returned, the valves had been turned off and the slaves unchained. Lady Sally wrapped a fluffy white towel around her and led them out of the engine room. It was surprising how opportunities for new and imaginative methods of sadistic torment presented themselves. She considered the experiment to be a great success.

29

The journey from the site of the crash to the Ottoman Empire was a long one. The captain maintained a high altitude to keep them safe from the clutches of any Russian Empire airships, except Lady Sally insisted on flying low over Kiev to appreciate the glittering, gold domes of its many churches.

When she wasn't entertaining herself with her slaves, she often stood at the great glass window in her playroom gazing at the clouds as they flew past below her, or admiring the scenery from afar as the patchwork fields and villages sped by.

They passed over the Crimea and then turned south-west across the Black Sea, heading towards Istanbul. They covered the final stretch in the early hours of the morning, and Lady Sally got up at dawn, taking up a place at the front of the gondola to gaze upon the sun rising, and the approaching minarets of Istanbul.

She sighed, wrapping her silk dressing gown around her, whilst still allowing for a peek of cleavage, "This is a magnificent view is it not?"

The captain's eyes could not fail to stray to Lady Sally's breasts, "It certainly is," he agreed.

As the airship slowed to make her descent, they both admired the sun dancing on the blue waters of the Black Sea, and the view of the isthmus on which the exotic city of Istanbul perched.

Although the Ottoman Empire had experienced grander days and was past its peak, it was still the point where eastern and western trading routes met. It required careful manoeuvring because, as well as being a busy airship station, it was a chaotic one. The captain weaved the giant dirigible through the traffic of airships from across Europe and the Far East to seek out an empty mooring mast with enough space to accommodate the vast bulk of *The Corseted Domme*.

He saw from the cockpit how Lady Sally's airship was causing a stir. He flew low and watched the awe struck looks and excited waves as the giant, silver dirigible circled around the airship station looking for a berth. Lady Sally, who had retired to get dressed ready for her shopping expedition, would have been pleased to see the furore her airship was creating. Eventually, he found a suitable mooring mast, and the rigger-men hooked up the lines from the tip of the airship to pull her in. After the enforced landing in the Russian Steppes it was good to have her secured to a proper mast. The captain was relieved to find hydrogen filling stations so the air bags could be refilled.

The people of Istanbul had never seen an airship as huge and magnificent as *The Corseted Domme*. A crowd gathered at the foot of the mooring mast to find out who owned this most magnificent of dirigibles. There were men in turbans, women with their heads covered in silk scarves, and bare-foot children. By the time the party were ready to disembark, an impromptu market had formed around the airship, the merchants not wishing to miss an opportunity to sell their wares.

When Lady Sally emerged, she was the perfect image of the calm, implacable, Edwardian gentlewoman in the midst of the scene of chaos that now surrounded the airship. As soon as they stepped out of mooring tower they were greeted with a blast of heat. Of course, Lady Sally was prepared, having insisted on taking most of her wardrobe, including her summer dresses. She was in an elegant, cotton dress in cream, which displayed her hour-glass figure to perfection. Perched on her head was a wide-brimmed hat secured by a wide bow of material tied under her chin.

Victoria, sweltering in her maid's dress, huge bustle and layers of petticoats followed with a large fan to cool her mistress down. The captain who had brought no wardrobe with him whatsoever was in his working clothes, his normal white roll neck jumper and flying boots. Luckily, his wide-brimmed fedora hat shielded his face from the sun, but he still looked distinctly uncomfortable in the scorching heat.

A crowd gathered around the party, and they were welcomed with cheers and waves. The children were as excited as those back in Yorkshire who greeted the launch of *The Corseted Domme*. They were familiar with airships but had never seen anything as grand as this.

At first Lady Sally felt pleased at the welcome she received, but as the crowd bustled around her, she soon changed her mind.

A kebab was thrust in her face, "Lady… you want kebab. Good kebab. Good price…"

A hand covered in jewellery waved in front of her, "Lady… you want bangle. Finest silver. Two for one, good price."

Offers of food and goods were tolerable though barely; other offers were definitely not.

"Lady… you want man, give you good fucky. Come with me. Good price."

"Lady… you want fanny sucky. I take you. How much you offer for good fanny sucky."

The attention soon became wearisome, and Lady Sally was relieved to be approached by Mustafa Shagazade's man with a steam-driven carriage to transport them to the Grand Bazaar. There was a full entourage as the men, dressed in smart linen suits, were required to help carry Lady Sally's shopping. The carriage was laden with several trunks, for the safe packing of said shopping. The captain, melting in his roll neck jumper, was extremely envious of the cool suits. He wanted to stay behind and supervise the filling of the hydrogen bags, but Lady Sally insisted all available hands were needed for the shopping expedition.

They were dropped off at the merchant's offices off Sultanahanet Square in the heart of the old city. This was Lady Sally's first visit to Istanbul, and she was thrilled to be there. She had travelled to Samarkand before, to seek out a special weave of silk with aphrodisiac properties she had read about in the third Earl of Rudston's journal, and to discover more about her silk route heritage. She loved the exoticism and sensuality of the east.

Mustafa Shagazade was a portly middle-aged gentleman with a black moustache that curled up at its ends, dressed in a turban and light blue kaftan

"Ah, Mr Mustafa, how delightful to meet you after all these years. I trust business is good."

"Lady Sally, it's a pleasure," he enthused, whilst lasciviously eyeing up her perfect figure and abundant décolletage bursting out of the cotton dress. "But I'm afraid to say business is only average. There is less trade going across land along the silk route, and more being transported by airship. There's now an airship route direct from Ishfahan to Berlin, bypassing Istanbul. And then there's been the Balkan Wars, and the threat of new wars…"

"Oh, I'm terribly sorry to hear that," offered Lady Sally.

"I know you are here for the shopping, so let me be your guide around the bazaar. But first you must join me in a glass of mint tea."

"That would be delightful, Mr Mustafa," replied Lady Sally with alacrity. It may not be China or Indian tea, but it was still tea, and mint tea was exceedingly refreshing. At least he was well enough acquainted with her tastes not to offer her Turkish coffee, which would have been simply vile.

The party settled onto the divans outside the merchant's trading emporium. They were served glasses of mint tea from a huge silver pot and accompanied by sugared almonds. They reclined on the seats to sip the sweet liquid.

"Please, Lady Sally, before we go into the bazaar, let me offer you a delicacy of the region."

A servant brought out a brass bowl containing an unappealing ball of meat swimming in a thin, white fluid. Lady Sally did not wish to offend her generous host by declining it, but had no intention of sampling it.

"Oh, but my maid tastes my food for me. You see, I'm afraid I have such a delicate stomach, and she will judge if it's too rich for me.",

Victoria looked on horrified at the brown lump of gristly meat in the dish but, nonetheless, obediently took a mouthful. Lady Sally smiled wickedly as she saw her maid's expression.

"May I ask what the dish is made of?" she enquired.

"Why yes, Lady Sally, it's horse testicle braised in ewe's milk infused with cardamom pods. It's a speciality of the region."

"Oh my, but that sounds simply delightful, Mr Mustafa. I'm just so sorry my delicate English stomach will not allow me to partake of any. You must jot the recipe down for me and I'll give it to cook."

The captain chuckled. He could imagine cook's reaction to such a recipe, and she might just have the nerve to tell Lady Sally where to shove her horse's testicle!

The entourage headed for The Grand Bazaar with the four gentlemen, Victoria and the captain carrying three huge chests between them, brought on her travels specifically for this purpose.

The Grand Bazaar was a huge covered market of massive colonnades with a network of smaller passages leading from them. The captain, for one, was relieved to get under cover out of the searing heat of the sun. The market was jammed full of crafts and antiques of every description.

"Now, Mr Mustafa, I am minded to build a Turkish bath in one of the ante rooms in Rudston Hall. I've already sourced a company that can supply the heating system back in England, but what I require are authentic Turkish majolica tiles."

"I know just the stall for you."

She pulled out a piece of paper with a sketch showing the dimensions of the room in question. After a brief discussion with the stallholder about the number of tiles required, she set about choosing from the abundant range of beautifully glazed blue, green, turquoise, yellow and white tiles with geometric patterns in the Islamic style. Having made her choice and negotiated a good deal on such a huge quantity, she paid and instructed the trader to have the tiles delivered direct to *The Corseted Domme* forthwith. The men let out a collective sigh of relief at this point as they had visions of having to cart thousands of heavy tiles back to the airship themselves.

Lady Sally was an organised and ruthless shopper. She had a vision for what she needed and set about her purchases with determination. She was also a tough negotiator and bartered hard with the traders to get a good, and fair, price. This was, of course, only what they would have expected, but if they thought this rich, aristocratic English woman was going to be a soft touch, that illusion was soon dispelled. Lady Sally used a combination of hard bargaining skills, along with her undoubted charm, to secure a good price.

They went from block to block in the bazaar, each zone specialising in a particular craft. She wanted hand-woven Turkish rugs and bought several of them, with brightly coloured geometric patterns. She purchased ceramics, copper bowls, hukkah pipes, silver tea pots, decorated glasses and lamps. That was before she even got to the section selling materials and clothing where she bought silks, cottons, kaftans, gowns, silk slippers and an abundant supply of silver jewellery. Then there were the spices and incenses, and last, but not least the teas. There were stalls selling a vast range of teas, many blends she was familiar with, but she also purchased pomegranate and jasmine teas, which she'd never tried before.

The chests filled up quickly, and it wasn't long before the six men found themselves carting the laden trunks around the bazaar with them. Lady Sally shopped like a whirling dervish, and it wasn't until it was time for tea that she finally stopped.

They retired to a tea shop recommended by Mr Mustafa. Lady Sally was sipping green tea whilst inhaling enormous drafts of smoke from a huge hukkah pipe. She was in a good mood... an exceedingly good mood.

She was giggling manically and telling them tales of her colourful past.

"Did I tell you about the time in Samarkand when I got fucked on the tomb of Tamerlane the Magnificent by my silk merchant?" she announced, proceeding to relate the story in graphic detail.

Then she told them about her poison garden at Rudston Hall, and how she'd fucked her gardener, and about how she punished Lord Melchiot on her automaton horse.

She was in fits of giggles.

"Oh, I've had such marvellous adventures." She turned to the merchant, "So tell me, Mr Mustafa, is this what is called 'hashish'?"

"Yes, Lady Sally, the very finest... and potent."

"Well, I must say, this is wonderful stuff. My last purchase will be to stock up with some to take back to England."

By now the whole party was well and truly stoned, except for Victoria, who had a 'gippy' stomach from the horse's testicle, and had declined the offer of smoking hashish. In between reclining on the divans collapsed in a constant state of giggles, they managed to demolish a huge plate of flatbreads, lamb kebabs, chickpea dip, dates and other delicacies.

A young, veiled woman approached them.

"Come here, my dear," called Lady Sally. "What a lovely necklace. It's so shiny. Oh, my goodness, I've never seen anything so shiny! I don't think my poor eyes can stand the brightness."

"Please, are you the famous English lady, Lady Sally Rudston-Chichester?"

Lady Sally was not averse to bit of flattery, "Oh, famous, well yes, naturally my reputation does proceed me."

"I've read about you in the Istanbul Sun. You are a strong lady who will stand up to males and protect women. I have come to plead for your help."

Victoria's ears pricked up. Alarm bells rang.

"Yes, do tell me more," Lady Sally encouraged.

"My name is Nisrahur. You see, my sister has been picked up from the streets by the sultan's guards where she has been taken to his harem as a slave. I know the girls are badly mistreated. I was hoping a lady of your standing could negotiate with the sultan to get her released."

"I will do better than that," exclaimed Lady Sally. "I will rescue her!"

Her maid tried to intervene, "Madam, is this wise? This could end up as a disaster. I see more explosions and being chased out of Istanbul."

"Victoria, let it not be said Lady Sally Rudston-Chichester will not leap to the defence of her sex for a noble cause."

30

The full trunks were loaded onto the steam-driven carriage, and they returned to the airship with the girl to plot a strategy for the rescue attempt.

The captain, used to a disciplined and frugal life style from his time in the army, was the most affected by the hashish.

On returning to the mooring mast, he waxed lyrical about the airship, "Hey, wow, she's like so huge, and silvery."

Lady Sally looked askance at him, "Captain, if we need to make a quick getaway, will you be capable of steering *The Corseted Domme*."

"Well, yes, that's no problem. I'll just take her floating up into the stars, milady."

To Victoria, this latest escapade had the makings of a disaster.

Even the girl, Nisahur, looked alarmed at the help she'd enlisted. She wanted somebody important to use her influence on the sultan, not the full-scale raid on the royal palace the English lady was intent on.

Lady Sally's goal was to infiltrate the Topkapi Palace (the official residence of the Sultan of the Ottoman Empire, Al Bin Kinkjani), seek out the harem, find Nisahur's sister, and rescue her and any other harem slaves who wanted to come with them.

She pondered on the logistical difficulties before exclaiming, "Aha, I have a plan!"

"A cunning plan?" asked Victoria.

"Don't sound so sceptical, maid. Yes, an ingenious plan. I am an English lady who has procured women for the sultan's harem. We simply go to the front gate of the palace, and I will use my charms to persuade the guard to take the girls to the harem; failing that, I have other means. The captain will be a snake charmer; he will carry an Ali Baba basket with blunderbusses, in case we need them."

"But, what girls?" asked Victoria.

"Well, that's where the ingenuity comes in. You, and the four gentlemen, dressed in belly-dancer costumes I purchased at the market. I intended them for some exotic play, but this is a far better use."

"But, we're all men, and we have beards, moustaches or whiskers."

"Yes, but I have veils to hide those."

"But madam…"

It was too late. Lady Sally was already rummaging in the trunks of her purchases from the Grand Bazaar to find the belly-dancer outfits.

They made for a bizarre troupe. Lady Sally, in order to portray herself as the perfect English gentlewoman, and despite the searing heat, opted for a velvet dress with a huge bustle with an ivory, cameo brooch at her neck. Victoria and the men looked ridiculous. They had material stuffed under their tops for breasts, whilst their skimpy costumes left their embarrassing middle-aged midriffs bare. Their costumes were vibrant colours, and decorated with tiny, silver cymbals, which tinkled with every movement. Their heads and faces were covered with silk veils though their assortment of facial hairs was all too evident. They looked comical, their absurd dress only emphasizing their strange mixture of body shapes–the bishop tall and thin, the banker, fat and round. Even Victoria, who was, of course, used to wearing women's clothes looked preposterous in such a skimpy costume. Only the duke, who had a slightly effeminate look, was remotely capable of pulling off the deception. Meanwhile, the captain was dressed as a snake charmer in traditional Turkish dress; baggy pantaloons, and a fez.

The effect of the hashish on the men was starting to wear off and, what had originally seemed like a wizard jape, suddenly looked distinctly outlandish. But having conceived of the venture, there was now no stopping Lady Sally.

They were soon at the gatehouse of the Topkapi Palace. Fortunately, the Turks were not in the same state of military readiness as the Prussian Empire, and the security was minimal to the point of lackadaisical. On being stopped at the gatehouse by a guard, Lady Sally set off on an elaborate explanation about how she had been instructed by the sultan to procure English ladies for his harem, and now she was delivering them.

Not surprisingly, the guard noted, "But, surely they're men?"

"Yes but, *I'm all woman*," said Lady Sally, unbuttoning her dress and thrusting her breasts in his face.

The mesmerised guard stared straight down her cleavage. It worked every time. Within seconds he had been kneed in the balls, tied up, gagged and bundled into the back of the guard house.

They gained entry into the palace grounds and headed straight for the harem, Nisahur leading the way. Luckily, they encountered no more guards. They burst through a gateway in a crenelated portico, and into an open courtyard with a fountain in its midst. Facing them was the elaborately carved, sandalwood door of the sultan's harem. Triumphantly, Lady Sally and her merry men crashed into the main chamber of the harem.

Lady Sally gasped. It was a spectacular sight, a massive hall decorated in blue, turquoise and white tiles with Arabic script and intricate geometric patterns glazed onto them. There were rows of elegant columns lining it's four sides. In the centre was a sparkling fountain with several cool pools surrounding it. The tiled floor was covered in sumptuous, brightly coloured rugs whilst the divans, dotted around the hall, were festooned with embroidered cushions. At one end was a huge divan covered by a carved, wooden canopy.

The women, dressed in attire similar to the men, though it had to be said with the body shape and sexual allure to pull it off, looked up in amazement at Lady Sally's wild and surprising intrusion.

Nisahur spotted her sister and rushed over to her. They gave each other a hug.

"Sehra, I'm so pleased to see you again. The English lady has come to rescue you from the sultan's clutches."

"Oh sister, it's been horrible. We're the sultan's sex slaves and he, and his family, subject us to all manner of perversions. This is astonishing. I can't believe you've broken into the sultan's palace to save me."

Lady Sally strode into the centre of the chamber, her presence commanding the harem girls' attention.

She spoke in broken Arabic, but with an upper-class English accent, "I'm here to rescue any who want to escape the sultan's attentions."

Scores of big, brown eyes turned towards Lady Sally, and stared over their veils at the strange English woman.

She continued, "Now look girls, I'm not one to judge. Maybe you are happy with your lives here, maybe you enjoy getting fucked every night, and indulging in sexual perversions. I'm an open-minded strict English dominatrix; lord knows I'm not averse to kinky sex myself. But if you are being treated badly, and you want to leave then I will take you away from here. Those who want to come with me, gather around the captain here," she said pointing to Captain Wyndham in the fez.

Most came over to Lady Sally, whilst others pondered the situation carefully. Eventually all the girls, about twenty of them, opted not to stay as sex slaves and be mistreated by the sultan. Life outside the palace's harem had to be better than that.

The troupe were about to make their exit when they heard a commotion from one of the arched porticos. It was Sultan Al Bin Kinkjani. Dressed in a tunic embroidered with gold and silver thread and bejewelled turban, he swept into the hall with an entourage of followers and family members. No doubt they came to enjoy an evening of pleasure with the harem girls.

He hesitated for a moment, wondering what on earth was going on.

Lady Sally, thinking on her feet as always, leapt into action, striding forward to meet him. Her velvet dress, still unbuttoned from the incident at the guard house, gave her a distinct advantage.

"Hello sultan, what a pleasure it is to meet you at last," she announced, greeting him as if he was a long-lost friend. "Let me introduce myself, I am Lady Sally Rudston-Chichester, strict English dominatrix. Your reputation proceeds you, sir, and, as we share an interest in the sensual and sadistic arts, I've used my contacts to gain access to your harem, so we can have a mutually rewarding discourse on exotic eroticism."

Sultan Al Bin Kinkjani was bemused by the English woman who had managed to infiltrate his palace. He was attracted to her pale skin, piercing blue eyes and voluptuous shape, so different from the other harem girls. He was also drawn to her erotic presence and commanding tone of voice.

The captain, alert to the precarious nature of their predicament, wasted no time in surreptitiously distributing the blunderbusses to the men whilst the sultan and his entourage's attentions were being diverted by Lady Sally.

Lady Sally pressed home her advantage, not allowing him to interrupt as she proceeded to describe her dungeon at Rudston Hall, how she was an expert in the erotic arts... and then describe what she could do to him. Without pausing for breath, she ran her fingers along his body, brushing them against the growing tumescence under his pantaloons. Taking his hand in hers, whilst lifting her dress up with the other hand, she placed his fingers on the wet patch on her satin knickers. She found it distasteful, but it was necessary for the greater good.

"I can see you've got a hard cock. You can have it inside me if you let me have my fun first. You can have whatever form of perverted sex you want with me if you are prepared to indulge an English dominatrix for a few moments. I would love to have that hard cock between my lips so I can suck on it, but I must do it whilst you are tied to one of the columns. I can assure you, surrendering control will make the experience more erotic."

Lady Sally had captivated him. He was caught, now all she had to do was reel him in. Within seconds his tunic and pantaloons had been stripped off and discarded on the tiles. Lady Sally produced coils of thin rope from within the confines of her dress. There were certainly advantages to being overdressed at times.

The captain watched and waited patiently for the right moment.

The sultan succumbed to Lady Sally's charms, and was willing to submit himself to the domineering English woman in exchange for a cock-sucking, and the further delights promised. He thought it curious she began by tying him facing the pillar with his arse exposed, rather than his groin and erect cock.

With the sultan co-operating, she soon had his ankles and wrists, which were pulled around the front of the pillar, securely tied. Lady Sally's knots were tight, and he was not going to wriggle out of that bondage any time soon.

The other men in the party looked on, fascinated by the behaviour of the self-proclaimed strict English madam. As soon as the sultan was tied-up, the captain made his move. He signalled for the men to raise the blunderbusses and train them on these other men.

"Ok, up against the pillars. Now!"

He tried to sound commanding, but was conscious of how ridiculous they must have looked. A group of men dressed as belly-dancers holding blunderbusses up to their eyes. The captain had little confidence any of them could actually shoot. Perhaps the duke who would no doubt have been on hunts, but the bishop, judge, banker and Victoria had no idea what they were doing. Luckily, the blunderbusses looked extremely fearsome and, of course, the captain was an expert shot, despite still being under the influence of the hashish.

To show he meant business, the captain pointed the lightning rifle at one of the pools and fired. Purple light shot out from its barrel into the tranquil water, causing it to seethe and bubble.

The other men were not going to argue with that demonstration of firepower. They were soon obediently lined up against the columns, being tied up by Lady Sally. She stepped back and admired her handiwork.

"Quick, let's make our getaway now," called the captain.

Lady Sally arched an eyebrow, "Now, but I'm only just starting to have fun."

"Oh madam, please," pleaded her maid.

"Oh, come now, when I've these arses lined up ready for a spanking. Let me spank the sultan at least, after all, it's not every day I get to inflict corporal chastisement on a sultan."

Lady Sally was incorrigible, and there was nothing the others could do but indulge her whim. She rolled up the sleeve of her dress, raised her arm and brought her hand down on the sultan's backside with a loud slap.

"Ouch!" he yelped. "You will not get away with this. I will have the whole Ottoman Amy chasing after you."

Her hand whipped his flesh even harder.

"Oh really. You will have to catch me first."

She whacked the sultan again, and he howled in pain.

"And your entire fleet is no match for my airship."

She raised her arm higher still and brought her hand crashing down. The flesh of the sultan's arse wobbled with the ferocity of the stroke.

Lady Sally had not finished. She administered whack after whack to the sound of the sultan's yelps and howls of pain. Her upper arm strength, acquired through numerous whippings and beatings over many years, was something to behold. She could spank relentlessly for long periods and not get tired… or bored at all. By the time she'd finished, the ruler of the Ottoman Empire was sobbing, and his backside a throbbing red.

"There, now you know what it means to be punished by a strict English mistress," proclaimed Lady Sally contemptuously, as she marched out with her belly-dancers and harem girls in tow.

31

They rushed out the gates of the palace, crammed into the steam-powered carriage, whose engine had been left stoked up in anticipation of the need for a speedy getaway. The carriage bounced through the narrow alleys of Istanbul at top speed, the chauffer honking its horn at any unfortunate person who got in his way.

The girls were dispersed into the alleyways of the city along the way, to be reunited with friends and family. Since the eunuchs of the harem kept no record of where the girls were picked up, or even their real names, the chances of the sultan recapturing them were slim. The girl Nisahur and her sister Sehra were effusive in their gratitude to Lady Sally, their earlier misgivings about the venture completely forgotten following the daring rescue.

They sped back to the airfield and hurriedly embarked onto the airship. They were just in time. Clearly the bound sultan and his entourage had been discovered, and the alarm sent out. The sultan's guard, armed with curved scimitars, swamped the airship station. The captain smiled. It was quaint, swords against lightning guns and the fastest airship in Christendom.

Fortunately, the captain ensured the crew and rigger-men were prepared for take-off before they departed for the palace, suspecting, with justification, they might be making another hasty departure. *The Corseted Domme* was ready just in time. The guy lines were already released so once the engines fired up the majestic dirigible swept up into the air, leaving the sultan's enraged guard on the ground.

The captain still had the fez on. As the airship rose up through the sky, he looked around him, and gasped, "Oh wow, that's just amazing, the sky's so bright and the clouds are so fluffy."

After the escapade, he'd come over ravenously hungry. He hoped cook had a decent dinner prepared, he could stuff a whole saddle of lamb.

Meanwhile, Lady Sally had taken up a position at the viewing window to the rear of the gondola. She laughed as she watched the comical spectacle of the sultan's guards in their turbans, tunics, and pantaloons receding into the distance as they waved their scimitars angrily at the airship

Lady Sally Rudston-Chichester had done it again. She completed the mission of freeing the harem slave girls from the clutches of the sultan. Who knows what debauched activities they had been forced to do. Not that Lady Sally was opposed to debauchery in principle, quite the contrary. It's just that, at least her slaves consented to her methods of exquisite domination. They were free to leave at any time. It was a testament to her charisma and skill that none ever availed themselves of that option; they were perfectly willing to submit to her.

Lady Sally was not one to miss a chance for erotic play and, seeing the men still dressed as belly-dancers, her mind turned to how to make best use of the opportunity. It would be rather wonderful to see them dance for her though she considered they might need an incentive to do so. She had just the device for that.

The wooden box she needed was in the playroom as it was her intention to use this particular toy next, and it was perfect for what she planned. She opened it and peered at a mass of wires with rubber-coated, metal clamps attached. The box consisted of a battery and a dial for adjusting the current. The principle of the design was not dissimilar to the electro-vibrator Lady Sally had already used, but with the sole attachment being the clamps. These she could attach to any sensitive part of the male anatomy, nipples or balls being the obvious candidates.

"I'm going to have a little competition to find the best belly-dancer," announced Lady Sally.

"But I can't dance, mistress," complained the banker.

"That's irrelevant. I shall make you dance. I expect you to enter into the spirit of the competition."

She started with the banker, removing the padding from inside the top of his costume and attaching a clamp to each nipple. He flinched as it squeezed tight onto the sensitive bud, the rubber-coated metal digging into his sensitive flesh. Lady Sally pushed his skimpy skirt to one side, attaching another two clamps to the sac of his balls.

She turned the dial on the box. At first the results were disappointing, so she had to turn the current up higher. The box buzzed, and the little clamps began to vibrate. The effect was highly entertaining for Lady Sally as the banker twisted and jiggled before her. The vibrating clamps generated a pricking sensation that made it impossible to stand still. The nipples were especially sensitive as the throbbing clips drove the banker to a frenzy of distraction.

"Now dance for me," she encouraged.

He attempted to gyrate his body and twist his hands in the fashion of a genuine belly dancer. Watching the roll of fat around his belly rotate and wobble was comical though. Lady Sally was in hysterics at the performance. He had at least given it a try.

She tried the device out on her other slaves with mixed effects. The judge was rather good, much to Lady Sally's surprise. He took off the veil and twirled it around him to good effect. The bishop was gangly and uncoordinated, and definitely came last in the competition, the banker at least having made an attempt to entertain her.

Not surprisingly, it was the duke that excelled at the game. He had the build of a dancer and, furthermore, he revelled in the opportunity to dress as a girl and perform for his mistress. She turned the current up to its highest setting for the duke to induce him into an ever more extravagant display. The clamps buzzed and vibrated, but he used the throbbing pain to drive him into a wilder, more seductive dance. He held his arms above his head and wiggled his hips, he fluttered his eyelids at Lady Sally, then removed the veil to incorporate it in his dance, using it to feign a sexual tease.

"A new vocation awaits you, duke," she applauded. "If the family's fortunes go into decline, you will be able to work in the gentlemen's clubs of Soho as a transvestite, erotic dancer."

She called on Victoria to bring the other electro-vibrating toy from her quarters so she could use both devices at the same time.

The captain appeared from the control room to get directions from Lady Sally for her next destination, following their enforced flight from Istanbul. He had changed back into his working clothes and was wearing his long, oil-splattered canvas coat as he'd just come from the engine room.

"Ah captain, have you come to do a dance for me?"

"Well, not really your ladyship."

"Oh, come now, you must join the fun." She held up the vibrating clamps and teased him with them, "Or do I have to attach these to induce you to dance for me."

Captain Wyndham was embarrassed. He didn't consider himself to be much of a dancer, but he didn't want to let Lady Sally down, and neither did he want the vibrating clamps on any part of his anatomy. He had learnt dances from native warriors during his time in the Zulu Wars so took it upon himself to perform one of these.

It was the most astonishing and energetic display. It was a war dance, performed by Zulu warriors before going into battle. He leapt around the dungeon equipment, his long coat flying around him. He took up one of Lady Sally's canes, incorporating it into the dance and wielding it like a Zulu spear.

Lady Sally was surprised. The captain's manner was usually so respectful, so to see him act out this wild, extravagant dance was quite an eye-opener.

She applauded, as did the other men, "Bravo captain. That's splendid, we've seen another side to you today."

"Thank you, madam," he mumbled, shocking himself at the extroverted display, which he'd forced out to please Lady Sally. "And where is your ladyship's next destination? We're flying over the Aegean Sea, heading towards Greece at the moment."

"Well, you can't get a decent cup of tea in Greece, so I'm not stopping there. We are heading for the Italian Empire, and Naples. There's a bronze statue of me for Rudston Hall that's awaiting collection, and I fancy examining the erotic frescoes at Pompeii. I should take on the role of tourist for at least one of my destinations."

"Very well, madam," he stood waiting to be dismissed when Victoria returned with the other wooden box containing the electro-massager.

Lady Sally wasted no time in getting the device out. She fitted the copper wire attachment with a view to using it in conjunction with the vibrating clips. She placed the wooden box on the rack and stood by it, her back to Captain Wyndham. She was ready to turn the crank around to get a strong current flowing, but on merely touching the handle blue sparks sprayed out from it, and she was propelled straight across the room. The captain, seeing the electric shock from the box, leapt forward to catch Lady Sally in his broad shoulders before she fell onto the floor.

The four men jumped forward to see how she was, concern etched on their faces. Victoria was in hysterics.

"Madam, oh madam, are you ok? What happened?"

Lady Sally lay in the captain's arms, her eyes closed, her usually immaculate hair turned into a frizz by the electric shock. The captain took her pulse… it was weak.

He sprang into action. She was still trussed up in the velvet dress she wore for the raid on the harem. He wasted no time in unbuttoning it. Underneath were the laces of her corset, pulled tight. He frantically began loosening the cords.

"You can't touch her corset," gasped Victoria.

"I must. It's restricting her breathing. Now everybody stand back and let her get air."

"Is mistress alright?" asked the judge anxiously, echoing the concerns of all of them.

The captain ignored him, pressing on with what needed to be done. There was no time to waste. Having completely untied the corset he folded the dress back and pulled the corset away from her body, slinging it behind him aimlessly. Victoria picked it up and was fingering it nervously whilst she looked upon her unconscious mistress.

Lady Sally's bare breasts were under the captain's nose, but this was no time to admire them. He cupped the white flesh in his hands, pressing hard-on the bottom of her breast against her heart. He pumped vigorously for a minute. Then he leaned over her, opened her mouth and put his lips to hers to give mouth to mouth resuscitation. After a minute he pulled away. He was pumping her heart hard, and his lips were at the point of touching hers again when Lady Sally's eyes flickered open.

"Mm," she mumbled, "don't stop captain, that feels rather nice."

"You're alive," shouted Victoria in relief.

Captain Wyndham crouched over Lady Sally, her tit in his hand, his eyes staring into hers, the hint of smile on her red lips. She looked dishevelled, and vulnerable for once, but sexier for that. He released hold of her boob.

"Are you alright, Lady Sally?"

"Yes, thank you, captain."

By now the other men were fussing around her, Victoria in particular. They were relieved to see her sat up again, breathing, and heart beating. Indeed, it was not long before she was back to her normal self.

"Really, stop fussing. It was just a little electric shock. I'm perfectly alright. It was just an accident. These things happen with electricity."

The captain receded into the background. He had other thoughts.

He examined the wooden box. There were fresh scratches on the wood near the screw holes. It had been opened... and recently. He cursed. With the adventures in Istanbul they had not been paying enough attention to the stowaway. The crew had been on guard whilst *The Corseted Domme* had been moored, and nothing untoward was reported, but the intruder was still at large. He got his screwdriver from his coat pocket and opened up the base of the electro-vibrator. His suspicions were confirmed. The wiring had been tampered with. Lady Sally's electric shock was no accident... it was deliberate.

32

Once the alarms calmed down, and her maid and gentlemen had finished fussing around her, Captain Wyndham drew Lady Sally to one side.

"Your ladyship," he whispered, "it was no accident, the electro-massager was tampered with. There's no doubt our stowaway has broken into your private quarters, seen the device and switched the earth and live wires."

Lady Sally was furious, "Bugger me! When I catch the blackguard, I'll cut his bloody balls off. What are we to do captain?"

"There'll be little sleep for the crew tonight, most of them will have to stay on watch. We've narrowly averted two threats to your life, your ladyship. You're at serious risk until we catch this stowaway. First thing tomorrow morning we start another sweep of the whole airship, and we won't stop until we find him."

"Yes, captain, we must. I'll join the hunt. I will devise such tortures for this miscreant when we capture him."

"Is that all, Lady Sally?"

"Oh, one more thing, captain. Thank you for your decisive actions back there. Victoria is a loyal maid, but a blithering idiot when it comes to a real crisis. Tell me, captain, did you save my life?"

Their eyes met. Captain Wyndham looked into hers with admiration and affection.

"Honestly, madam," he replied, "I don't believe so. Your heart was weak but still beating. I only did what had to be done. I'd have done the same for anybody, though I've got to say I was mightily relieved when you recovered consciousness. We all were. We all... revere you so much, Lady Sally."

"You are too modest, captain. Still, you did get an opportunity to grope a tit; not many men are afforded that privilege," she said, a provocative smile spreading across her red lips.

"No, indeed, madam. I'm a very lucky man."

Lady Sally went back to the dungeon and told her gentlemen to retire for the night. It had been an exciting day. Meanwhile the captain gathered the rigger-men and crew to organise shifts for watching the airship. It was the early hours of the morning before he got back to his quarters for a sleep, but he didn't get much before there was an excited knocking on the door of his cabin.

There had finally been a breakthrough in the hunt for the stowaway. One of the rigger-men posted outside the kitchen spotted a tiny figure creeping out of it and go scuttling along one of the gangways. He followed but the figure mysteriously disappeared into a ventilation shaft before he could catch up with him.

The captain put a guard on entrance to the ventilation shaft.

He reported this news to Lady Sally first thing in the morning, and they met with the rigger-man and Victoria where the culprit had mysteriously disappeared into the tube of galvanised tin.

"Did you see the scoundrel?" asked Lady Sally.

"It were dark, milady, so I couldn't make out any features. It were just a shadowy figure. What were strange is it were so small, like a little animal... and it had short, stubby legs, and kind of shuffled along the passage as it were."

"A little animal, how odd," pondered Lady Sally.

"And look at the ventilation shaft," the captain pointed out, "it's far too narrow for a grown man... or woman to squeeze into."

"Indeed, captain. It's most curious. And where does this shaft lead?"

"It goes back into the fuselage and the hydrogen bags. It draws fresh air into the living quarters. The good news is I've had it guarded overnight, so we know that whatever it is, it's trapped inside the fuselage."

"Excellent. Let the hunt begin. I will not rest until it has been caught."

Lady Sally entered into the spirit of the pursuit by dressing in her red hunting jacket, jodhpurs and riding boots, the lightning blunderbuss slung over her shoulder.

"There we are, Victoria. I'm so pleased I packed my hunting apparel; I knew I'd get the chance to wear it during my adventures."

"Yes, madam. You look incredibly sexy in it."

"Really, Victoria. This is a serious business. This is no time to get aroused."

Captain Wyndham unlocked the padlock on the metal door leading from the gondola into the fuselage. Victoria, the captain and a band of the crew entered.

Lady Sally recalled the day of the maiden flight, her tour of the fuselage and her chief engineer's detailed description of the airship's construction.

She gazed around in awe and wonderment. The duralumin frame of the airship was vast; it was like stepping into another world of gleaming metal. There was a hard, erect girder, rounded like a massive pole, stretching the whole length of the airship's frame. Lady Sally wrapped her hand around it, its girth too thick for her fingers to stretch around it. It felt firm in her grip, but surprisingly light with a certain amount of flex in it. Duralumin was an incredibly light metal; it would have been impossible to construct an airship this size with anything else, but it was its ability to bend with stress or strong winds that provided the airship with its durability.

The pole penetrated a series of holes. These were the joints around which the polygonal frames were centred. There were a whole series of these along the length of the structure, reducing in size at the front to produce the airship's distinctive, bulbous tip. The sensual curves of shining duralumin filled the fuselage. They were supported by both a wheel of girders and a series of wires. This was the sub-structure which gave *The Corseted Domme* its pleasingly, sleek, bullet-like shape.

Between, each of the polygonal structures were a network of walkways and steps. It was like being in a massive puzzle or three-dimensional version of snakes and ladders. Lady Sally was reminded of the work of one of her favourite artists, an Italian engraver named Piranesi, who produced a series of prints called *Le Carceri* which depicted prisons with stairs and walkways that led nowhere. She had a signed set of these engravings on the wall of her dungeon in Rudston Hall to remind her submissive slaves that, once they were in her clutches, there was no escape.

The gangways and stairs provided access to every part of the frame, for the purposes of servicing and maintaining both structure and air bags. Between each polygonal frame was an air bag, twelve of them in all, on two levels.

Another feature of the airship's frame was the feeling of silence and calm, in marked contrast to the engine room. The only thing that could be heard was the wind blowing against the silver-coated linen covering the frame which engendered a sense of eerie calmness.

"You see our problem," the captain pointed out, "there's a maze of gangways in here and we have to search them systematically because the view through the frame of the ship is obstructed by the air bags."

"Yes, indeed, I can see. And the whole frame is so vast. It's quite incredible," said Lady Sally.

The captain divided them into four teams, two went left to sweep the rear end of the airship whilst the other two (one team consisting of himself, Lady Sally and Victoria) scoured the front end. They had to cover systematically every walkway and stairway. Meanwhile, the ventilation duct was permanently guarded, so there was no escape from the airship's frame.

They set out on their task. It was exhausting work. They went up and down stairs, along what felt like miles and miles of gangways and then up and down yet more steps. They had been conducting this painstaking search all morning and were getting demoralised, having seen no evidence of the mysterious stowaway.

Suddenly, Lady Sally discerned a ripple of movement along one of the air bags, which was strange because they were usually so still. Suspecting she might be on to something, she rushed ahead of the others where she could see around the corner and beyond the air bag. She paused, standing there in her red, hunting jacket, pulled the sight of the lightning blunderbuss up to her eye, and started to squeeze the trigger.

"Right, I've got you now. I'm going to zap you to kingdom come!" she shouted in triumph.

"Lady Sally, nooooo!"

"Madam, nooooo!"

The captain and Victoria called out in tandem.

"You'll blow us up!"

Lady Sally arched an elegant eyebrow, lowered the lightning blunderbuss, turned to the captain and said, "Well, yes, captain, of course I knew that. Do you take me for a fool?"

The captain had his doubts, he reckoned Lady Sally was about to shoot, though he certainly wasn't going to contest the issue with his employer.

"Did you see him?" asked the captain, rushing up to her side, with Victoria following behind.

"Yes. It was a funny looking thing. Definitely human, though small. I didn't see a face because it was wearing a duffle coat with its hood up."

"Small, madam?" queried Victoria.

"Dwarf-like. Yes, my maid, I have my suspicions. But we must capture the thing first to be sure."

The captain looked around. He was familiar with the structure of the airship's frame, and he was working out a strategy to trap the stowaway.

"Lady Sally, you follow him along this gangway," the captain explained pointing to where she had spotted the figure. "Victoria, you take the steps up in that direction, and I'll go down the other walkway. I'm hoping we can force him into the cone of the frame where there's no way to escape."

"Him?" questioned Lady Sally, "How do you know it's not a *her*?"

"*It*, then. Why, do you think it's female?"

Lady Sally shrugged, "I believe all will be revealed when the *thing* is caught."

They set off in their respective directions. After clambering down a set of steps, the captain looked up to see a black, hooded figure scuttling along one of the gangways above him. This was the gangway Lady Sally had followed and, sure enough, she soon emerged from behind one of the air bags in pursuit of her quarry. The captain ran on ahead hoping to cut any means of escape by blocking one set of stairs, hopefully Victoria would reach the other gangway in time.

He lost sight of it momentarily but as he turned a corner, there it suddenly was, a short, stocky figure facing him. It was close enough for him to make out the snarling gaze it threw back at him. Beyond it, Lady Sally was in pursuit, whilst Victoria stumbled down one of the staircases to block off another direction. There was only one route away from them, and that was into the tip of the airship… where there was no escape. They had it trapped.

The figure dashed along the one walkway that wasn't blocked, not realising there was no exit from it. It ran along, its little legs trying to go as fast as possible, but no match for the captain's long strides and Lady Sally's determined dash to confront her enemy. It realised the error when it saw the curves of the duralumin frame looming ahead.

It turned to face them. A tiny figure framed against the shining, duralumin curves at the very apex of *The Corseted Domme*. There was no way out; only a leap off the walkway to plunge deep into the bowels of the airship's frame, and certain death.

"Aha!" exclaimed Lady Sally as she drew up alongside the captain. "Now I have you."

33

The mysterious stowaway was pinned into the duralumin cone at the tip of the airship, with no route for escape.

Lady Sally stepped up. Towering over the diminutive figure, she pulled back the black hood. A cascade of auburn hair tumbled over the black duffel coat. The *it* was a woman... and *it* was a dwarf.

"Ha! It's as I thought. Has Madam Bellowhead sent you?"

The dwarf only shot back a hostile stare with beady eyes like black pin-pricks, refusing to answer.

"Who is Madam Bellowhead?" asked Captain Wyndham.

"She's head of the UK Society of Lesbian Dwarves.

"Oh, not them again," groaned Victoria.

"Yes. I suspected as much when the rigger-man said he'd seen a thing that looked like a creature. And only something small, such as a dwarf, could climb through the ventilation shaft."

"But why?" asked the captain, bemused at the bizarre discovery, and Lady Sally's vitriolic response to it.

"UKSOLD is a secret society of lesbian dwarves. My feud with them is long standing. It began when Madam Bellowhead, chairwoman of the society, had the temerity to criticise the style of my whipping when, many years ago, she invited me to one of their meetings as guest dominatrix to inflict cruel punishments. Well, I ask you! Nobody criticises Lady Sally Rudston-Chichester and gets away with it... and me a guest dominatrix too! So, I administered the severest whipping I possibly could, and she refused to pay me. Well, I wasn't having that, so I kidnapped Madam Bellowhead and two of her colleagues, had them brought to Rudston Hall to put them in bondage and punish them. Then they tried to impugn my reputation by making complaints about me in *The London Gazette*. Well, I couldn't have that. So, I got the lawyer to sue them for libel. Naturally, I won the case, because I was able to prove in court how severe my whippings were... believe me, the judge will never forget that case! And then..."

"...It's ok. I think I get the idea. How long has this feud been going on?"

"...Well, around ten years now."

"Ten years! But even so, trying to blow you up and electrocute you? Isn't that extreme to settle a dispute over how severely you whip?"

160

"Certainly not!" exclaimed Lady Sally, indignantly. "Besides, they are a miserable, joyless, vindictive bunch, especially that Madam Bellowhead. Now, I don't hold grudges, but if someone dares criticise me, then I will defend myself, it's a matter of honour... especially for a severe, lady dominatrix. I'm afraid you just don't understand the seriousness of the matter, captain."

The lesbian dwarf listened to the exchange, thoroughly bemused, as if she knew nothing of the history of these altercations.

"Ok, but what are you going to do with her now you've captured her?"

"Torture and torment her until she confesses."

Lady Sally retrieved coils of cord from her hunting jacket and tied the young woman's wrists together. The midget looked on, stubbornly determined but, having been caught, doing nothing to resist being restrained. Lady Sally pulled her through the maze of gangways and stairways out of the fuselage where she could deal with her.

They emerged into the dungeon playroom. Lady Sally's submissive gentlemen clustered around her, both surprised at, and curious about, the nature of the culprit who had attempted to sabotage the airship and electrocute their mistress.

Eventually, the dwarf spoke up, in a pronounced German accent, "You are Lady Sally Rudston-Chichester?"

"Yes, of course."

"Ze famous British spy-mistress?"

"Spying, no. The famous English, lady dominatrix, yes!" exclaimed Lady Sally. "Now, who are you? Have you been sent by Madam Bellowhead? And why are you trying to sabotage my airship?"

The dwarf was defiant, "I vill say nothing. I am under strict orders to keep silence. You can torture me all that you like. I vill tell you nothing. I have been trained to resist pain."

Lady Sally smiled, a wide, disconcerting smile. Her wicked imagination clicked into gear.

"Ah, trained to resist pain, are you? But are you trained to resist pleasure? Strip her boys," she ordered.

The gentlemen set about the task with relish. The black duffel coat was dragged off her back, jumper pulled over her head, trousers brought down, and knickers and bra ripped off. Her clothes were thrown onto the floor. The dwarf did not protest or resist, maintaining the stoic acceptance of her capture. Once stripped of the grubby clothes she had worn to crawl through the ventilation shaft, her appearance was surprisingly attractive. She was young, with a pretty face, alert grey eyes and striking auburn hair, though her build was obviously squat and stubby.

Lady Sally soon had her on the rack, wrists secured, legs raised, and ankles tied to a harness, making her orifices accessible. Meanwhile, Victoria had gathered an array of her steam-powered and electric sex-toys.

Lady Sally squeezed the midget's nipples to make them hard, which barely registered a flicker of discomfort in her, before attaching the vibrating clamps onto the pert nubs of flesh. She took up the box with the electro-massager and fitted it with the brass bullet attachment. She inserted a finger in the dwarf's arsehole, massaging until it could accommodate a second, then third, digit. The dwarf didn't flinch or moan, responding only with deeper breaths as Lady Sally worked her fingers up her back-passage. Satisfied her arse was stretched enough for the challenge of the brass bullet, Lady Sally eased it inside her. The dwarf was so controlled there was hardly any reaction even though the object was inserted deep inside her.

Lady Sally turned the dials and sent the electric current pulsing through the wires. The toys purred with a gentle buzz. She checked the oscillating needles. They were vibrating at a sensuous throb which was precisely the pace Lady Sally wanted for this particular exercise.

"Hand the men the ostrich-feathers, Victoria."

"Ostrich-feathers, madam?" queried the maid.

Even the girl looked surprised. She was steeling herself to be whipped, tortured, subject to all manner of corporal punishment, or worse... *but ostrich-feathers?*

"Why yes, don't concern yourself, Victoria. She will talk after I've finished with her."

The duke, lawyer, banker and bishop gathered around the rack, holding an ostrich feather, each dyed a different colour.

Lady Sally cranked the wheel to increase the tension of the ropes tying her onto the rack. It pleased her to see the dwarf's stunted frame stretched to its limit. But it wasn't her intention to use the rack as a device of torture, to stretch and pull limbs, only to tighten the flesh, thus enhancing its sensitivity.

"Well, I'm ready. It's quite simple. I want to know who you are working for, and why you've tried to sabotage my airship?"

The dwarf snarled, "I've told you, I'm trained to withstand torture... and you think you can get me to talk with ostrich-feathers?"

"Ostrich-feathers are merely a start. Besides, these are plucked from the most magnificent examples of the species from my own ostrich farm on the savannahs of Tanganyika. They're the very finest, used for feather boas in burlesque clubs around the world. You say you are trained to resist pain, but can you resist pleasure, I wonder... a surfeit of pleasure."

The four men ran the soft feathers over her taut skin: along her arms, over her shoulders, across her breasts, down her abdomen, up her thighs and, most deliciously of all, over her pubes. The touch of the feathers was exquisitely soft, the merest brush causing goose-pimples to form on her skin. The feather was so sensuous it triggered her juices to flow. For the first time, there was doubt in her eyes as she wondered if Lady Sally's counter-intuitive strategy for getting her to talk might have some substance.

Lady Sally bent over her, strands of her raven hair dangling across the midget's crotch. She sniffed.

"When was the last time you changed your knickers? The crawling around ventilation shafts has given you a sweaty crotch. Tis no matter, it's lucky I find the musky smell of a sweaty cunt something of a turn-on," she said, burying her face into the dwarf's sex.

Lady Sally's tongue delved deep into her hole, licked the folds of her flesh, and rolled over the hard bud of her clit. All the time, the brass bullet in her arse throbbed, and the vibrating clamps on her nipples thrummed, whilst the soft ostrich-feathers teased her flesh to distraction. Beads of sweat formed on her brow. Her breaths became deeper and heavier as the tingling pleasure spread over her. However hard she tried to restrain herself, little moans of desire and need emitted from her lips.

Lady Sally came up for air.

"Come, what association do you have with UKSOLD? I know you're a lesbian, so the pleasure a *woman* gives must be the most exquisite for you," she taunted, leaning over the dwarf.

Her cleavage burst out of her hunting jacket, the phoenix tattoo, in fiery reds and oranges, visible above the low-cut line of its collar. She gazed into the dwarf's eyes, lowered her face, puckered her red lips, and planted a kiss onto hers. She tasted of lipstick and the saltiness of the dwarf's own juices. Lady Sally's tongue pushed into her mouth to seek hers out.

Lady Sally was soon down at her crotch again, her tongue probing the dwarf's slippery hole. She strained every muscle to ward off the waves of pleasure, but to no avail. The tip of Lady Sally's tongue was rubbing against her clit in frenetic motions. Every sinew of her body was trying to fight off the inevitable climax, knowing that to succumb to it would give the English dominatrix a victory. It was impossible. Within moments she screamed out, her body bucking and twisting at her restraints. The dwarf hoped to get some respite, to compose herself or find a way to resist the torment of pleasure, but there was none. Having gained an advantage, Lady Sally ploughed on, her tongue working into the dwarf's sopping crack, rubbing the nub of her pleasure until her body strained again, and she gave in to another orgasm. The dwarf was panting and groaning now.

Lady Sally did not to offer any break in her torture by pleasure. Whilst she was carrying out her sadistic seduction, Victoria had gone back to her dressing room to fetch the automaton.

"Let me introduce you to Borghild, my automaton sex-toy," announced Lady Sally.

Borghild stood over the dwarf. She was dressed in her kinky red latex, with the black, rubber strap-on protruding from her waist. It was a fearsome object, the thickest and longest strap-on Lady Sally owned from the extensive collection in her possession.

The dwarf gasped. Her eyes watered at the sight of what was about to be thrust inside her.

Lady Sally fixed her gaze on Borghild. "Pleasure her," she ordered with a dismissive wave of her hand before nonchalantly strolling across the playroom to take up a grandstand seat on her throne for the performance.

Borghild mounted the rack. The giant, rubber phallus hovered tantalisingly before the dwarf's gash. The automaton drove the strap-on into her slippery hole. She was still aroused and sopping from the attentions of Lady Sally's tongue. The dildo stretched her and filled her... filled her like she'd never been filled before. Once the object was nestled deeply inside her, it wasn't painful, far from it, it was gloriously arousing.

Borghild pumped the strap-on into her cunt. The midget soon felt another orgasm welling up inside her.

Lady Sally sat sipping a cup of tea. After all, it was tea-time by now.

"You see, the thing is, even I get tired, and need to partake of refreshment, but Borghild can keep fucking and fucking. She won't stop until I order her, or until her charge runs flat, and I can assure you she's fully charged. She'll just keep giving pleasure until I tell her to stop, which won't be until you answer my questions. Time is no issue; I have all night. So, it's a case of how much pleasure you can stand."

The dwarf was going to say something when her fourth orgasm burst over her with a euphoric scream. Every sinew of her body pulsed with wave after wave of climax.

Lady Sally decided to take another turn fucking her with a strap-on after that, before handing over to the automaton again. She had to hand it to her, the dwarf was stubborn.

But after the tenth orgasm, and with no prospect of any break and the rest of the evening and night of rip-roaring climaxes looming before her, she relented. It was too much for her: she was in a daze, every muscle in her body ached with the exertion, and her throat was sore from her continuous moans, groans and screams. She couldn't take any more, yet weirdly she wanted more.

She burst out, "Please, please, you win. I give up. I can't take any more. Please, stop the machine. I'll talk."

Lady Sally strolled over to Borghild and quietly told her to stop fucking. The strap-on was still lodged inside the dwarf's cunt, a warning the automaton could be switched on at any time.

She paused to allow the midget to get her breath back and recover her composure before quietly asking, "So, do you know Madam Bellowhead?"

"No, no" she gasped, relieved at getting respite from perpetual orgasm. "Only by name. I never met her."

"So, how is it you've heard of her?"

"I'm a member of the Hanoverian Society of Lesbian Dwarves. We know of your UK Society, but I never got any instructions from Madam Bellowhead."

"Who did they come from then?" Lady Sally persisted.

"I'm a spy. I work for the Prussian secret service. They use dwarves because we can hide in confined spaces."

"But why are the Prussians spying on me?"

"My mission was to stowaway in your airship. I was to study the machine, make plans of it, bring it down on Prussian soil if possible, and destroy it if I could not. They believed your airship carried secret weapons."

Captain Wyndham interjected. "I found this in the pocket of her duffel coat," he said holding up a notebook containing sketches of the airship. "These drawings confirm she was after technical details of the construction of *The Corseted Domme*."

"So, when did you join my airship?" asked Lady Sally.

"I got on board whilst you were moored at Potsdam. The Archduke had no idea. It was a secret service mission. I didn't know he also had plans to capture your airship. You left so quickly, I never got the chance to bring the airship down on Prussian soil."

"And was this the sole reason for your mission? Was there nothing personal against me?"

"The second part of the mission was to track Lady Sally Rudston-Chichester, the notorious British spy."

"But I'm no spy," protested Lady Sally indignantly.

"This is where Madam Bellowhead came in. She provided the Prussian Secret Service with that information. She said you were a British spy, and the purpose of your flight was to fly over Prussia to spy on the Empire's war preparations."

"Piffle," exclaimed Lady Sally. "*The Corseted Domme* is a vehicle for pleasure only... *my pleasure*. I don't care tuppence about spying and war."

"Madam Bellowhead told the secret service you were a spy, and they certainly believed it."

"Poppycock. She is a liar and a blackguard, and I will get my revenge on her. You have been deceived, I'm afraid."

The captain asked a question, "Had you any idea how dangerous your sabotage of the airship was. You could have killed us all, yourself included."

"I was desperate. I knew if I returned to Prussia without completing the mission and disabling the airship things would go badly for me. The prisons in Prussia are full of failed dwarf-spies."

"What are you going to do with her?" asked Captain Wyndham.

"That's a good question, captain. I haven't decided."

"You must punish her, madam," offered Victoria. "After all, she tried to kill you,."

"Yes, there is that I suppose, though my anger is more directed at Madam Bellowhead and UKSOLD, and the Prussian Secret Service."

"Keep me. Please keep me. Take me again."

"What! You've not had enough?"

"I've never had orgasms like these before. Now I've had a rest I could definitely come again. Please," she begged, "please, fuck me with your strap-on again, whilst I'm still in bondage. Please, Lady Sally."

"What a splendid suggestion. I can see you are a convert to the Lady Sally methods of sadistic pleasure. But, there must be an exchange. I know, you must allow me to sit on your face whilst you make me come. How does that sound?"

"Yes please, Lady Sally. I should love to have my tongue up your cunt. Let me serve you."

"Excellent. If you are prepared to submit to me, then I'm ready to dismiss the other unfortunate incidents, you know... spying, sabotage, attempted murder..."

"I can certainly do that, Mistress Sally," the lesbian dwarf agreed with relish. She had been won over.

"Well, that's all settled then!"

34

The fun went on into the evening, and ended with the dwarf being invited back to Lady Sally's bedchamber, much to the envy of Victoria, the four gentlemen and, though he was reluctant to admit it, Captain Wyndham. The squeals of pleasure from the room echoed through the passages of the gondola through the night.

The dwarf was an enthusiastic convert from spying to debauchery.

Her name was Frau Kina Linguzh. She was born in Poland, moved to Germany where the Hanoverian Society of Lesbian Dwarves was known to be especially active, and through them recruited into the Prussian Secret Service. It turned out she had many humorous stories about hiding in wardrobes, cupboards and drawers spying on British, French, Russian and Austrian Empire diplomats, and their sexual shenanigans. She promised to introduce Lady Sally and her gentlemen to the exciting erotic delights of voyeurism, which she had acquired from her experiences as a spy.

Overnight they flew over the Adriatic Sea heading towards their next destination, the Italian Empire, and the city of Naples. Lady Sally was excited. Other aristocratic tourists visited Venice and Florence, attracted by the wonders of Renaissance art and architecture. Lady Sally's tastes were more exotic; her ambition was to see the erotic frescoes at Pompeii.

The Corseted Domme took a route following the Amalfi coast, over the elegant Italian resort of Sorrento towards the port of Naples. As the airship descended, Lady Sally took her place in the cockpit alongside the captain and Clarissa. She insisted on flying the airship over Mount Vesuvius.

"Over a volcano," queried her maid, "isn't that dangerous?"

"It's ok, Victoria. It erupted in '06, it won't blow again for decades," explained the captain.

The maid looked sceptical as she stared into the crater at the seething lava and wisps of steam and smoke floating up into the sky, "Yes, but you know stuff happens when madam is around."

"Cheer up, Victoria, you know what they say, *See Naples... and die!*"

"Thanks, that's all I need," she groaned.

Captain Wyndham sought out the mooring mast on the dockside. Naples was a huge, sprawling port-city, dominated by its massive, medieval fortress, the Castel Nuovo. It was also extremely poor. *The Corseted Domme* was a revelation to the city's residents. As usual, the airship attracted attention, and soon a horde of curious, bare-footed street kids surrounded her.

"I'm simply ravenous. Captain, go ahead and order pizzas from a stall on the dockside. We'll join you in a minute when we're ready to disembark. Mine is a Pizza Napoletana, and make sure it's made with *San Marzano* tomatoes, they grow on the volcanic plains below Vesuvius... oh, and order plenty of carafes of red wine. I think we deserve a celebration after surviving so many alarms and exposing our stowaway."

"What's pizza?" asked her maid, suspicious about her next culinary experience after the horse's testicle.

"You'll love it. It's thin bread with tomato and cheese and different toppings. Everybody loves pizza! Besides it's the local fare, so we must partake of it."

The party, which included their new companion, Frau Kina Linguzh, sat overlooking the harbour at simple tables with checked table-cloths laden with massive pizzas, drinking copious amounts of wine.

They were soon joined by cook who, hearing of mistress's impromptu meal on the dockside, was on the warpath.

"Milady, what's this muck you're eating. I've kitchens full of venison bred on your Scottish estate, Gressingham duck and corn-fed spatchcock chickens. I've fresh vegetables from your kitchen garden. I tell you, this stuff will bung you up, milady. I remember from when you were a child, you always needed brussel sprouts to make you fart. Peasant food, that's what it is, milady. It's beneath an aristocratic lady like yerself."

"Really cook, that's way too much information. It's merely a snack of the local delicacy. And I will eat what I wish. Now get back to the kitchen and prepare dinner."

Cook stormed back to the airship in a huff.

"Ah, this is the life. My enemies are left far behind, so we can relax, safe in the Italian Empire, eating pizza and drinking wine. I just need to wait at the dockside and take delivery of my statue. You know, I've commissioned a bronze statue of myself for the courtyard at Rudston Hall. My agent here has arranged for me to collect it."

"A bronze statue?" Captain Wyndham smiled. "I presume that, as well as a brass mine, Lady Sally has a bronze mine too?"

She looked askance at him with an expression of disdain, "What are you talking about, captain? Are you making fun of me? Everybody knows bronze is an alloy of copper and tin, so a bronze mine is quite impossible. I'm most surprised at you captain. I thought a man of the world like yourself knew such things."

Captain Wyndham was left open-mouthed, before spluttering, "But, wait a minute, what about your bra…"

He was cut off in his protestations by a dismissive wave of Lady Sally's hand and the sound of wheels rattling ponderously along the cobbled streets of the docks. A cart, pulled by twenty horses, turned the corner and came into sight

And what a magnificent sight it was. Mounted on the cart was an enormous bronze statue, lines of rope securing it into place. The representation was at least four or five times larger than the real-life Lady Sally Rudston-Chichester, which was a scary prospect. It was a remarkable and unmistakable likeness, which captured her in a dominant pose with a fearsome expression. She was depicted wearing a corset and thigh-length boots, a whip grasped in her hand, its bronze thongs dangling menacingly

"How splendid," exclaimed Lady Sally. "I'm overwhelmed. What an accurate characterisation. I love the bronze moulding on my cleavage, and they've even managed to capture my phoenix tattoo."

"*Bonjourno*, Lady Sally. What a delight it is to meet-a you again. You look-a more stunning than ever. You-a English ladies are *bellissima*."

He was introduced to them as Signore Giovanni Fellatio, a Neapolitan gentleman with a closely shaven beard, dressed in black. He was burly and muscular, with an aspect like the dockers at the port, yet, in contrast to this there were obvious displays of wealth, a gold fob watch and silver-tipped cane. He strode up to Lady Sally and demonstratively kissed her on both cheeks.

"Thank you, Signore. You flatter me. And how is business?"

"Ah, well-a this is Napoli, my lady, everything is chaotic! But it's-a always a pleasure to do business with the dominant-a English ladies. Your-a crates of wine are-a following in another cart."

Captain Wyndham studied the man with suspicion. He had been to Naples before, had stopped there briefly on the way back from Khartoum after fighting for the British Empire in the Sudan. He noted the lion-headed ring. He recognised the striking markings: a rat, a key, and a line of women's names (almost certainly his mistresses), tattooed on the back of the Italian gentleman's hand… and he was concerned. Lady Sally certainly kept strange company.

"And what-a are your plans whilst your ladyship is in-a Napoli."

"Tomorrow I'm planning a visit to Pompeii to examine the erotic frescoes. It's always been an ambition of mine. I don't much care for Renaissance art, but one cannot beat fine erotic etchings."

"An excellent-a choice, my lady. But do you intend to go alone with just your friends?" he asked, glancing disdainfully at the four strange gentlemen, Victoria in her French maid's uniform, and a lady dwarf. "I do not-a recommend that. I will a offer-a you my protection."

"Do you believe that's necessary, Signore Fellatio?"

"Most-a definitely. The bay of Napoli is lawless. A rich-a English lady is a target for thieves. And-a you know the motto of my brethren, *Loyalty, Honour... Revenge.* You know-a we look after our friends-a."

The captain looked alarmed. His suspicions were confirmed.

"Well, that's most kind of you. And quite right too; *Loyalty, Honour... Revenge*, that is, indeed, a creed I follow in my own way... and expect my submissive slaves to adhere to, especially the loyalty. You are very generous. But your protection will be discreet, won't it?"

"Lady Sally, our-a brethren are always discreet."

"Excellent, so that's settled then. You must join us for dinner on *The Corseted Domme.*"

"It would be-a pleasure, but now I have-a more business to attend to. *Bonjourno, mia bellezza.*"

Lady Sally poured herself another glass of red wine, "There, you see, what gentlemen the Italians are."

Captain Wyndham did not look impressed, "But, madam, surely he's a member of the *Camorra?*"

"What's the *Camorra?*" asked the bishop.

The lawyer and banker certainly knew, they looked as alarmed as the captain.

"Well, the *Camorra* is a society of criminal gangs; basically, they're a Neapolitan *Mafia,*" explained the captain

"Oh, don't be such a fuss-pot, captain. I've had a partnership with Signore Fellatio for many years. It's impossible to do business in Naples without dealing with the *Camorra,* everything entering and leaving the port is controlled by them. How else am I going to get wine from my Tuscan vineyards shipped to Rudston Hall? If Signore Fellatio says they will protect us, then I believe him. Besides, they're extremely loyal to their friends."

"...And extremely murderous to their enemies," the captain muttered under his breath.

35

Seeing how enamoured Lady Sally was with the *Camorra*, Captain Wyndham held back from expressing his concerns regarding an organisation with a reputation for ruthlessness and violence that surpassed even the *Mafia*.

His immediate problem was loading the massive statue onto the airship. It was too tall to stand upright anywhere in the gondola. Luckily, the airship did have a hold for storage. The statue was hauled into this (an operation requiring the crew and lots of rope), wrapped in sheets of linen to protect it, laid on its side, and secured into position by the ropes. The captain hoped Lady Sally would not need a speedy getaway because, what with the statue which weighed tons, and the thousands of tiles for her Turkish Bath, the airship was going to be sluggish.

Dinner time was lively. The party drank lots of wine, including many bottles of *Brunello di Montalcino*, Lady Sally's favourite wine from her Tuscan vineyard, crates of which had been loaded onto her airship for the wine cellars of Rudston Hall.

The captain joined the party just as Signore Fellatio was showing off his tattoos to Lady Sally. This included the one on his chest which depicted the back of a naked woman with the inscription (in Italian) *in your anus I have lost half of my cock*, which she found highly amusing.

In the morning, they prepared for the outing to Pompeii. Signore Fellatio generously arranged to supply a procession of horse and carts for the party and their lavish picnic-lunch.

The dock-side was busy, the flamboyant English lady in her cool linen dress and parasol with her strange entourage attracting lots of attention. Once again, the captain, in his roll-neck jumper, fedora hat and flying boots, envied the lightweight suits of the other gentlemen.

His curiosity was aroused by observing people at the docks. Most of the seething throng were the locals who had greeted the airship so enthusiastically. There were the burly Italian dockers in their working clothes, the pedlars selling their wares, the women in peasant clothes and headscarves, and the bare-footed children trying to scrounge sweet cakes from the crowds.

Amongst them were figures who didn't fit in. There were individuals sat at the cafes who clearly weren't natives of Naples. Others appeared to be engrossed in Italian newspapers, yet every so often they dropped a corner to observe surreptitiously what was going on at the dock-side. The captain got the distinct impression Lady Sally and her entourage were being watched. Perhaps these were the members of the *Camorra* offered to provide 'discreet' protection, but he doubted it.

"Should we take the lightning blunderbusses with us?" he suggested to Lady Sally.

"I don't think it's necessary, captain, but if you think so, then by all means, go and get one."

For some inexplicable reason, the captain felt uneasy, so he scurried back to the airship to collect a rifle before the carts set off for the archaeological site.

Lady Sally toured the remains of Pompeii with interest. She marvelled at how perfectly the streets and buildings had been preserved by the volcanic ash. She was fascinated by the petrified bodies, frozen in time at the point of their deaths. She wondered at the eerie sensation of walking the empty avenues of the deserted city. She imagined what its inhabitants must have felt when they were, unexpectedly, pummelled with volcanic rock and then suffocated in layers of ash.

Having taken in the wonders of the site it was not long before Lady Sally was leading them to the locations she most wanted to see; the baths and the brothel, with their notorious erotic frescoes. She paid the guardian a handsome sum to unlock the gates and allow her access.

Lady Sally stood in the stone chamber which acted as the entrance hall for the brothel. The walls were surrounded by erotic figures painted in ochre, in earthy yellows, browns or greens, and bold reds. They were well-preserved.

"How wonderful," gasped Lady Sally. "To think these have been preserved for over two thousand years, and they are still perfectly clear. The Ancient Romans certainly appreciated sexual indulgence. What magnificent images. I should convert one of the rooms in Rudston Hall and have the wall painted with scenes of me punishing my slaves."

"Yes, I can just see that, madam. Imagine what future archaeologists would make of it," offered her maid.

"What an interesting thought, Victoria. They would speculate on what sadistic pleasures took place in the house, on whether they were real or the products of someone's perverted imagination. They would look at the pictures of me and marvel at the seductive female capable of entrapping men into scenes of bondage and flagellation."

"Indeed, madam," added Victoria, encouraging Lady Sally in her flight of fancy.

"Look here," commented the lawyer as he pointed to a mural of a naked woman reclining on a couch, his classical education coming to the fore, "she must surely be Venus."

"Yes, that would be me–the Goddess of love and fertility, but come to dominate and enslave."

"Look at this one, mistress," commented Kina Linguzh, pointing at a bearded figure with an outrageously huge cock.

"That's Priapus," explained the judge. "The Greek God of fertility, nature and male genitalia, always portrayed with a ludicrously over-sized erection."

Lady Sally was impressed by the size of his member, "The men don't understand, they have such small cocks. What I would give to have a Priapus to serve in my dungeon to pleasure me."

The four gentlemen looked deflated at their mistress's description of their manhood.

"I have our entertainment for the afternoon," she announced. "We should try to recreate the ancient Roman Empire, and re-enact scenes in the frescoes. I've paid the guardian handsomely for private access so we will not be disturbed."

The submissive gentlemen were enthusiastic and soon had their clothes ripped off. With the zeal of the new convert, the lesbian dwarf was up for it. Lady Sally stripped down to her ivory chemise, threw her silk scarf over her shoulders, and reclined on the stone bed, like Venus, to direct the proceedings.

"Come, captain. Don't be coy. You should enter into the spirit of my re-enactment of the debauchery of Ancient Rome. I'm sure you have no reason to be ashamed of your naked body. I promise I'll not do anything to humiliate you, if that's your concern; besides, I have plenty of men willing to subject themselves to that for me."

"Very well, madam," he replied gruffly, torn between his reluctance to expose himself, and a desire to please Lady Sally.

He pulled his jumper over his head, relieved to divest himself of the heavy, woollen garment if the truth was known. His trousers, flying boots and goggles were soon dispensed with until he stood there in just his underpants.

"And your knickerbockers, captain." Lady Sally gestured with her finger.

He slid his underpants over his muscular legs. It was as Lady Sally observed, he had nothing to be ashamed of. Beneath his pointed face with its straggly goatee beard was a well-toned body. His time in the army had given him a powerful physique and, as an aviator, it was necessary to keep a high level of physical fitness to endure the hardships of flying bi-planes.

Lady Sally cast him an appreciative glance. "Mm. There, you see, you have nothing to fear. What a delicious body you have. Come here, captain," she said, beckoning him over.

The captain shuffled forward until his groin was eye-level with Lady Sally's face. She reached out a hand and ran a finger along his shaft.

"And look, you must certainly have the longest cock of my submissive men, and it's not even erect... yet. You can be my Priapus."

The captain's pulse raced. He had succumbed to Lady Sally's wiles. Not that there was any doubt in his, or her, mind he would surrender to her demands. She had the power to do that; few men were capable of resisting it and Captain Wyndham recognised he was not one of them. He stood naked in front of the woman he had admired from their first meeting, even from the fleeting glance of her in the grandstand at Doncaster Aerodrome, which seemed an age ago now. He had shared such adventures with her and, through them, his respect, submission, and love for her had only blossomed. And now he stood there, trying to resist her teasing fingers but knowing resistance was futile. The blood surged into his cock as it swelled to an erection.

Lady Sally's eyes met his, and she smiled. She allowed a fleeting moment of intimacy between them before turning to recreate the scenes of Bacchanalian debauchery of a Pompeii brothel.

She orchestrated proceedings, taking the images from the frescoes and reproducing them in a present-day Dionysian orgy of sexual ecstasy. She reproduced the painting of the satyr seducing a maiden by having the judge who had the right amount of body hair for the role, to grope her breasts. The mosaic of a woman crouched over a man, fondling his cock was replicated by her and the dwarf with the men. The fresco of Pan, yet another god of fertility (the Romans liked their fertility gods) was acted out with the banker who was made to strut about as if he had the legs of a goat. The scene of a man performing oral sex on a lady as she reclined on a couch, her legs splayed to offer up her sex to him, was enthusiastically joined by the bishop. The men were made to copy the scenes of homosexual acts, which principally showed men bending over a reclining partner to suck cock.

A series of frescoes depicting the sexual act was re-enacted by Lady Sally. This involved many positions: bent double as the banker took her from behind, reclining on the stone divan with her legs on the duke's shoulders, lowering herself onto the judge as he lay on the couch, crouched on the floor 'doggy' style and many others, as they took turns to enter her. She had several satisfying orgasms in the course of the action, and much spunk was spent by the men during an afternoon of frenzied fucking.

Lady Sally noted, with irritation, that most of the frescoes depicted the men in dominant positions, but that could not be helped if she wanted to recreate the images faithfully, and certainly didn't detract from her enjoyment.

The dwarf was an enthusiastic participant in the proceedings. She declared that though she may be a lesbian she was not averse to sex with men. Victoria remained fully clothed in her maid's dress, and had to clean up after them, as was fitting.

Sensitive to the captain's hesitancy about entering into her sexual games, Lady Sally didn't involve the captain in the orgy. His role was to represent the fresco of Priapus with the over-sized cock as the god of fertility inspiring them to new levels of depravity. It intrigued her to observe the captain's reaction, as he was clearly tortured between keeping himself distant from the other submissive men and the desire for intimacy with her. The frustration of his predicament was etched over face, much to Lady Sally's interest, and amusement.

The entourage was exhausted and sticky with sweat, and other body fluids. They could have done with a relaxing Roman plunge bath, but unfortunately the sauna at Pompeii had not been in use for millennia. Frau Linguzh, complaining she always needed to pee after sex, sneaked out of the stone house to find somewhere secluded. The others got dressed, ready to leave the Roman brothel and its frescoes to have their picnic. By the time they were ready, the dwarf had still not returned. They waited longer, but she still didn't appear.

"Perhaps, this has been a ploy to give her a chance to escape from you," suggested Victoria.

"No, I don't believe so. I'm an excellent judge of character, and I can tell her conversion to my service is sincere. She has been gone too long, and Signore Fellatio did warn us of robbers in this area. I'm concerned for her, I must confess."

36

The captain agreed with Lady Sally, there was something wrong. He grabbed the lightning blunderbuss, feeling justified in bringing it with him. The men set off in different directions along the dust-covered streets of Pompeii calling her name, "Kina Linguzh... Kina Linguzh... Kina Linguzh... Kina Linguzh."

Captain Wyndham's approach was more focused. He followed the dwarf's footprints in the dust. He was an experienced tracker, having pursued warriors across the Kenyatta Plain during the Zulu Wars. The tracks led to shrubs behind the former brothel, into which she must have gone to find somewhere private to pee. When the captain inspected the ground there, his concerns were confirmed. There were various prints, only one set of them the distinctive, small feet of the midget. There was evidence of her having been ambushed and dragged away.

The captain called Lady Sally over. The conclusion was inescapable... Frau Linguzh had been kidnapped.

They caught the attention of the others who scurried back to join them.

"What are you going to do, madam?" asked Victoria.

"There is nothing else for it. We must rescue her," pronounced Lady Sally. "Let it not be said that Lady Sally Rudston-Chichester does not rush to the aid of a companion in trouble."

The captain studied the confusing set of footprints in the dirt.

"I think she was taken by at least four people, possibly five."

"Well, that's no problem, captain. There's seven of us. We can take them on."

The captain was not so convinced.

He led the way, the footprints being easy to follow in the dust. They led back to one of Pompeii's streets which they followed for several hundred yards, and then into one of its villas, one called *Casa di Amori*. The captain proceeded cautiously under the portico onto a floor tiled with mosaics where the trail became less clear. It led them into a ruined courtyard with the remains of a pool at its centre. It was there they heard muffled voices. The captain tried to hold Lady Sally back and urge caution, but she ploughed on ahead. There was a series of rooms beyond the colonnade of the courtyard, and she burst into one of these, the others followed.

In the corner of a bare-stone room was the dwarf, tied up and gagged. There was nobody else there. She looked wide-eyed and agitated, nodding furiously. Lady Sally stepped forward, untied her, and released the gag. Frau Linguzh had just enough time to blurt out that it was a trap before the room filled with four men pointing rifles at them. Caught by surprise, they were soon overwhelmed. Realising Lady Sally was the real prize, they took hold of her first, placing a pistol to her head. With the mistress being in imminent danger, the captain had no choice but to surrender the lightning rifle.

Their leader gloated. "We've got our traitorous dwarf-spy, who we'll take back to Berlin to interrogate, and we have the bonus of capturing the British spy, Lady Sally Rudston-Chichester."

They were Prussian Secret Service men.

Lady Sally thrust her breasts out, proclaiming in her most imperious voice, "How ridiculous. I'm not, and never have been, a spy. I am a strict English dominatrix!"

"We'll go back to Naples where you will show us how to fly your airship, so we can take it back with us."

"You will do nothing of the kind. I will never surrender *The Corseted Domme* into your hands," insisted Lady Sally.

"It looks to me like you have very little choice."

They were in a predicament. It did appear Lady Sally's fortunes had changed, and that enemies she made on her adventures across Europe had finally caught up with her.

There was a commotion in the entrance to the chamber which suddenly filled with another group of men in khaki uniforms and helmets, with rifles trained on the Prussian Secret Service men.

"I don't think so, old chap. Release her now and hand her over to the British Army. Lady Sally is an English gentlewoman, and a citizen of the British Empire. She, and her airship, are returning with us."

The Prussians were not going to surrender their hard-earned quarry without a fight. They set upon the British soldiers. A scuffle ensued. A pistol shot went off, and a bullet ricocheted off the ceiling of the villa.

The Prussian officer holding Lady Sally made the fatal mistake of releasing her to join the scrap with the soldiers. Seizing her opportunity, a Prussian and British soldier were soon doubled up in agony groping their groins, having been kicked in the balls. She scooped up the lightning blunderbuss from the ground where it fell and clutched it against her chest. She wished she'd worn her steel-tipped boots, which would have caused serious damage.

In the commotion, she gathered up her entourage and pushed them towards the entrance. Their way was blocked by a British soldier, a rifle at his eye, trying to pick out a target from the melee of fighting men.

The captain swung his fist at the soldier's jaw, flooring him with one mighty punch.

"Sorry, old chap." The captain felt bad about flattening his compatriot.

The way was open for Lady Sally and the others to escape the chaos of the fight. They dashed through the courtyard, the dwarf's little legs running like the clappers, the banker heaving his belly along, desperately trying not to get left behind. The sounds of fighting continued. More shots rang out.

They ran back through the vestibule and tumbled out of the villa into the sun-scorched streets of the petrified Roman town.

They'd made it.

The captain fell, crashing into the dust. He was dazed, but managed to scramble back onto his feet where he was confronted by a fearsome man with a huge moustache wearing leather boots and wielding a massive knife. The captain was disorientated, but quickly weighed up the situation. Boots... Cossack style boots, in Pompeii? There was only one conclusion he could draw, they'd been ambushed by Russian Secret Service agents.

They had been caught by surprise. The Cossacks must have jumped on them from the roof of the villa as soon as they emerged from its portico. Two of them grabbed hold of Lady Sally by the arms. She remained undaunted.

"Unhand me, you blackguards!"

The others were confronted by Cossacks wielding long knives.

Lady Sally's trail of destruction across Europe was finally catching up with her.

The leader of the gang shouted at them in Russian. Lady Sally understood enough of the language to know they were going to drag them back to their horses before the fight in the villa was resolved, and either the Prussians or British arrived.

She was having nothing of it. Her arms were in the clasp of one of the Cossacks but her hands were still free, forced behind her back. She still had enough flexibility to make handy use of them. She grasped the Cossack by the balls and twisted them. This was a manoeuvre acquired through years of experience. She knew exactly which part of the male anatomy to squeeze to inflict the maximum discomfort. The Cossack, tears coming to his eyes as Lady Sally squeezed and twisted, loosened his hold long enough for her to break free from his grasp.

At that moment, the shots started.

The first bullet whizzed past the captain and struck the Cossack, who'd just let go of Lady Sally, in the thigh. A second hit their leader in the shoulder. A third missed its target and lodged in the crumbling stone of the villa wall. A fourth hit the ground right by a Russian's foot.

The captain smiled grimly. *You expected shoot-outs in the wild west, not in ancient archaeological sites.*

Instinctively, the captain leapt forward onto Lady Sally, and they both went crashing into the dust. He covered her body with his, forcing the whole of his weight onto her to protect her.

More shots rang out. Another two Russians fell to the ground, hit. The captain dared to look up and saw wisps of smoke from firing rifles on the opposite side of the wide avenue, and shadowy figures dressed in black. It suddenly dawned on him; it was the *Camorra*. Signore Fellatio had made good on his promise to protect Lady Sally. The captain was reassured. This was their land, and they would allow no-one, Prussian, British or Russian, on their patch. They were murderous rogues of course... but murderous rogues on their side. They had no compunction in gunning down anyone who encroached on their territory. The captain understood, it was a matter of honour... Signore Fellatio had given his word to protect Lady Sally.

"Captain, you are squashing my boobs! I know you would simply love to get intimate with me, but that is no justification for jumping on top of me."

"I'm sorry, Lady Sally. I was only trying to protect you," he protested.

He rolled off her. Lady Sally stretched an arm out to pick up the lightning blunderbuss, which had fallen within reach, and leapt to her feet.

A few of the Cossacks were on the ground, wounded or dead, whilst the others retreated under the portico of the villa for cover. They'd been taken completely by surprise by the *Camorra*, hidden in the roofs of the villas on the opposite side of the street.

Through the opening in the front of the villa, Lady Sally saw a group of men rushing through the courtyard towards them, British and Prussians. Perhaps they'd heard the gun shots and broken off their fight to see what was going on, only to discover a band of Russian Cossacks, who were hated equally by British and Prussian.

Lady Sally wasn't taking any chances. She stood astride, her hat cocked to one side, her fine, cream, cotton dress covered in dirt, the sight of the blunderbuss at her eye. The Russians saw what she was about to do, diving desperately into the courtyard at the feet of the onrushing men.

There was a sizzle and a blast of blue light. It struck the key stone in the arch of the portico and exploded. Stone and dust flew into the air. The entrance of the villa collapsed into rubble before their eyes.

The villa had survived the eruption of Vesuvius, being pelted by volcanic rocks, and being covered in volcanic ash for two thousand years, but did not last one afternoon in the presence of Lady Sally Rudston-Chichester.

Lady Sally was livid. "Really, captain. Look at my dress. It's covered in dirt. Those marks will never come out. It's totally ruined!"

37

"We'll go into the rubble and shoot-a the bastards."

The band of the brotherhood of the *Camorra* emerged from their hiding places. Tough, hardened, burly Neapolitans, dressed in black with roughly tailored jackets and bowler hats, the distinctive tattoos of their brethren on their knuckles.

"Really, there's no need. Leave them to fight it out amongst themselves," said Lady Sally.

"Just say the word-a, my lady, and we will-a slaughter them for you. It's a matter of honour."

"That's very kind of you, I'm sure, but I'm happy honour has been satisfied, after all Lady Sally Rudston-Chichester has emerged victorious over her enemies again. Who would have thought so many empires would send their agents half way across Europe just to pursue little me? I'm most flattered."

The men and Victoria were still shaken. Shoot-outs were not what they had signed up for when they enlisted for Lady Sally's erotic, airship adventure. The dwarf was exhilarated at having seen so much action though, saying it was a refreshing change from hiding in wardrobes.

They didn't hang around to discover the outcome of the ensuing fight between the Prussians, British and Russians. The *Camorra* accompanied them back to the port of Naples.

"I think it best we depart Naples as soon as possible," said Lady Sally. "Besides, I need to leave at once because I have an important engagement in Paris. We should be safe there, I don't believe I have any enemies in the French Empire."

"Yet...," mumbled Victoria.

Lady Sally gave her a hard stare.

"What's the engagement you are attending?" enquired the captain.

"I have been awarded *Le Prix D'Honeur De La Republique* for services to airship technology. I was nominated by members of *La Societé D'Aviation Et Les Dirigeables* for the technical specification for *The Corseted Domme* prepared for me by Mr Barnes-Wallis, and for my sponsorship of flying events. The presentation is tomorrow night at a gala ball in my honour."

Captain Wyndham was impressed, "That's a great honour. *La Societé* is the most illustrious organisation for the promotion of aviation in the world. And it will be richly deserved, of course."

"Thank you, captain."

"I just hope we can get off the ground with the extra weight on board," he added.

"Well, I'm certainly not leaving my statue behind!"

Luckily, during her travels, the crew had got more than used making emergency launches, and had everything prepared for take-off, just in case. Lady Sally offered her thanks to the band of the *Camorra* and asked them to pass on her gratitude for their help to Signore Fellatio.

The airship's engines fired up, and they were soon on their way again. As *The Corseted Domme* rose majestically into the air, the street urchins on the port side jumped and waved at her departure. The captain hoped Lady Sally didn't want a quick getaway, or get into any further scrapes that might lead to one, as the weight of the bronze statue definitely impeded her acceleration.

Cook, disgusted at the party's flirtation with Italian 'peasant food' as she called it, delivered a hearty feast that evening, which was considered most welcome after the excitement of the afternoon. The main course was roast boar with roast and mashed potatoes, a choice of vegetables, lashings of gravy and a special treat of Yorkshire puddings. The vegetables included asparagus, this time steamed to the required levels of firmness. Lady Sally took great delight in waving an asparagus tip through the air to test it.

"Look, it should be stiff enough to insert into a lady's vagina without disintegrating. My dwarf will demonstrate," she said, passing an asparagus to Frau Linguzh.

The dwarf duly obliged and followed up by threading the tip into the bishop's mouth to prove how firm it was to bite into.

The next morning *The Corseted Domme* flew over the French Riviera heading for Paris to meet a tea-time deadline. Lady Sally was due to be met at the airship station by representatives from *La Societé D'Aviation Et Les Dirigeables*.

Conscious this was likely to be their last full day of travelling, Lady Sally planned an extravaganza of sadistic sexual torments for her gentlemen. She produced the dastardly devices she'd brought with her for the journey: the electro-vibrator and it's attachments, the steam-powered rubber phallus with a new boiler, the electric-powered masturbating machine, and the steam-powered spanking device. They were available to her, along with the many whips, canes, and straps for corporal punishment and rope, chains, and cuffs for bondage, all of which lined the walls of the dungeon.

Borghild, the automaton was there, still dressed in the red rubber chosen by Victoria when she was first unloaded from her crate. Lady Sally chose a corset embroidered with intertwining lines of dark-green poison-ivy she had especially tailored in an homage to her walled garden of poisonous and prickly plants at Rudston Hall. She wore knee-length boots with it and nothing else, so her dark bush of pubic hair and beautifully rounded arse were in full view. She considered it a treat for the men on their last full day.

Borghild's mechanical eyes swivelled manically to take in the array of implements of torment available for her use. Her expression, far from being blank and robotic, was somewhat disturbing. It mixed resentment at being been locked in the crate for so long with a fervour to make up for lost time.

The four men and the dwarf were stripped naked in preparation for a day of sadistic fun, whilst Victoria was already tied to the whipping bench, her knickerbockers pulled down and petticoats rolled up.

Lady Sally set to work putting them into bondage.

The automaton zoomed in on Victoria's bare backside, which presented an excellent target. With a whip in one hand and a cane in the other, she set upon the maid with relish. She had mastered the ability to co-ordinate her movements so she could deliver alternate strokes with each arm. Her gears clicked and whirred into action as meticulously each arm was alternately raised and lowered with mechanical force, a slash of the whip being followed by a stroke of the cane. The robotic movements were steady and persistent at first, but gradually built up in speed and intensity until Victoria was wailing for mercy.

"Ouch, oh madam, please call her off," Victoria screamed.

Her concentration broken, Lady Sally looked up from the intricate pattern of knots she had weaved around the judge's stocky frame to tie him to the rack. She cared not for her maid's pleas for mercy but was, nonetheless, cross with Borghild for not assisting her in putting the men into bondage. Lady Sally glared at the automaton and gestured for her to strap Frau Linguzh to the wall board. She sighed. *It was so hard to get reliable staff these days, even automatons aren't attentive enough.*

It was Lady Sally's intention to put everybody into bondage before putting her particular brand of sensuous torment into effect. With Borghild now fully engaged in the task it wasn't long before they were in some form of restraint, the sensitive parts of their anatomy and vital orifices exposed. It was her aim for them to experience each of the dastardly steam and electric powered devices during the day, along with the more traditional forms of corporal punishment provided by her collection of implements. There were the strap-on cocks as well. Lady Sally secured a belt around her waist and an enormous black, rubber cock protruded from her crotch. She helped Borghild on with a red phallus. They were ready for serious sadistic play. By tea-time the gentlemen's nipples and backsides would be so sore they wouldn't know where to put themselves.

There was a special treat in store for the lesbian dwarf; a pair of vibrating brass balls, which Lady Sally had brought along for her own pleasure, but were the only device she had not yet used during her travels. She stretched the dwarf's gash wide open and pushed them inside, leaving the wires attached to the brass dial for adjusting the vibration trailing from her crack. Lady Sally was exceedingly pleased with the results. The controlling gauge hummed as the balls vibrated at an intensity capable of bringing Frau Linguzh to a state of arousal without tipping her over the edge into climax. Lady Sally could maintain this erotic suspense until she deigned to allow her to come if indeed she would.

For the rest of the day Lady's Sally's playroom was a maelstrom of activity. The sounds of the different devices filled the room. The electro-vibrator purred with an electric hum, the steam-powered pumping phallus thumped and hissed, the electric masturbating machine buzzed, whilst the steam-powered spanking device pumped and slapped. All of this, along with the gasps, groans, squeals and screams of pain and pleasure created a cacophony of noise which ebbed and flowed during the morning as the activity reached a series of crescendos. At the centre was Lady Sally like the conductor of an orchestra.

Every so often each of the protagonists was untied and placed into a different predicament so that everybody experienced the full range of Lady Sally's wicked devices.

Borghild's glass eyes glinted with an expression which could only be described as satisfaction; now fully trained, she was an enthusiastic participant in the sadistic orgy her mistress orchestrated.

For Lady Sally, it was a most satisfying day, and the culmination of her travels as her dastardly toys were being put to full use. She was enjoying herself immensely. She climbed up on the rack and was crouching over the duke to penetrate him with her strap-on. Her arse, a magnificent mound of peachy flesh, thrust into the air as she probed the duke's anal passage ready to penetrate him.

Lady Sally's arse was a thing of wondrous beauty, an orb of deliciously soft voluptuousness, and a source of both admiration and arousal to her submissive gentlemen. Positioned as it was, it was presented a marvellous target. It hovered in the air invitingly. Of course, however tempting, none of her guests dare touch it without permission. On a rare occasion she might invite a privileged slave to plant his lips on it as an act of submissive homage to his mistress.

Borghild's eyes swivelled around. They alighted on Lady Sally's posterior and lit up with a red glow. She had been trained to find arse... she had been trained to whip arse... and this was the most inviting arse she'd ever recorded in her photo-sensitive cells. It was there, suspended in the air in all its fleshy glory, just waiting to be beaten. What else could a well-trained automaton do?

Lady Sally's eyes widened. It came as a shock, the slash of leather thongs against her arse... and with one of *her own* whips! She knew what it felt like to be whipped. Purely in the interests of research she was not averse to experiencing the treatments she meted out to her slaves. But this was a complete surprise. It was undoubtedly a hard stroke but its impact was not without pleasure as Lady Sally felt her flesh wobble with the impact, and the prickly pain fan out across her backside. She took a deep breath. She cocked her head to one side to see the culprit, Borghild, standing behind her, whip in hand, a look of what could only be described as pleasure in her glass eyes. A look that Lady Sally had seen many times reflected in the mirror whilst she punished her slaves. The look of a dominatrix enjoying herself.

She waited to see what the automaton would do next. She felt a cold, brass hand run its fingers across her bottom. Borghild had observed and learnt well. This was precisely Lady Sally's art, alternating sensual play with severe hits. A second stroke came zipping onto her backside. The gentlemen, now aware of what was happening, gazed aghast upon their mistress receiving a whipping from her automaton.

A third stroke whipped with a loud smack. It was not unpleasant... quite the opposite, the glowing pain was rather nice. Lady Sally understood only too well the pleasure her slaves got from the administration of seductive pain inflicted by a skilful mistress. In different circumstances, she might have allowed Borghild to continue. Indeed, when she got home to Rudston Hall, she may well allow the automaton to play with her in such a way. But this was not the time. She could not allow an automaton to get the better of her, especially in front of the men. That would simply not do. Her automaton had to be brought under *her* control and disciplined like any other wilfully disobedient slave. She needed to be taught a lesson.

Furiously, Lady Sally swivelled around and jumped off the rack to confront Borghild. Could the automaton understand what she had done wrong? Seeing the fierce look and dominant posture her mistress assumed as she snatched the whip from her hands, the red glow in Borghild's eyes dimmed.

"Your behaviour is completely unacceptable. You must be punished. *Punished*. Do you understand?"

Borghild hung her head in shame.

Luckily, the whipping bench was free. Lady Sally grabbed the automaton by her brass hand and dragged her over to it. She pushed her onto her knees on the bench and, in moments, had her wrists and ankles cuffed. She pulled her head back by the blonde wig, stuffed a ball-gag in her mouth and tightened the strap. Lady Sally realised it was entirely unnecessary, but it was, nonetheless, a means of enforcing upon the automaton who was in charge.

Lady Sally lifted up the red latex skirt. She couldn't help but admire the shiny, golden curves of her backside. The artificers had done a wonderful job with the moulding, the shape of the mounds being remarkably lifelike even though they were fashioned from brass.

Lady Sally stood in front of the automaton, the leather tendrils of the whip dangling menacingly before her eyes. The men looked on in astonishment, none of them daring to comment on the bizarre spectacle of their mistress striding around the whipping bench to administer corporal punishment on a brass arse.

Lady Sally raised the whip high above her head and brought it slashing down on with a crack on the shiny metal. The automaton might not feel a thing but, nonetheless, she had acquired enough understanding from observing her mistress to know this was a punishment. Lady Sally felt it was imperative to establish her control to prevent any further disobedience from Borghild in the future. Lady Sally continued to thrash the automaton with her hardest strokes, beating her relentlessly with slash upon slash.

This was the scene the captain encountered when he entered the playroom to inform his mistress they were beginning their descent towards the airship station in Paris. He looked surprised, and not a little bemused, at the spectacle of Lady Sally delivering a vicious beating to a brass automaton.

"You many well wonder what has gone on, captain. All I will say is that it's a poor do when one has to discipline one's own automaton."

38

The Corseted Domme landed at the mooring station in Paris. This was familiar territory to the captain. He visited Paris often to meet with the tightknit band of bi-plane aviators, which included several prominent Frenchmen, and to compete at flying meetings. Lady Sally was a frequent visitor to Paris. She had investments in several *Parisien* burlesque clubs including *Le Chat Noir*, *Folies Bergère* and *Caberet Des Noctambules,* being a regular guest at their shows whenever she was in Paris.

The party was met with a rousing welcome. The airfield was decorated with bunting, and the tricolour flag everywhere fluttering in the breeze. They were greeted with a raucous rendition of *La Marseillaise* by a brass band.

Lady Sally, dressed in her most sumptuous and daringly cut velvet gown and brown, knee-length boots, stepped onto the airfield. As soon as her foot touched the ground her hand was swept up and a welcoming kiss planted onto it.

"*Bonjour*, Ladee Salee, it ees a pleasure to welcome you to Parees. You are an honoured guest of *La Societé D'Aviation Et Les Dirigeables.*"

"How kind of you. How delightful. What a marvellous welcome you've laid on for me."

The Frenchman oozed charm with his handsome looks, blue eyes, waxed moustache and oiled hair. He was dressed in a smartly tailored suit, a boater hat and carried a silver-tipped cane.

Captain Wyndham, following behind Lady Sally, recognised the suave tone of voice and reek of expensive perfume as it wafted towards him. It was Monsieur Saunier, his rival, who had beaten him in the bi-plane trials that memorable afternoon in Doncaster. He was turning on his charm and social ease, his arm threaded through Lady Sally's as he led her away from the airship... and her appearing to lap it up. If he had known Saunier would be there to greet Lady Sally the captain would have changed out of his working clothes into something smarter.

Saunier and Lady Sally led the way, arm in arm. The Frenchman turned back, commenting to her, "I see you 'av brought your servants with you, Ladee Sallee."

"They are not merely servants. This is my maid, Victoria, these are my submissive slaves, and this is my dwarf," she explained, introducing them.

"And then I have my airship captain with me. Why Monsieur Saunier, you must surely know Captain Wyndham?"

"*Bonjour* Weendham…"

"…*Captain* Wyndham."

"*Mais oui*. We have competed many times. I recall the last time was in *Angleterre* when your plane 'ad a leetle engine trouble, and I beat you to the finish post. But I don't believe that made any deeference to the result, I was always in control of the race," he boasted.

Captain Wyndham seethed. *Arrogant arsehole.*

"No, on the contrary, I was on the point of overtaking you when the engine cut out. I'll race you again, then we can prove who's the fastest. Look, there are a couple of bi-planes in front of the hanger."

Monsieur Saunier was taken aback. He was not expecting such an open confrontation, but recognised that to maintain his honour he was obliged to accept Wyndham's challenge.

"Very well, we shall toss a coin for choice of plane."

The two men marched off towards the two awaiting bi-planes, the seething Captain Wyndham leading the way.

A broad smile spread across Lady Sally's red lips. She turned to Victoria, "How amusing to have men compete over one."

"I thought they were racing to see who's the fastest."

"Oh, my maid, you can be so naïve. And who are you rooting for, Victoria?"

"The captain, every time," she said. "And you, madam?"

"…Ah, well, we shall see."

The two bi-planes stuttered to a start. Their engines buzzed, and they soon took to the air. It was risky for the captain to make such a reckless challenge without knowing how the aircraft handled. They were both the same model and, given similar planes, he was convinced he could beat Saunier for speed. Although an airship handled very differently, he had become used to flying at speeds of 100 mph or more, far in excess of what these machines could reach. It was invigorating being in a bi-plane again. There was no escape from the elements and the blast of chilly wind as the plane sped through the air.

Captain Wyndham wasn't going to play cat and mouse games this time, waiting till the last moment to overtake. Having flown for a few minutes to get used to the handling of the craft he intended to lead from the front. He kept close to Saunier's tail, but soon drew up alongside him, dangerously close, so the tips of their wings were nearly touching. The Frenchman stared across at him angrily. The captain could see he was rattled by his aggressive move, but that only pleased him.

He inched ahead, tilting his plane and swinging it into Saunier's path, forcing him to brake. The Frenchman was furious. The captain then swung back in front of his rival and, taking advantage of Saunier being forced to slow down, turned the throttle full-on. He visualised the escape from the Prussian airship fleet in *The Corseted Domme*, and the exciting burst of acceleration. The engine roared and spewed out a trail of black exhaust fumes. He left Saunier trailing in his wake. But he was not going to let up, he kept the throttle open, increasing the distance between the two planes with every second. There was no way Saunier was going to catch him now. He zoomed past the finishing line at top speed.

After they landed, they walked back to join the others, Captain Wyndham in smug triumph, Monsieur Saunier in angry silence. He looked less suave now he was defeated... and coated in black soot.

"Bravo, captain," exclaimed Lady Sally, as she applauded the two aviators on their return.

"That was crazee flying, Weendham. You could have caused a crash."

"Oh, I thought it was tremendously exciting," said Lady Sally.

The captain narrowed his deep-set eyes, "But I proved I'm the more daring... and faster pilot."

Saunier led the party to the club room at the aerodrome where Lady Sally was introduced to the other committee members of *La Societé*. She was offered a very welcome cup of tea, along with a selection of French *pâtisserie*. The chairman of *La Societé* explained the order of events for the evening whilst Lady Sally stuffed a strawberry *mille-feuille* into her mouth, its cream oozing out from between the crisp, buttery layers of sweet pastry over her scarlet lips. A cream covered strawberry squeezed out of the pastry and plopped onto one of Lady Sally's breasts.

"Oh dear, how careless of me. Would you be so kind as to remove that with your fingers for me?"

The red-faced chairman reached out and delicately picked up the fallen strawberry resting on its shelf of flesh.

"You may eat the strawberry if you wish," she suggested with a sly grin and mischievous twinkle in her eye. "And then if you would just wipe the cream off my breast with your napkin, that would be lovely."

"Yes, of course Ladee Sallee," he said as he carefully dabbed her boob with his napkin.

How she loved to make men squirm.

After tea, the party returned to *The Corseted Domme* to get ready for the evening event, which was to take place in the hall of the Palais-Royale. It was a formal ball in Lady Sally's honour so she had to look her best, taking an age deliberating with Victoria over her choice of dress.

When she swept down the magnificent staircase of the palace into the ballroom, all eyes turned to Lady Sally. She looked stunning in a cerise, taffeta gown accompanied by a silk *chinon* in a flowered print. Needless to say, the bust was cut low and exhibited her elegant neckline and magnificent décolletage to perfection.

Lady Sally took pride of place alongside members of the committee of *La Societé* and other dignitaries whilst her entourage was relegated to another table. Victoria had remained on *The Corseted Domme* to pack her wardrobe into trunks in preparation for the journey home. The captain felt distinctly uncomfortable; he did not like formal occasions, and he had to borrow a dinner-jacket, winged-collared shirt and bow tie from the duke who had spare ones. Unfortunately, the duke was a smaller build than him and it was a tight fit, making him feel more stiff and uncomfortable. He daren't do any dancing, for fear of splitting the pants.

Lady Sally was enjoying every moment. The captain had got used to seeing her in the relative intimacy of her airship but it was clear she revelled in being the centre of attention. Everybody wanted to be seen with her, speak with her, and dance with her. She was thrilled with the ceremony for the presentation of *Le Prix D'Honeur De La Republique*, and the receipt of a golden statuette in the shape of an airship. The speakers extolled the design, technical wizardry and magnificence of *The Corseted Domme*. They were gushing in their praise of Lady Sally's contribution to the promotion of aviation. Until then the captain was not aware of how much she had done, funding flying meetings and sponsoring races over France, including ones he'd competed in and won prizes at. It was strange to think that even before being taken on as her airship pilot he had already been the recipient of her largesse.

The captain felt uncomfortable at these big events and, if he was on his own, he would certainly have found an excuse to leave, but he was Lady's Sally's guest so felt obliged to stick it out. In addition to which, the most important thing was that Lady Sally enjoyed the evening, which she certainly was. The champagne flowed, and Monsieur Saunier insisted on filling her glass at every available opportunity.

Around midnight the ball wound up. Lady Sally had danced with numerous members of the committee and other dignitaries. It happened that she ended up dancing with Monsieur Saunier, looking suave and dapper again after washing off the trail of sooty smoke the captain had left him in. When Lady Sally approached the table to gather up her party to return to the airship, he was with her.

"I'm ready to leave now," she announced. "I've invited Monsieur Saunier to come back to *The Corseted Domme* with me."

39

Captain Wyndham was fuming. In the charabanc on the way back to the airfield Monsieur Saunier was all over her. Lady Sally was animated, tipsy from the bottles of champagne she'd quaffed to celebrate her prize. They were chatting and giggling in French, which she could speak fluently. Saunier's hands were everywhere, stroking her bare shoulders, up her thighs, under her ball gown, openly fingering her crotch. He kissed her on her lips and on her exposed breasts; in full view of the passengers, wantonly ignoring their presence.

On returning to the airship, Lady Sally dismissed them and led Monsieur Saunier to her bedroom... *to her bedroom.* The captain was shocked. He didn't know how to take it.

The teak door with its brass handle was closed shut behind them, shutting the captain, the four submissive gentlemen and the lesbian dwarf out. The other men looked as forlorn as Wyndham felt. It was their final night. The next day would be their last as they were setting off for England first thing in the morning. Perhaps they were hoping for an especially debauched treat for the final night.

Victoria appeared. She emerged from her mistress's changing room, separated from her bedroom by a partition door, where she'd been packing. Hearing Lady Sally and Monsieur Saunier arrive and the exuberant mood they were both in, she thought it politic to leave them to it.

They stood outside Lady Sally's door. The sounds of drunken giggles soon giving way to murmured endearments.

Frau Kina Linguzh knelt on the ground and peeked through the keyhole. It was an exceedingly large keyhole, providing the viewer with a panoramic view of the mistress's bedroom, and of Monsieur Saunier's seduction of Lady Sally.

"He's unbuttoning the mistress's dress," she whispered, peering through the hole.

Victoria was indignant. "You can't do that! You can't spy on madam."

The dwarf looked up, "But she wants us to. She gave her permission. She drew me to one side earlier and said she wanted to treat you to a bit of voyeurism. She wants you to spy on her."

The men's faces lit up. So, there was going to be a treat for them on the final night… an opportunity to watch Lady Sally in bed, being fucked by the Frenchman.

Victoria looked crestfallen, "Well if that's what madam wants…"

The dwarf peeked through the keyhole again, "It's a fantastic view. He's unbuttoning her gown, I think he's going to pull it off. Come on, take a look."

She turned away for the banker to kneel and take a look, continuing the whispered commentary, "Oo, he's pulled the dress off her back now. I can see her back and bare arse. Oh, mistress has such a beautiful bum."

"Let me look!" demanded the duke.

"And me…" said the bishop.

"Don't forget me…" said the judge, as they huddled around the keyhole waiting their turn.

They took it in turns to peek through the keyhole, each one sharing a whispered exposition of every move they saw in the bedroom.

He's dropping his trousers now. He's already hard. Oh, look at that, he's got a huge cock. Bigger than mine? I reckon so, come and take a peep. You think she'll let him fuck her? She's pulling his shirt off now. She's running her hands across his chest. She's touching his cock. See that look of lust. He wants her. Yeah, he really wants his cock inside her. He's pulling her face towards his. They're kissing now. Oh god, they've collapsed onto the bed. His hands are all over her. He's put a finger up her slit! She's moaning with pleasure. Yes, we can hear her. She's lying on the bed… she's spreading her legs for him.

"Enter me, Monsieur. I want you inside me. Fuck me!"

He's kneeling over her. I can only see her legs and back though. Oh, she's moved her head to one side, I can see her face now. He's got his fingers up her slit. She's ready for it. He's putting his cock in her cunt. Let me look! Yeah move over, stop hogging the keyhole! She's pushed his prick in her slit now. Can you hear her moan? Yes, yes.

"Oh, it's so good to feel you inside me, monsieur."

He's fucking her. He's really pumping it inside her now. Look at her face, it's contorted with pleasure. Yeah, she's enjoying that. She obviously wanted a good fucking. Oh, it's so sexy watching mistress get fucked. Have you got a hard-on. Yeah, of course I have… haven't you? Yes, my cock's like iron. Let me have a look now. Do you think she'd mind if we wanked? I'm going to have to. This is turning me on… I've got to get some relief. He's pulling out of her now. They're changing positions. Mistress is mounting him now.

The mumbled commentary continued as the four men got more and more excited. They looked on as Lady Sally and Monsieur Saunier changed positions several times, his cock thrusting into her from different angles whilst the men pulled on their erect cocks to give themselves pleasure.

"Captain, aren't you going to take a peep?" asked the dwarf. "Lady Sally won't mind. She was insistent she wanted to be spied on. I think the idea of it turned her on."

"No," he replied

The last thing he wanted was to watch Lady Sally getting fucked by the arrogant Monsieur Saunier. He'd heard too much of the noises of lovemaking, the groans and moans, the heavy breathing and panting, the squeals and shrieks. He'd had enough. He turned away and headed for the cockpit. He took solace in the company of Clarissa.

He was fiddling around, checking readings and adjusting dials on the automaton's control panel in preparation for a launch later that morning, it being way past midnight now.

It was impossible to escape the sounds of the raucous sex though. They reverberated through the gondola as far as the control cabin.

"Oh yes! Yes! Fuck me, monsieur! Fuck me!"

The captain was distracted by the sound of somebody moving behind him. He looked up. It was Victoria.

"You're not peeking through the keyhole either, then?"

"No, I'm not bothered. I've left the others to it. They seem to be having fun. Madam was amused at the dwarf's stories about spying on people having sex in hotel rooms," she offered by way of explanation of her mistress's choice.

"Oh! Yes. Yes. Yes. Give it to me *mon amour*!"

"Why Saunier? I can't believe it. I can't believe she's taken in by his smarmy, superficial charm. He's been wheedling up to her since the moment she stepped off the airship. When I think about it they've been all over one another throughout the evening. I saw him groping her backside when they were dancing..."

"Oh, oh, yes! I'm nearly there. Ram your cock up my cunt. Fuck me harder!"

"...and she's been taken in by him. All surface show. I don't understand. Why does she let him use her like that? Why doesn't she dominate him like she does every other man? I mean, I can accept what she does with her submissive gentlemen. I know what she's like. But to jump into bed with that odious Frenchman. I can't help it, and I certainly don't want to watch them going at it."

"Ah. That's it. Yes. Yes. Yes. Oh. Oo. Ah. Yes!"

Lady Sally had just reached her climax.

193

"You are over-thinking things, captain," said Victoria. "She's a law unto herself. Believe me, it's impossible to predict what she'll do next. But whatever you do, don't underestimate her. Good night, captain."

"Oh, oh, Ladee Sallee, Ladee Sallee. I'm coming. I'm coming. *Oui, oui! Sacre bleu!*"

"Thanks. Good night, Victoria."

The captain pulled out charts of Northern France and the English Channel. He knew the route well enough. He didn't need to check the maps, he just wanted something to do. After a while he dozed off, the charts spread over his lap.

"So, this is where you're hiding captain."

Captain Wyndham woke from his nap, unsure what the time was or how long he'd been asleep.

"Yes."

Lady Sally was behind him, a silk dressing gown wrapped around her, barely covering her chest. He dark hair was dishevelled, and she had an enigmatic smile. The captain couldn't help but note how ravishing she looked. The sex had certainly given her a healthy glow.

"Well, it's our last day. Later today we'll be back in Yorkshire. Are you sad our travels have come to an end? I am," she said, moving around to take up the spare seat in the cockpit next to the captain.

"Yes."

"How beautiful Paris looks," she says gazing out at the city's lights and the distant view of the floodlit Eiffel Tower.

"Yes."

"Come, captain. Why so monosyllabic?"

"Oh, I'm sorry, Lady Sally. I'm just in a bit of a reflective mood."

There was a pause.

"Are you jealous, captain?"

The question sliced through him like a knife. It laid bare his confused and conflicted feelings about Lady Sally. He was tortured over whether his admiration and respect for Lady Sally could be anything more, doubtful over whether it was possible to fall in love with a strict dominatrix, yet reluctant to succumb to the extreme submission of her submissive gentlemen. And he was angry at his caution in expressing what he really thought about her and whether it was a missed opportunity. Seeing Saunier jump in with no hesitation, knowing he'd been welcomed into her bed, had exposed his raw emotions. He took a deep breath and considered his reply.

"Yes. If I'm honest with myself, I'm jealous. You're an amazing person, Lady Sally. I admire you and revere you, and you mean a lot to me. I know you'll do what you want, but seeing you go off with Saunier like that…"

"I see. And do you truly wish you were in Monsieur Saunier's place?"

"I don't know. Maybe."

"Sorry, I still don't know your Christian name, captain?"

"Charles. Charles Wyndham."

"You are jealous of him fucking me. You wish it was you? You should be careful what you wish for, Charles?"

"I don't know, somehow I can accept the way you treat your slaves, it doesn't bother me. That's who you are. But seeing you go off with Saunier just hit a nerve."

Lady Sally laughed. "But don't you see. You have no reason to be jealous of your rival, Charles. He has been used. I've had my guests spy on him and our lovemaking for my amusement. Besides, there's always a price to pay for taking pleasure from Lady Sally Rudston-Chichester. He will find that out in the morning when he awakes dewy eyed and loving only for me to treat him like a whelp. You see, Monsieur Saunier means nothing to me. Later this morning he will just be another dominated submissive male, but you... you will still be my airship captain... and my friend."

The captain looked into Lady Sally's eyes. Her words were heartfelt and full of meaning. He nodded, "Yes, I see. I understand."

"Good. I'm glad we understand one another. I would not have us part in this moody silence after we've shared such magnificent adventures together."

Captain Wyndham smiled. "It's been amazing hasn't it, Lady Sally?"

"Indeed, it has, captain," she said, leaning over to give him a kiss, before heading back to her bed, and the oblivious, snoring Monsieur Saunier.

Lady Sally was true to her word. There was a price to pay for pleasure... and that was punishment and humiliation.

They were in the midst of tucking into cook's full English breakfast for their last morning when Lady Sally emerged from her bedroom, dressed in thigh-length, leather boots and matching black leather bra and pants. She gripped a dressage whip in her hand, it's long coil of cord brushing the floor. She looked every inch the severe dominatrix. She had secured a studded, leather collar around the dozing and compliant Monsieur Saunier's neck and was pulling his naked body along on all fours with a lead to his whining and complaining.

"Keep to your mistress's heel," she snapped, tugging at the lead to drag him along behind her. He scrambled behind her crawling on all fours.

"But please madam, *ma amour*. I beg you. Does all my expression of love for you last night mean nothing."

"You misjudge me. There is a reckoning to pay for receiving pleasure from me. You are well enough acquainted with my nature, you must have had an inkling of how this would turn out."

The cord zipped across his arse with a wicked crack.

"Ow. Please, that hurt," he whimpered. "*Ma Cherie*. Oh, please, you have seen how much pleasure I can give you. I love you, Ladee Sallee. Please, don't treat me like this. I know you are desperate for it. Let's go back to bed and make love. I know you want me."

The dressage whip was raised high above Lady Sally's shoulder and brought whizzing down with a hiss. The cord smacked across Saunier's backside leaving a long, reddening mark across his flesh. A second, even stronger stroke, struck him with a stinging zing.

"Ow! Oh, please, Ladee Sallee."

"You overestimate your skills of seduction, and your faith in your own prowess, monsieur. You think you can fuck me and I will fall into your arms to become your lover. You have the arrogance to think I will succumb to you because of your miserable little cock. No, monsieur."

The long cord cracked again. His face contorted in pain, tears welling up in his eyes. There was now a row of welt marks across his arse so raw you could almost see them throbbing.

"I will teach you a lesson in male arrogance and then send you packing so I can continue on my journey home. All of you, follow me!"

At her command, they jumped up from the breakfast table. Lady Sally turned on her submissive men.

"And did you enjoy watching your mistress being fucked?" They shuffled uncomfortably. "Did you watch through the keyhole? Did you get hard-ons?" They reddened. "Do not take me for a fool. I knew you were there. I heard your whisperings. I could even hear you jerking off."

They looked embarrassed. They guiltily shuffled from one foot to the other. They knew there was no point denying it.

She scalded them, "Yes, and there will be a reckoning for you as well. I may have given permission for you to peep through the keyhole. That was for *my* pleasure. The idea of you watching aroused *me*. But I never gave you permission to make lascivious comments about me, get erections… or wank. You are led by your cocks, all of you. What have you to say for yourselves?"

They mumbled their acknowledgments that she was right and muttered apologies.

Captain Wyndham witnessed the spectacle. He was amused at her reprimand of the four gentlemen, but enjoyed even more the predicament his rival had been put in. He understood her. He reflected on the question

Lady Sally had put to him in the night and, no, he would rather be Lady Sally's friend, and have her respect, than be in Monsieur Saunier's position.

She tugged at his lead to drag him into her dungeon playroom, striking him with the whip if he didn't keep to heel. She mounted her throne with him on his knees before her.

She pointed to her boots, "Lick them!"

"Please, madam." He whimpered a plaintive appeal.

Her voice was stern. "I said, lick them."

He got down at her feet and ran his tongue along the leather. She lifted a foot so he could lick the boot's sole and suck on its heel. She made him cover every inch of leather. He carried out the task wordlessly and thoroughly, knowing he had little choice, and hoping that in doing so he might avoid further stinging cracks of Lady Sally's whip.

When Monsieur Saunier completed the task to her satisfaction, she pushed him away and stood up. He was still on his knees in front of her. She put thumbs and fingers inside her black, leather pants and wriggled them over the white flesh of her thighs, over the folds of leather at the top of her boots, bending to lower them right down to her ankles. She towered over him, her bush of black pubic hair above him as he knelt. She took hold of a shock of his tousled hair and pulled his face up. He was forced to stare up at her. Her legs were parted, her slit visible, her cruel, blue eyes baring down on him. Her fingers pulled at either side of her crotch to open up her crack so he was staring into it. Then she relaxed the muscles of her bladder to let her waters flow. They gushed out in a stream over his onlooking face. They filled his gaping mouth with warmth and wetness as he gazed up at her. They burst over his head. He closed his eyes to let the stream of golden waters drip over his eyelids, along his cheeks and across his lips.

"There, I think you have been given an appropriate lesson in feminine domination. Now you understand what it means to submit to a strict English dominatrix."

"Yes, Ladee Sallee," he mumbled.

"Have you no more to say?"

He hesitated for a moment, struggling to find the right response. "Thank you, Ladee Sallee. It's an honour to submit to you and receive your golden waters," he said.

"That's better."

She leant over him and undid the collar around his neck. By now Victoria was by her side and handed her a bag with his clothes in.

"Now, Monsieur Saunier, it is time to leave my airship. I want to be back in Yorkshire and unpacked in time for dinner so we must be on our way.

When we meet again, I will expect appropriately submissive behaviour from you, monsieur."

"Yes, Ladee Sallee. Thank you Ladee Sallee," he said as he took the bag and backed away toward the exit to the mooring tower.

"Now, I have to punish you for your behaviour last night," she announced to the duke, banker, judge and bishop. I have a whole morning to deliver spankings and whippings. Borghild and my devices have been packed away but I still have an array of whips, floggers, and riding crops at my disposal. Captain, set the course for Yorkshire. We are going home."

"Yes, Lady Sally. *The Corseted Domme* is prepared for launch right away, madam."

He turned away to take up his position in the control room.

It had been an entertaining and instructive morning.

40

Realising their travels were finally over, the whole party was tinged with sadness when *The Corseted Domme* docked onto the mooring mast at the Howden Airship Station. It had been a fun-filled and action-packed adventure and everyone was sorry to see it come to an end. Lady Sally's submissive gentlemen were effusive in their praise of their mistress and appreciative of the magnificent escapade she'd provided them with.

They had been subjected to all manner of dastardly and perverted incursions into their bodily orifices, but that was, of course, precisely what they had signed up for. They had also experienced explosions, crashes, wild bears, daring rescues and shoot-outs, which they had not signed up for, but which had only added to the excitement of the adventure. Only last night the bishop had found a last sliver of copper lodged in his backside from the exploding boiler.

"It has been an honour and privilege to serve you on your airship, mistress," announced the duke, echoing the sentiments of them all.

"Hear, hear," the banker, judge and bishop called in unison.

"It has been a wonderful adventure," said the banker.

"We did wonder if we would get back to England alive," added the judge. "But I wouldn't have missed it for anything."

"Why, thank you. That's most kind of you. But you should show more faith in your mistress. Come now, it went entirely to plan. Was there ever any doubt that Lady Sally Rudston-Chichester would not prevail?"

"None indeed, mistress," replied the bishop.

The four gentlemen were the first to disembark and go their way, the duke having arranged for his carriage to meet them at the airfield. Frau Linguzh left with them, the duke having promised to show the dwarf the sights of London before returning her to Lady Sally's care.

The Corseted Domme was greeted by a flotilla of horse and carts, commissioned to carry Lady Sally's luggage back to Rudston Hall. She stayed on board to direct the operation with meticulous care. Cook supervised the removal of the kitchen utensils and what remained of the uneaten food and drink. Victoria looked after the trunks and hat boxes containing her mistress's wardrobe. Lady Sally took responsibility for the boxes of her dastardly steam and electric powered devices, whilst Borghild was already returned to her crate. She would be kept at Rudston Hall as a permanent tool for inflicting erotic punishment. The captain was in charge of packing Clarissa, his automaton co-pilot, and for ensuring the airship was left safe and secure. The crew remained on board to assist with carrying everything down the mooring mast into the waiting carts.

They started with the bronze statue. This was lowered carefully from the airship's hold into the largest and strongest cart available, pulled by several shire horses.

"My statue will look simply magnificent in the courtyard of Rudston Hall," commented Lady Sally.

This was followed by the tiles for her Turkish bath and her trunks of shopping from the bazaar in Istanbul. The bulkiest items having been unloaded first, the contents of the kitchen came next. This was overseen by cook who ordered the crew around, insisting she did not want any of her saucepans 'dinted' by careless handling. Cook was the next to leave the airship, needing to get back to Rudston Hall to prepare dinner for Lady Sally.

"And have you enjoyed your airship adventure, cook?"

"No I ain't, milady! Next time you goes on travels, you can count me out. I ain't ever worked in such conditions... and as for them explosions!"

Lady Sally arched an eyebrow and rolled her eyes, "You seemed to manage perfectly well, cook. I recall your roast boar the other night was especially fine."

Cook grunted, though she was obviously pleased with the compliment, before stomping off to accompany the cart carrying the kitchen utensils.

Victoria supervised the unloading of the trunks for Lady Sally's wardrobes, which he'd lovingly packed over the last couple of days. Whilst she was doing that, Captain Wyndham checked the airship was left in good working order by ensuring the air bags were left fully inflated.

He hung from the top of the mooring mast with a team of rigger-men. They were grasping a massive hose in an attempt to thread it into the slit at the cone of the airship. They were finding it hard work as the rubber pipe was wobbly and unwieldy. They had their hands gripped around it but were experiencing enormous difficulty getting it into the hole. The captain gave an order to blast hydrogen through the hose to make it stiff. The tactic worked, and once the hose was rigid, it was easier to penetrate the hole in the tip of the airship. Once threaded into the frame of the airship it was attached to the air bags for the hydrogen tank to inflate them.

Soon everything was ready. The crew was dismissed and Lady Sally, Victoria and Captain Wyndham were the last to leave *The Corseted Domme*.

Victoria was close to tears, "It's been totally marvellous. It's been such a pleasure to serve you, madam."

"Thank you, my maid. That is, of course, how it should be, Victoria."

The captain was no less emotional about parting though he showed it somewhat less, "It has indeed been a privilege and honour to pilot *The Corseted Domme* and to be a part of your travels. It has been a fantastic adventure with a remarkable lady and I shall never forget it... or you."

"Oh, thank you captain, your comments are most kind and appreciated," she said leaning forward to give the captain a heartfelt hug.

Lady Sally slung her lightning blunderbuss over her shoulder and the three of them set off to disembark from the airship for the final time.

They descended the steps of the mooring tower in reflective and companionable silence. They tramped along the airfield heading for Lady Sally's charabanc and her chauffeur, who was waiting. Curiously, there were two other official looking, black cars parked alongside her vehicle.

They were prevented from reaching the perimeter of the airfield, and the charabanc, by two men, one in a black suit and bowler hat, the other in the uniform of the British Empire airship fleet.

The former introduced himself as Mr Blenkinsop-Smythe, from the Ministry of War and his companion as Lieutenant Digby from the Ministry of Aviation.

"Lady Sally Rudston-Chichester?" asked the representative from the Ministry of War.

"Yes indeed, that is me," replied Lady Sally in a tone of complete indifference.

"Have you any idea of the trouble you have caused?"

"I have an inkling, yes."

"You've caused major diplomatic incidents wherever you've gone. We've received complaints from the Austro-Hungarian Empire of insults to the Archduchess Labiastein, from the Prussian Empire for attacking their airship fleet, from the Russian Empire for blowing up the Alexander column, from the Sultan of the Ottoman Empire for breaking into his harem, and from the Italian Empire for blowing up a villa at Pompeii. Our diplomatic service has been on twenty-four-hour alert whilst you've been on your expedition causing mayhem across the continent. We've had to use all our diplomatic skills to prevent war being declared."

"I don't know what you are fussing about, Mr Blenkinsop-Smythe. The Archduchess insulted me by serving coffee at tea time. The Prussians tried to capture my airship, so I had no option but to defend myself. I confess my collaboration with the Russian anarchists was perhaps a moment of drunken rashness, but a revolution has long been overdue in that backward empire. And I merely rescued an innocent young girl from a life of sexual slavery at the hands of the Sultan. The destruction of an ancient monument was regrettable, but entirely necessary as a matter of self-defence. Besides, it's a poor do when a Lady of the realm and strict dominatrix cannot have adventures!"

Mr Blenkinsop-Smythe looked accusingly at Lady Sally, "You've also defied an order of the government of the British Empire, and assaulted a soldier of the British Army."

Captain Wyndham reddened. That was his doing though he had apologised.

"I do not believe you have the power to take the property of an English Lady, sir."

"But we do. I have here," he said, waving a signed and sealed letter from the Minister of War before her eyes, "an order for the requisition of your airship. Lieutenant Digby has been ordered to fly her back to the Saffron Walden Airship Base with immediate effect."

Lady Sally was defiant. Her eyes blazed, and she thrust her breasts out, "*The Corseted Domme* is a vehicle for pleasure. I will not have her used for the purposes of war. She is my property and I will do what I wish with her."

As she was speaking she slipped the blunderbuss off her shoulder into her hands.

"I'm sorry Lady Sally, but the order to requisition your airship is official. I'm going to have to order you to surrender her, by force if necessary."

"I assure you that won't be necessary," said Lady Sally as she swivelled around, raised the sight to her eye and aimed at the mooring tower and *The Corseted Domme*.

Captain Wyndham looked on aghast. *Surely, she wouldn't?*

The brass muzzle was directed at its target, and Lady Sally gently squeezed the trigger. There was a sizzle and fizz from the wires within the barrel as the electrical circuits sprung to life, and then a blaze of blue light shot across the sky towards *The Corseted Domme*. The light hit the top of the mooring tower where the hydrogen tanks and hose feeding the airship's air bags met. At the exact point where there was several hundred square feet of hydrogen in close vicinity.

The captain knew what it meant. He'd seen airship explosions before. He wasted no time in leaping on top of Lady Sally and pushing her onto the grass, sheltering her with his body to protect her.

"Not again, captain," she gasped as his weight squashed her breasts against the ground.

The others hadn't anticipated and were slow to react. They stood immobile, frozen in expectant silence before the inevitable blast. It took an age as if time had been suspended. Then the explosion set off with a deafening roar which thundered across the airfield, audible for miles around.

A fireball shot several hundred feet into the sky. The debris from the airship and mooring tower flew through the air. There were shattered girders of duralumin from the fuselage, clusters of burning wood from the gondola, and shards of torn silver-coated linen from the airship's covering. One piece of material, still etched with the word *Domme*, was carried by the wind and landed miles away. Years later it was sold at auction for thousands of pounds, being the only part of Lady Sally Rudston-Chichester's famous airship to survive the explosion intact.

Luckily, they were on the perimeter and out of the reach of the flying metal but they couldn't escape from the cloud of soot, dust and grime which billowed across the airfield. The men from the Ministry looked shocked and dazed. They stood there for ages until the cloud had settled or dispersed. They were covered in a layer of thick, black soot, their faces like singers in a minstrel show. Victoria, who hadn't responded quickly enough, was also coated in grime. Her white blouse and petticoats, clean on that day for disembarkation, were blackened with a thick layer of soot.

After getting up, the captain's back was coated with a layer of dust, but other than that he had not fared too badly. He reached out a hand and pulled Lady Sally up from the ground. She nonchalantly flicked a piece of grass from her velvet dress and pulled back a single strand of hair that had fallen out of place. She looked completely unperturbed, the skin of her face as elegantly pale as it ever was.

"Really, Victoria, look at you. How can you possibly serve as my maid in that state!"

"Sorry, madam," she mumbled, too covered in grime to even consider contesting the justice of her mistress's reprimand.

She turned to the two men from the Ministry. "Well, that's settled then. I told you I would never surrender *The Corseted Domme*," she pronounced triumphantly.

"But your airship…" gasped Captain Wyndham, "your beautiful airship!"

Lady Sally shrugged, "Well, my view is that the age of the dirigible is coming to an end. *The Corseted Domme* was the finest example of airship technology in the world. We shall never see her like again. She will go down in legend. Ah well, I suppose I shall have to find another project to amuse me. I understand the technology of submersibles is advancing."

She marched towards her charabanc with her maid and airship pilot in tow. The men from the Ministry of War and Ministry of Aviation were too shell-shocked and dumbfounded to stop her.

Before climbing into her vehicle, she caught Captain Wyndham with her piercing gaze, "You know, you are welcome at Rudston Hall anytime. It will be a pleasure and honour to receive my airship captain. You will visit me, won't you?"

"Thank you, Lady Sally, and yes, of course I'd love to visit."

A wry smile spread across the captain's lips as Lady Sally's charabanc roared away leaving him covered in a layer of dirt.

Also from S. Nano

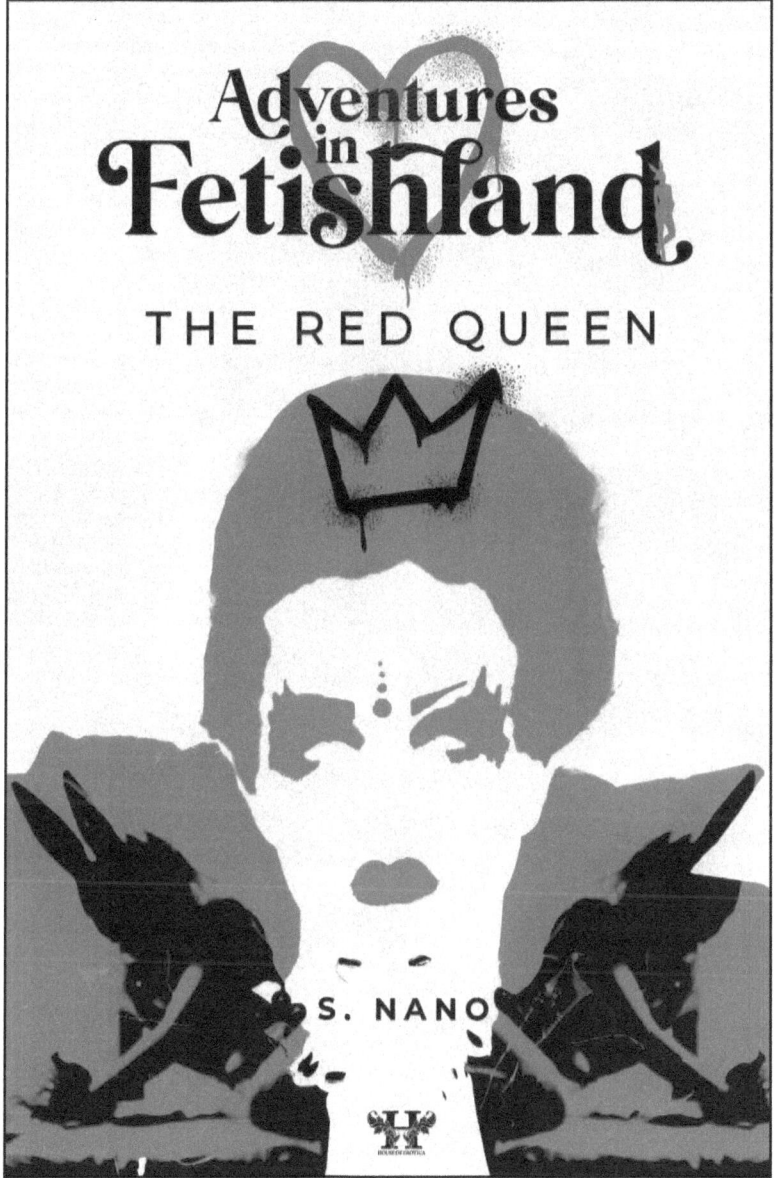

Also from S. Nano

www.ingramcontent.com/pod-product-compliance
Lightning Source LLC
Chambersburg PA
CBHW020951180626

46814CB00003B/1037